Black Heart Auctions

TAKING CHANCES

JAYCE CARTER

Taking Chances
ISBN # 978-1-80250-586-3
©Copyright Jayce Carter 2023
Cover Art by Kelly Martin ©Copyright November 2023
Interior text design by Claire Siemaszkiewicz
Totally Bound Publishing

TAKING CHANCES

Dedication

To my children, who should be embarrassed of
me but somehow aren't.

Chapter One

Kenz

Sometimes my brain stopped working—it took one look at the situation I found myself in and just fucked right off. It had happened when I'd found out about the murder of my mother and sister, again when my father had tried to kill me and it happened again now, as I faced a man I'd trusted, one I'd relied on, only to realize that he'd been behind everything I'd suffered recently.

"So we officially meet," Grisham said, taking his phone from his ear, a soft smile on his face as though he didn't truly mind being exposed. "I didn't expect you to be the one to figure it out."

"How could you?" I whispered, trembles running through my body, fear swamping me as I tried to connect the man who had helped me so often with the monster I'd heard about, the nightmare from my dreams.

He tilted his head, making no attempt to rise or do anything but stare back at me. "I've already told you—

you just didn't read between the lines. I saw your work at the entrance exhibit, and I knew, right away, that you were the one for me."

I took two steps closer and slammed my palm on the top of his desk. "You didn't even *know* me! If you actually gave a damn, why didn't you do something normal like ask me out? What sort of psychotic idiot has their soulmate abducted and sold at an auction?"

His chuckle came out soft and unconcerned. It forced me to look into his eyes, the ones I thought I'd known, and recognize an overwhelming emptiness in them. They seemed to lack a part, as though a vital piece of him had gone missing at some point.

Or maybe he'd never had that piece at all.

"I tried to get closer, but you never allowed anyone near. You had a wall up no matter what I did, kept me at a distance that I couldn't cross. We are *soulmates*, Kenz, and if you only give yourself the time and space to recognize it, you'll see it, too."

A click behind me made me freeze. The safety of a gun flipping off was a sound no person ever really forgot.

Grisham — *Lorien*? — peered over my shoulder but no change to his expression suggested he worried at all.

"It was you all along?" Hayden asked, rage in his voice that terrified me as much as the man before me.

"You were so close," Lorien said with a laugh, "but you never saw it. You never managed to put the pieces together to find me. Sometimes, I wondered if you and the others' incompetence was a sign that you didn't really want to find me. The four of you should have managed it, yet in five years, you've never gotten close enough for it to matter."

"Who cares?" Hayden fully entered the office, then shut the door without ever removing his gaze from

Grisham. "A bullet between your eyes doesn't require much time, after all."

Grisham shrugged and sat back in his chair. "You won't shoot me."

"Do you really think that? After what you've done? After I've chased you this long?"

"You're smarter than that. If you couldn't find solid proof about me, do you think the police will? Or do you think that if you kill me here, in my office, in a place where others will come quickly at the noise, *you'll* be held responsible as a murderer?"

"So? I'm ready to throw my life away," Hayden assured him, no hesitation in his voice.

It brought back the same crushing pain from last night, the realization that the men I loved didn't value or even want their lives.

"But are you ready to throw hers away?" Grisham gestured toward me.

He sure knows where to aim that threat.

Hayden hesitated, his lips pressing together, but he didn't lower his gun.

Grisham's smile spread wider. "Kenz has enjoyed a quiet life this last year because her existence isn't widely known. If anything happens to me, her identity will get out. I have ensured that every person who might wish to make use of her will know *everything* about her. Her ability to live as she wishes will disappear if that happens, assuming she survives it."

Hayden lifted his lip, a look of pure disgust on his face. "And you claim you love her, that you're soulmates, but you would do that to her?"

"I'm a practical man. We're soulmates, and that means if I go, her time should come soon after. Besides, if something happens to me, do you think my mother would sit back quietly? She may be a meek woman, but mothers are notoriously vicious. If I'm harmed, she will set her sights not only on Kenz herself but on those Kenz cares about as well. I know you don't value your own life, but you are far too easy to predict, and you'll value the life of others."

My stomach rolled as I thought about Nem in danger because of me. Not just her — she was tough, as were the Quad — but others. What about Sasha? What about those who worked for my sister? I'd lived in this world long enough to know exactly how much death came from a real war, when there were no innocents — just the victors and the dead.

Hayden still didn't lower his gun, but the look in his gaze said he'd taken the threat seriously. "So what now?"

"Now we appear to be at an impasse, don't we? We both have something to hold over the head of the other. It seems we are at a standoff at the moment." Grisham moved his gaze from Hayden to me, and I had to fight the desire to take a step away from the intensity of it. "I am not backing down. I *will* have Kenz."

"I'm not something to own," I whispered.

Grisham gave me an indulgent smile. "Everyone is something to own. Even me. And don't mistake me, you will have me as well. If I wanted a slave, I could have that. Instead, I've given you time to get to know me, to realize we're meant to be. My patience has limits, however. I suggest you do not push me to that point." His threat sent a shiver through me.

"This isn't over," Hayden said.

"Of course it isn't. However, I will admit, this is the most fun I've had in a while. Jobs are too easy anymore, no challenge, no real risk, nothing to make them interesting. At least this has become interesting. So go on, and think carefully, Kenz. The longer you draw this out, the riskier it gets. I don't care who dies, who suffers as we drag this you, but I have a feeling *you* do."

I swallowed hard, my throat tight and dry. So many faces flashed through my mind, all the people who might pay the price for this, not the least of which were the men I loved.

Was I really worth risking so many people?

* * * *

Char

I rubbed my eyes, exhausted after all the hours I'd spent on the phone and staring at the bright screen of my laptop.

I was used to research — it was a necessary evil in my line of work — but I wasn't sure it had ever mattered quite this much, that I'd ever done it with so much focus.

A water landed in my lap, and I groaned when it smacked me in the groin. A glance up showed Vance without an ounce of regret.

Instead of snapping at him — he'd only enjoy annoying me, after all — I gave him my best fake smile. "Thanks."

"Anytime." He twisted the lid off his own and tipped it back, gulping it down.

Despite the sun having set a little while before, the heat hadn't let up. Sweat had soaked into the back of my shirt, and when I moved my hair from my face, I found droplets on my forehead. The cold water was a welcome treat, though I could have done without the crotch-shot.

"Anything new?" Vance asked.

"Just a lot of bad," I admitted. "Even if there was a doubt before, there isn't now. Grisham is Lorien."

"How did he land a job at a college? That's a hard background to fake."

"Looks like his mother and father made sure he was never connected to them by anything official. So, officially, from birth, he's been Grisham. He went to college under that name, got his degree in Fine Arts and the History of Art. If you follow his official name, he's lived a perfectly normal life."

"Why would they do that?"

"It's not that uncommon, especially for second kids. It lets them hide an heir," I explained. "If no one knows who he is, no one can target him."

"But with his brother and father gone, he's set to take over, so why keep hiding him?"

"I get the feeling he likes it, that he wants his other life more than he wants to lead. In fact, I think the only reason he's taken an interest in his family business at all is so they don't stop him. I doubt he wants to run it."

Someone sat beside me, and I fought the urge to jump.

Damn Tor, the sneaky bastard. I wondered at times if he just enjoyed freaking people out by sneaking up on them. It was like a reminder that if he wanted to slit my throat, he could.

He set a hand behind him and leaned back, his gaze going up to the dark sky. After hearing his voice the other day, it still echoed in my head. It was quiet, but it was there.

Given I lived my life by talking, by twisting facts and people into useful forms, by twisting *myself* into whatever I had to be, his silence always unnerved me a bit. Yet, there was something oddly comforting in that quiet, as though I didn't have to be on during that time.

"Water?" Hayden huffed softly as he shut the slider behind him. "I figured tonight would be a night for alcohol." Even as he made the joke, however, he held water as well.

I suspected none of us wanted to let our guard down, not tonight, not now that we realized just how close the danger to Kenz really stood.

Instead of Lorien being some faceless voice over a phone, a name without form, we'd discovered he was closer than we'd ever thought. The idea that Kenz had met with him right under our noses, that we'd never even thought to suspect him, ate at me.

I was supposed to read people well, to know when they lied, and yet I hadn't even considered he could be the one we searched for.

"How's Kenz?" Vance asked Hayden.

Hayden pulled a chair over from the seating area and sat in it. "She's okay. She showered, barely ate, but she's sleeping now. Hopefully a full eight hours will help her feel more ready to deal with this tomorrow."

"What's there to deal with?" I muttered. At their looks, I let out a rough breath. "He's got us, doesn't he? He knows that we can't move against him, not as long as he threatens Kenz. We're stuck."

"He can't move, either," Hayden pointed out. "Now that we know who he really is, he can't attack her directly or we tear apart his life."

My phone buzzed, and just like Hayden and Vance, I pulled it out to peer at the screen. *Even if we don't have proof to turn him over to the authorities, we know plenty of enemies of his who would love to get his real name.*

"That doesn't help," I snapped. "It means we're both stuck right here, at a place we can't stay. Kenz is still in the middle, and no one can move, can do anything. We can't get our revenge, he can't get Kenz, so what? We just stay like this until we die?" I carded my fingers through my hair, pushing it out of my face so roughly that I accidentally yanked at least a strand or two.

I made my life by reading others, by tricking them, by creating plans that got me what I wanted, but I couldn't figure out a plan right now.

I couldn't see a way forward, a path to what we wanted most. Each time I went down another rabbit hole, each time I explored some new method, it led to the same.

Kenz paying the price for our revenge.

I rubbed my palm over my face as I let out a humorless laugh.

"What's so funny?" Hayden asked.

"I was thinking about that first night Kenz got here. Remember how scared she was? I took one look at her and was ready to do whatever it took to get what we wanted. The idea of using her didn't bother me at all, and if she got hurt because of it?" I shrugged. "Funny how that changed, how now the idea of her left holding the bag just isn't acceptable."

"I know what you mean," Vance said. "I've spent five years wanting nothing more than revenge. I wanted to make Lorien pay for what he'd done, and each time I saw my mangled hand, it only made me more desperate for that. Now?" He shook his head. "I go days without thinking much about it. Even when I look at that hand, I don't feel the same hatred I did before. Hell, sometimes I wonder if I couldn't just walk away from it all, if I couldn't move on."

I nearly scoffed and said there was no way that was possible.

However, I couldn't quite get that out.

I used to see my wife's smiling face in my dreams. I used to dream of her almost every night, waking up panting, having to remind myself she was gone. The anger and sorrow that would overcome me at times like those had only been soothed by my thoughts of revenge.

However, those dreams had slowly been replaced by something else, something calmer. I'd started to dream about Kenz, to see her sweet face, to hear her laugh in my mind, to think of her. Worse, a part of me even had fantasized about a future, about what could occur in the future with her.

It wasn't that I'd forgotten my wife so much as Kenz had built a foundation beneath me, had allowed me to stand instead of drown, and I wasn't sure what that meant.

"It doesn't matter if we'd be willing to give up our revenge," Hayden pointed out, his voice soft. "Lorien wants her, and he's willing to get her killed if he can't have her. Even if we were willing to walk away from this all, we can't. We started on this path and the only way Kenz can be safe anymore will be to deal with Lorien and the threat he poses."

Nice idea, but we still don't know how to do that, Tor wrote.

"I have an idea," Vance said.

I lifted an eyebrow in his direction. Of all the people who might have an idea on what to do, I sure would have placed Vance last. He was smart, of course, and his network of information was impressive. His connections due to his art and family meant if we needed to know someone, if we needed to get close to someone, he could manage it. Still, he'd never been the type to plot much, especially when it came to situations like this. "Oh yeah?" I asked, not expecting much.

He snorted softly, the sound implying he could guess my line of thought. "Yeah. Why does Lorien's threat matter?"

"Because of Kenz," I said.

Vance shook his head. "No. I mean why specifically does it matter if he threatens Kenz?"

Because he can carry it out, Tor wrote.

"That's right. See, Lorien has the backing to do what he says. Grisham doesn't have much power, but Lorien does, and he has that because of his family. He's dangerous as an individual, sure, but he's only dangerous the way a man is. It's his family that gives him the power to threaten Kenz, though. His leverage is there because of his mother, because she'll follow through on his wishes if something happens to him."

It hit me then, and I cursed at myself for not having thought about that before. Worse, the fact that Vance had beat me to such an obvious solution bothered me. "The way to deal with an enemy is to cut off their resources."

Vance nodded. "That's right. If we can strain that relationship, if we can sow doubt between them, it lessens his ability to carry out his threat."

"She's his mother," Hayden said. "Mothers don't just abandon their kids, no matter how terrible those kids are."

"Are you sure about that?" Vance asked. "Because as someone who constantly gets threatened to be disowned, I can assure you that parents aren't quite as perfect as we like to pretend. Besides, we don't need her to throw him to the wolves, exactly, just to withdraw her support of him. Without her backing, his threats mean nothing. He's made his life on his own, worked on his own, only using her connections, so without her, he's got no one to help him carry out his plan. If we want to take him out and not risk Kenz, we've got to split him from his mother."

I thought about it, trying to come up with a reason why it wouldn't work, but I couldn't come up with anything. It wasn't that it would be easy, of course, but it was something.

It was a hell of a lot more than we'd had before, at least.

I glanced up at the house, toward Kenz's dark window. She'd been the key to finding him, to get this far, but at the same time, she was the thing standing in the way of ending it quickly.

And for the first time, I wished we could all just walk away, could forget this all, but a tightness in my chest assured me it wasn't possible.

Maybe this was all my punishment for wanting things I didn't deserve. I might not get what I wanted, but I'd do whatever it took to make sure Kenz could have what she wanted.

She deserved at least that much.

Chapter Two

Kenz

The most amazing thing about humans was how quickly we bounced back, how fast we moved from fear or grief or confusion to our own sense of normalcy.

I'd felt that after the death of my mother, when within a week, I sat at a table, eating dinner and talking about my day like that hadn't happened. I found the same thing now, when after discovering that Grisham was Lorien, when figuring out just how trapped I was, I tended to the flowers as though nothing had changed.

I dragged my arm across my head, wiping away the sweat.

My trips to the school had been put on hold. I hated that, but I couldn't really argue with it, either. Now that we realized how much power Lorien wielded, that the school was really his territory, going there wasn't a great idea.

Plus, I had no desire to see him. I'd ignored his call the night before, unable to even consider hearing his voice—his real voice, because there would be no reason to hide it anymore.

He'd sent a text, telling me he understood and would give me time to come to terms with the truth. He'd told me goodnight, and the words had blurred as tears had threatened to fall.

It felt like since that auction, the noose around my neck had tightened with each passing day. No matter what I did, my options only disappeared, and I had a feeling that anything I did only pushed me closer to the point where I could no longer move, no longer breathe.

Lorien's words played in my head—not so much about my future, but about Nem.

She'd risked everything for me—I could do no less for her.

What if I went through with what I'd thought about before? I'd tried to turn myself over to Lorien once before, but the men had stopped me, had told me not to do that, and I'd listened.

Weak, as always.

"Don't you dare." Hayden's rough voice made me look up to find him standing beside me, his expression tense. "I know that look on your face, now. You're thinking about doing something stupid like turning yourself over to Lorien again."

Maybe the smartest idea was to lie, but I didn't have the strength. "It'd solve everything, wouldn't it? You all could have your own lives again and Nem wouldn't be targeted. I could do my part, and everyone I care about would be safe."

Hayden sat on the edge of the flowerbed beside me. "You always talk about how we don't value our lives, but neither do you."

"You're wrong."

"Then why are you always trying to give yourself up? Why do you think you're worth so much less?"

I sighed and leaned forward. "You don't get it. I value life so much, and I don't want to die, to give up my freedom, but I know it's the only choice I have. If I were someone else, if I were Nem or the Quad or Jarrod, I could *do* something. I could fight, could protect everyone I love, but I'm not strong enough for that. This is all I'm capable of, the only thing I can do to protect those around me."

As I said that, the crushing reality of it hit me. It forced more words from my lips. "I *hate* that I'm not strong, that I'm not like everyone else. Nem went through what I did—she was almost killed by our father, but she grew stronger. She came back a force of nature, unwilling to let anything stand in her way. If I were her, I could take on Lorien myself, could do whatever it took to remove him. I'm *not* her, though. Despite growing up around so many amazing people—I don't measure up."

Hayden said nothing at first, and I couldn't stop the heavy sigh that escaped me. What had I hoped for? That somehow, he'd take away the doubt that had plagued me my entire life? That he'd magically know what to say and I wouldn't feel the way I felt?

If it had been that easy, wouldn't I have rid myself of this upset long ago?

"You really don't see it?" he asked.

I twisted to peer at him, his brows knitted together and his gaze down on the dirt before us.

"You're right that you aren't your sister, that you aren't any of those other men you know, that you aren't even like us. We all went through tragedy and came out the other side vicious, jaded, *angry*. We all traded any softness we ever had for something darker, something uglier. When Nem was almost killed, those broken parts inside her, she sharpened to lethal points. You didn't do that."

"Because I'm weak," I whispered.

"No, because you're *strong*. Stronger than the rest of us. When life shattered you, you dulled those edges so you wouldn't cut others with them. You kept that sweetness of yours, no matter how hard the world tried to drive it out of you. Instead of lashing out at others, you keep putting yourself out there, keep risking yourself for others even when they've given you no good reason to. Even now, instead of focusing on revenge, you're willing to give yourself up just to try to ease the burden of the people around you. If that isn't strength…"

Hayden sighed softly. "I spent most of my life protecting others, but when things got hard, when things went wrong, I lost a part of myself. I lost that desire to protect and the person I saw in the mirror didn't feel like me anymore. Don't ever mistake kindness for weakness. It's a lot harder to be kind than it is to be vicious."

He offered those words up like they were obvious and easy, as though I should have known them already. It was strange, because they were exactly what I'd wanted to hear without even realizing it.

I thought about Nem, about Jarrod, about the Quad. They'd all pursued revenge the moment they could, willing to kill and hurt anything in their way to get what they wanted. They took life without a second thought, and I'd grown up believing that was what it meant to be strong.

But maybe I was wrong about that? Maybe I'd mistaken that?

It felt too convenient, like the answer I'd wanted to hear all along. Sometimes what we really wanted wasn't the truth though—it was just easy.

Fingers touched my chin, and Hayden turned my face toward him. He'd pulled his lips into the smile that always made my heart beat a bit faster, and now was no exception.

He ran his thumb along my cheek. "You've got dirt on your face."

"Gardening isn't for the weak," I said with a laugh.

Except, he didn't pull back. He didn't remove his fingers from my chin, and after clearing away the smudge, he moved his pointer finger over my bottom lip as though memorizing the texture, the way it gave beneath the gentle pressure.

I knew what he was thinking. It didn't take experience to guess, not when he stared at my lips as he touched me like that. I recalled my kiss with Vance, the fact that I'd crossed that line already.

I've crossed a lot more lines than that.

And I didn't know how else to thank him for what he'd said, for offering me a ladder when I'd been so deep into the pit of self-loathing that I could no longer see the sun.

No, that's not it. Saying what I wanted was due to gratitude ignored all the reasons I really wanted it. It made it about him, made it not about my own desire, and that was cowardly.

So I leaned in, closing my eyes, wondering if he'd stop me.

To my amazement, he didn't. He moved his finger from my lip but kept his grip on my chin. The press of his lips to mine made me melt more than the hot sun or humidity. He was gentle, careful, treating me as though

I were precious. He tilted his head, then used the grip on my chin to tilt mine the opposite way.

His breath tasted of mint, as though he'd had one just earlier, and it almost made me laugh to think he'd done that for me. Or, rather, it might have made me laugh if he didn't part his lips slightly and suck softly at my bottom lip, the sensation drawing a moan from me.

Vance had kissed me so suddenly — both times — that I hadn't really gotten the chance to enjoy it, to savor it. It had been over so fast that he'd left me with a slight tingle and bewilderment about what had just happened.

Hayden did the opposite, his kiss like a light in the distance that drew me deeper and deeper into a dark forest. Yet, I chased his light happily, content to follow him anywhere so long as he kept doing *that*.

I curled my fingers in the front of his shirt, trying to get closer, to feel more of him. He clouded my mind and my rational thoughts, making it so I couldn't think about anything except this. How was it that just a kiss could turn me so mindless?

Because it's him.

He broke the kiss, teasing my bottom lip with his tongue before whispering, "Promise me, Kenz, that you won't do anything foolish."

I opened my eyes, finding him embarrassingly close, his words a rude wake-up call in the middle of the passion.

"Even if you gave yourself up, we wouldn't stop, we wouldn't give up. We wouldn't just let him have you, so doing it would really just put us in more danger."

"I lived my whole life until a year ago expecting to just become the trophy wife of some man. I never wanted that future, never would have been okay with it, but for you?" I licked his bottom lip, finding the warm skin damp from our kiss. "I think for you it'd be worth it. It was the future I expected all along, but for the first time, it'd be worth it. I'd accept it happily if it meant you all could move on, could have the futures you deserve."

He blew out a long breath, as though my words exhausted him. "Any future where you're suffering isn't one I want or could tolerate. Trust me — trust *us* — we've got an idea." He pulled back, turning his gaze from mine.

It didn't feel like a rejection, though, and having his eyes off me helped my mind sputter back to life again. Without him staring at me, I could think again.

"Promise me that you won't do anything rash," he pressed.

"I can't promise I won't do what I think is best. If I don't see another way, if I feel like it's the only option, I'll do whatever I have to to protect the people I love."

"And you're still saying that's us?"

I linked my arm with his and rested my head against his shoulder. "No matter how confusing or difficult life gets, no matter how many questions I have or how little I understand or am sure about anything, I know that much at least."

* * * *

Lorien

I tried to breathe slowly, to not let the frustration boiling inside me show on my face. The control I had over my emotions had always been one of my biggest strengths, after all. People who allowed their feelings to rule them made mistakes, allowed others to take control.

I would not be a slave to anything—least of all my own emotions.

"Enter," came a familiar voice through the door after I knocked.

I turned the handle, then walked into the large office to find my mother seated at her desk.

She was lovely, at least for a woman of her age. Her hair had started to gray at thirty, so now at sixty, the salt and pepper tones had spread so not a strand of the old black remained. She somehow didn't appear frail, as so many people her age did, but rather had a sharpness in her gaze that made others take notice.

She wore a loose black dress that hung to the floor, having passed the age where she attempted to show off her body.

Those serious eyes of hers softened however when they rested on me. "Lorien," she said, a fondness to her tone reserved for her children.

"You called me, Mother?"

Uncertainty danced in those eyes at my use of mother. How many times had she asked me to call her Mom?

As many times as I ignored the request.

Who could blame me, though? I'd been raised only seeing her from time to time, forced to grow up with relatives to ensure I remained a secret. I was the spare, the extra kept hidden in case anything happened to my brother.

Then I thought about my father and my brother, at the way the light had gone out of their eyes, at the look of surprise when they'd realized I was behind it.

How could they be surprised, though? After all they'd done, after they'd barred the doors of this family against me, how could they not expect me to do something? To react? To break down those barriers?

Because they were weak fools.

And now running the family fell to my mother. She did well, something I would never have expected. When I'd killed the male heirs, I'd expected the entire family to fall into disarray. I'd thought that other families would rise up and attack, and that my mother would be unable to hold it together.

Ten years down the line, however, she had not only held on to our power but increased it.

Pauline Hatchet was not a woman to be underestimated. If I had any ties to family, any sense of accomplishment due to those I shared blood with, I might have felt a certain pride from that.

As it was, however, I felt nothing but reassurance that I still had the benefits of her position.

She rose from her desk and went to the large antique couch against the wall then patted the spot beside her. I did as she requested but kept a good distance between us.

"How long will this go on?" she asked.

I could have pretended not to know what she meant, but how would that serve me? "Not much longer now."

Even if I didn't know how it would end, I still held a confidence that it *would* end, and soon. There was a tension that occurred with anything important. It was like pulling a rubber band, stretching it bit by bit while feeling the way the material reached its limit.

That was the feeling I got, that all of us involved were approaching our limit.

One way or another, that band would snap and things would settle. Who would survive it, who would get what they wanted, that I didn't know.

Which excited me more than it should have.

"You need to come home," she said.

"This isn't home."

"Of course it is. You are *my* son, so this has always been your home."

I thought back to all the years I'd spent by myself, when she'd come to visit me in secret. I'd known she was my mother even if I'd had to keep it quiet.

Being a child who was forced to face his mother but pretend she was nothing more than an aunt — that was a weight no kid should have to carry.

"You've run this family fine. You don't need me."

"Of course I do. I don't know how many years I have left, and I have to know that this family is left in good hands."

"So find a successor, but it isn't me. What about one of your daughters?"

"I have run this family in my husband's name only because the men already knew me. Do you really think they'd accept a woman as the new head? Your sisters wouldn't be able to hold it together."

Sisters.

The two girls were younger than me, the results of her husband insisting on more kids no matter my mother's feelings. I'd met them, of course, but I hardly considered them sisters.

Family was a foreign concept to me, something not tangible, something too elusive to understand. I'd never had it, so it meant little to me.

However, my mother didn't agree, and she constantly attempted to turn us into some picture-perfect fantasy of family.

"There are women who run families," I pointed out, my thoughts moving to Nemesis, the red-haired vixen who controlled most of the west coast.

And Nem's sister.

She was nothing if not proof that women could be every bit as dangerous as their male counterparts.

"There are," my mother agreed, "but they are rare. I have allowed you freedom to do as you want, to behave as you wish, to sow your oats and feel as though you had time to yourself. However, things need to change."

"Why?"

"Because my health is failing, Lorien. I need to know that I leave things in good hands, that I can rest easy. That is why I've helped you with Mackenzie, because she is the steadying force you need to take over. With her by your side, you have the backing to take over."

I pulled in a slow breath, then released it, using it to center myself. I knew well that the reason my mother hadn't objected to my *little obsession,* as she liked to call it, was because of Kenz's true parentage. With her by my side, even my history as second son would hardly matter. I could step into her position, and no one would raise a word against me.

I didn't care for feeling as though others planned my life, however.

"You rarely take this long to complete anything," she pressed. "Normally, anything you put your mind to is done in a matter of days, yet this drags on. We have spent so much money and yet you seem no closer to a resolution than you were at the start."

"I am closer," I argued, hating how it made me feel like a teenager whose mother scolded him. "However, if I simply take her, she will never truly relent. She'll fight me, forever, and that would serve no one."

"And you think you'll win her like this? That you'll eventually wear her down?"

"That's how people are."

She shook her head as though pitying me. "That may be men, but you know little about women. Women

28

do not wear down. We remain quiet, we submit, but we do not forget or forgive."

"If you don't think I can win her over, then why allow me to do this at all?"

"Because her agreement or love isn't needed — only her obedience. I married my husband because it was expected of me, because I needed to. It had nothing to do with what I wanted, with my feelings, and at least he had the decency to know that. He never believed or pretended as though I loved him. That honesty made for a strong union."

I pressed my lips together, an unease creeping into me. Was she right? Was it possible that Kenz would never really accept me? I thought about the times I had seen my mother with her husband, when I'd come with my fake parents, with my mother's sister, me posing as my mother's nephew. They hadn't smiled at each other, hadn't seemed as though they cared for each other in the least.

It had turned my stomach, the game one that I never wished to play.

But what if she were right? What if Kenz never did fall for me?

I shook my head. I couldn't think like that. I'd been born with nothing, not even with my real name, raised by a family who hadn't birthed me, who didn't want me, and forced to watch the place I belonged get along just fine without me.

I'd gotten where I was by sheer determination, by never giving up, by never allowing anything to get the best of me.

So the idea that I might fail here, that I might not obtain the one thing I really wanted — my soulmate — wasn't possible. It wasn't acceptable. I could not even entertain such an idea.

So I shoved it away like a spider that scurried beneath the couch—so long as I couldn't see it, I didn't have to acknowledge or think about it.

"I will win her," I said, infusing as much confidence into the words as possible. I would because I had to, because no other ending was acceptable.

"And if you don't? If this doesn't work? Will you return home and take your spot?"

I nodded. "Yes, I will."

Such a promise was fine because it would not happen.

I would ensure it. Not even Kenz could keep me from what I wanted.

Chapter Three

Kenz

The sight of Vance without his gloves gave me pause when I walked into his room. Even though I knew about his hand, he still hid it from me.

Not just me, of course. He hid from everyone. He wore those gloves and the prosthetic with the same fervor as a girl at the beach in a bikini, as though his modesty demanded it.

Though I knew the truth. It wasn't modesty—it ran so much deeper.

So when I strolled into his room without knocking—I didn't want him to ignore me—and found him with a towel wrapped around his waist and neither his gloves nor his prosthetic on, I went still.

Vance turned toward me, his hand frozen midair, his other on the place where the towel folded over to keep it up. He swallowed hard, then offered me a strained smile. "Were you hoping for a peepshow, Kenz?"

The words were playful, but his tone let me know the truth. It screamed his unease, and the flicker of his blue eyes toward his dresser, where the prosthetic and gloves sat, waiting, said he wanted to retreat, to hide, to wipe away what I'd seen.

If we were playing this game, I could go along with it. "Well, a girl has to do what she's got to do," I answered. "It isn't like you've stripped for me any other time."

"Seems to me you've seen more of me than anyone else," he whispered.

And I knew damn well he didn't mean his body. Countless women had seen that, had touched him, had felt every inch of his body all save for his hand, for the wound there that even five years couldn't heal.

I knew the jealousy I felt was petty and pointless, but I couldn't shake it. Every interview I'd seen, every magazine article, every tabloid cover where Vance had stood there with some beautiful model on his arm came back to me.

Even though that bred insecurity inside me, I couldn't pull back, couldn't look away. His skin was so pale, and it made the blue of his eyes stand out. The black towel wrapped around him made his skin seem even brighter, and my fingers itched to pull at the waist of it, to tug where the fabric was tucked to keep it up.

"It's amazing that a girl as innocent as you could have a look that lewd on your face," Vance said, his right hand lowering as though he'd forgotten about it for a moment. "Of course, given what I heard from Hayden, Tor and Char, I'm not sure innocent is a word I can use for you anymore, can I?"

My cheeks burned, not only at the reminder of what we had done, but the idea that they'd all talked about it, that he knew.

I opened my mouth to explain myself—though what I'd say I didn't know. How did a person admit that they'd done *those* things with other men without making themselves sound like some sort of whore?

He *tsk'd* softly, then walked up to me. Fingers touched my chin, forcing me to look up and into those beautiful blue eyes of his—using his left hand, of course. "You need to work on your poker face. Everything you think gets screamed out through your expression. You think I'm mad about that? I'm a little annoyed I got left out, but that's it."

"How can you not be mad? Most men—"

"I'm not most men. Seems neither are the others, because yeah, we talked about it. Turns out I don't mind you playing with them even a bit, not so long as you keep looking at me with *this* look." He leaned down, but he bypassed my lips to press a kiss to my neck.

At least, that's what I thought it was at first. A sharp sting as he sucked had me arching against his bare form, and I couldn't believe it when even that excited me. He released me with a noisy pop, then dragged his tongue over the sore spot.

His gaze locked onto where he'd sucked just as he smirked. "I don't think I've ever wanted to mark a girl before. In fact, I was always happy if they forgot about me the moment we were done, so leaving them with a memento never even occurred to me. You, though? I like the idea of you wearing my mark as someone else fucks you. I wonder why that is…" He whispered the last part as though he wasn't entirely sure, either.

"Because you're a pervert," I offered.

Vance stepped backward with a soft chuckle. "Well, it's hard to deny that. I think I like pervert better than man-whore."

"You're that, too."

"I used to be that, maybe, but since you've come along?" He shrugged. "I haven't had anyone else, so does that title even fit anymore?"

His words made me pause, looking up and into his eyes to judge if he meant it. I thought back at all the times he'd left, when I'd figured that he'd been out with women.

He sighed as though not surprised by my reaction. "Is it really *that* hard to believe?"

"A little," I admitted. "Where have you gone at night, then?"

"I have a life still, you know? Even if I haven't done any new work in a few years, I still have backlogs of work, exhibits, interviews, meetings with my manager." He frowned. "You really thought I was out with other women?"

"It wouldn't be that big a shock, would it?"

"I guess I deserve that. You were at least my fake girlfriend, though. Would I risk that for a fling?"

"You can be discreet when needed."

"You have too little faith in me. Still, if you thought that, why didn't you push me away more?"

"Because I thought some of your time was better than none of it."

He shook his head. "You don't give yourself enough credit, Kenz. You deserve a hell of a lot more than just a little of someone's time, and if anyone doesn't get that, they don't deserve any of yours."

"Thanks for the pep talk." Unable to help it, my gaze moved down again, drawn by his damp skin, by the way his nipples had tightened after he'd left the heat of the shower, down to the damn towel that kept the rest from me.

"You want to see?" he asked in a whisper. "Well, if you want to see more, you're going to have to make the move." He moved his hands out as though offering me the chance.

And despite my nerves, despite my hesitation, I knew I couldn't resist. Before all my doubts could gain a foothold, my hands moved as though working on their own.

The muscles of his lower stomach twitched beneath the pad of my finger as I traced the line of his towel. He groaned, the sound deep and desperate and lacking any sense of control. It should have made me nervous, having a man so much larger and stronger and hungry making a sound like that, but it didn't.

It made me feel wanted, something I desperately craved.

I tucked my finger beneath the edge of the towel, then pulled to untuck it. The fabric floated away, falling to the ground without Vance attempting to stop it.

Which made me damn jealous of men. Why was it that they didn't have the same hang-ups over nudity as women were trained to have?

Then again, look at him. He has no reason to be uncomfortable.

Every last bit of him was perfect. That *V* of muscles dipped down toward his groin, with light hair trailing from his belly button to his pelvis. It wasn't a lot, not that thick, and against his pale skin it was hard to even notice. His muscles all stood out, as though tensed, and the urge to bite into them took over me.

I wanted to feel them twitch at my touch, to feel as they shifted beneath his flawless skin, to leave marks of my own. I recalled how it had felt when Tor had pushed his cock past my lips, and I wanted the same again. I wanted to lick his hip bones, to wrap my hand around his shaft, to claim all of him in a way that made him feel like mine.

"You expect me to stay unaffected when you look at me like *that*?" Vance said, his voice having dropped lower and deeper. It had lost some of that playful edge to it from before, betraying his true feelings.

And that excited me more than anything else, that he wasn't just playing a game with me, that he seemed as ravenous as I felt.

I placed my palm on his chest, my hand flat and my fingers spread out. His heart beat hard and fast, and it drew me closer. I leaned against him, the feeling of him naked while I was dressed odd. It seemed like a reversal from usual, when I always felt as though I were in an inferior position.

"What's got you so worried?" Vance asked, trailing his fingers against my side, slipping them beneath the fabric of my top to touch my heated skin directly.

"I feel like I'm in control because you're naked and I'm not," I admitted.

"Doesn't that excite you? The idea that you could do *anything* to me?" He pressed in closer to me, his cock grinding against my stomach.

I shook my head. "It makes me feel anxious. I don't know what I'm doing, and I don't know what I'm supposed to do and—"

He silenced me with a kiss, bending down to capture my lips and stop my tailspin. He wiped those worries away, this kiss deeper and more passionate than our last one. "You know just want to say," he whispered between those kisses, "to drive me crazy, don't you? You don't even do it on purpose. You just can't help it, I think." He twisted us, then walked me backward.

I went happily, drugged by his touch and the promise of his voice. My calves touched something a moment before I fell backward. I grasped at Vance, afraid to hit the ground, but I hadn't needed to worry. My butt hit the bed as I sat.

It made me look up at Vance—especially because I didn't want to just stare at his crotch.

Or, maybe the better way to say that was that I didn't want to get caught ogling his cock like a cat in heat. I wanted to look, but I didn't need him to know that.

He ran his thumb over my bottom lip and it had me guessing what he wanted. I reached forward to wrap my fingers around his shaft, to take him past my lips. That's what *all* men wanted, wasn't it?

And I don't mind it one little bit…

Except, he stopped me. He shifted his hips back slightly, out of my reach, his lips twisted into a smirk. "Not so fast there, sweetheart."

"But I thought—"

"Don't think. You didn't want to be in charge, right? So just listen to me and do as I say."

Someone telling me that at any other time would have set me off. It would have woken all those fears I had about having to be a good girl, about others controlling me, but somehow having a naked man telling me what to do was exactly what I liked.

So I found myself nodding, giving myself over to him, refusing to worry or think too deeply about anything.

"Good girl." He bent forward, but instead of a kiss, he traced my bottom lip with his tongue. It left a tingling sensation behind, one that made me part my lips and breathe in sharply.

Vance set his hands on my knees, through the loose fabric of my skirt, and spread my thighs. He dropped down to kneel there, seeming to take no notice of his own lack of clothing.

He touched the back of my ankles, then shifted his left hand up, over my calves, lifting the fabric of my skirt as he went. When he reached my knee, however, he didn't move it up anymore. Instead, he touched my thigh beneath the skirt, the sensation more teasing than if he'd exposed me entirely.

It felt naughtier, like we were doing something more taboo, as he shifted his fingers from the outside of my legs to my sensitive inner thighs.

The use of one hand occurred to me, just for a moment. However, his touch was so hot, I couldn't hold on to that worry for long. He used his shoulder on one side and his hand on the other to spread my thighs wider, then dipped down, moving beneath my skirt.

It meant the fabric covered his head, the sight so alluring I moaned softly before slapping my hand over my mouth to silence it.

His chuckle said I hadn't done a good job.

I held my breath, waiting, until warm hair brushed across my cunt through my panties. *His breath?* I didn't have time to think about it before something warm and wet moved up the crotch of my panties, pressing the fabric in slightly. Even I knew what that had to be, and I struggled between excitement, embarrassment and disappointment.

I enjoyed the sensation of his tongue against me, but I wished I could see him. I wanted to watch as that pink, talented tongue of his moved against me, to see the lust in his blue eyes, yet the movement of my skirt as he was beneath it turned me on, too.

He moved his hand up my thigh, to my hip, and grasped the waist of my panties. A soft tug had me lifting my hips to let him slide the underwear down. He moved back enough to pull them off entirely.

"I like this," he admitted, his voice strange since I couldn't see him. Worse, each word he said blew another stream of warm air against my pussy, making me crave more. "I like to touch you beneath your skirt. It makes me think about doing this in a room full of people, maybe when I slip beneath the table at a restaurant. Your thighs quiver and shake as you want more, your hips thrusting forward just a bit, like you're wet little pussy is begging me." Something solid ran up my folds, pausing just before he stroked against my clit. "Do you want more, sweetheart?" His lips pressed against my inner thigh, his teasing words making me desperate.

"Yes," I whispered back, not giving a damn about my pride. "I want more."

He chuckled. "What a good girl. Then lie back because once I get my mouth on you for real, I'm not going to let you go until you're *crying* for me to stop."

And that sounded like a good damn idea to me.

Vance

I breathed Kenz in, drowning in her sweet, feminine scent. It felt like forever that I'd fantasized about this, that I'd wanted to touch her so intimately, that I wanted to see all the parts of her that she hid from others. I wanted to lose myself in her and let it make me feel as though I was normal, that things between us were normal.

They weren't, but I'd let this fantasy hold me a little while, at least.

I kept my right hand on my own thigh, ignoring the missing fingers, the way even I couldn't quite stomach the touch of it. If I thought about that too much, I'd lose this moment, and nothing was worth that.

So instead, I pressed a line of kisses against her trembling thighs, up toward her cunt. The skirt blocked out the light—I did wish I had her naked and spread out before me, a feast for the eyes—but the added fun of doing this blind was worth it.

She'd leaned back, and if I could see her, I'd bet she looked like a virgin sacrifice on an altar, just waiting for a beast to devour her.

And I plan on being that beast.

I ran my tongue through her folds, careful not to press too hard, not to go too deep. She'd never done this before, so the last thing I wanted was for her to freak out, to startle her. I didn't deal much with virgins—I preferred not being remembered and most people remembered their first time—but that didn't mean I couldn't figure it out.

Slow and careful, that's what she needed.

At least, that's what I thought before I felt her clutching hand on the back of my head, pushing me closer, urging me to get with it.

I don't mind following that order at all.

I laughed softly at her eagerness, then ran the flat of my tongue directly against her clit. The noise she let out went straight to my aching cock, as though it were some mating call and I were helpless to resist. Hell, I'd bet if I slid up her body, wrapped her legs around my waist, I could plunge my cock into her waiting cunt and she'd only hold me tighter, demand more.

Go slow, you asshole!

I shook the thought away, focusing my attention on her hard little clit. At the same time, I brought my left hand up and pressed two of my fingers into her. She was hot and wet and tight, but her body gave so easily, surrendering to me. The walls of her pussy clutched at my finger, gripping it as though she didn't want it to escape.

"Vance," she moaned, the name quiet and breathy. No doubt she kept her voice down out of embarrassment, not wanting to risk anyone else overhearing.

Which was incredibly adorable. It made me want to break that fear, to shatter whatever resistance or restraint she held on to. I wanted her so mindless with want and pleasure that she screamed, not caring who could hear it, who else was around.

Which was a strange thought, given I never before cared about a claim, cared about anyone else beyond myself and the moment.

I shoved the thought away and wrapped my right hand around my hard dick, too turned on to care that it was my mangled hand. I pictured that it was my cock inside of her instead of my fingers, matching the timing of my hand on my shaft along with how I fucked her. Even during that, my tongue never let up on her clit. Even when she shifted her hips, when she seemed torn between evading my touch and demanding more of it, I never let off.

The need to shatter her was too strong, like an instinct drawn forth by her scent, by the noises she made.

I added a third finger, and she hissed as though the thickness stung. Even still, she thrust her hips toward me, telling me she wanted it. I happily gave it all to her, tormenting her clit, fucking her as deep as I could with my fingers, held in place by her hand as I stroked my own cock.

She cried out when she came, the sound so musical and filthy that I couldn't help myself from toppling right over with her. My cock jerked as I spilled on the floor between my thighs, my lips nursing at her clit with gentle kisses.

She panted hard and loud, then went to sit up as though we'd finished. I chuckled at the thought.

"Oh, sweetheart, you better buckle in. We're not anywhere *close* to done."

"What?" The question came out confused and more than a little turned on, which was all I needed to hear.

"I told you I wouldn't let you go so quickly, didn't I? So be a good girl and let me devour you."

"But I already…"

"And you will again and again and again." I proved my words by dragging my eager tongue along her clit, rewarded by her jumping.

Ah, they're so pretty when they're this sensitive. I had a feeling I was going nowhere for the rest of the night.

Chapter Four

Kenz

I covered my mouth as I yawned, the action so large that my jaw ached at the end of it.

"You look like a fish when you do that," Char whispered to me. "Did you not sleep well?"

His question brought up exactly *why* I was so tired, and remembering the way Vance had kept me up late the night before had my cheeks burning.

Please, don't let Char notice.

Except, he let out a dark chuckle that said he had a pretty damn good idea what exactly had kept me awake until the early morning hours. Actually, come to think about it, I wasn't sure when I'd actually gotten to sleep.

At some point, I'd just passed out, unable to handle another orgasm crashing through me. When Vance had said I'd beg for him to stop, he hadn't been joking. My entire body ached when I'd woken this morning, as though I'd done a million crunches the day before and my muscles needed rest.

However, rest wasn't in my future, it seemed, since Char needed my help on a job.

"I thought you said they'd be here at nine," I complained before taking a sip of the unsweetened iced tea that I'd ordered at the trendy little shop. The place sold all vegan items, and even Char had struggled to keep a straight face when he'd spotted a sandwich piled high with green alfalfa sprouts, avocado and no meat or dairy of any sort.

"They come here after a yoga class. Sometimes the class runs long. Drink your tea and behave yourself."

I rolled my eyes and looked around the shop, at the women who all carried expensive bags that shops kept behind locked glass cases normally. They laughed with one another, eating weird raw foods that I didn't recognize.

What would it feel like to be that carefree? To just go to places like this without a single worry?

It was strange, but ultimately a worthless thought since I didn't think I could ever have that. Even if I kept my false name, even if I got out of this mess with Lorien, I always had to keep watch over my own shoulder, worry that someone figured out who I was, that someone would try to use that against me.

At least Char found me helpful, though. When I'd asked why he needed me, he'd explained that this wasn't the sort of place men could go on their own. They tended to stick out, which was the last thing Char wanted.

Just then, the bell above the door rang as two women walked in—the ones we were waiting for.

Rachel and Dilaura Hatchet, the only two surviving siblings of Lorien. Despite being siblings, they really didn't look much like him. They smiled together, yoga mats hung over their shoulders from straps, wearing trendy and expensive workout clothing that didn't look as though they'd ever sweated in them before.

The sight of them took me back for a moment, because they were just like me. Daughters of a crime family, girls born into a world that didn't respect them beyond their ability to create heirs for men in power. They didn't look all that bothered by their position, of course, but I hadn't either before I'd known better.

Anything can be accepted if someone doesn't know they have other options.

The girls went to the counter, but the woman working in the back had already started their drinks. As usual, Char's information proved flawless, the action showing they came here often.

After they paid, they turned toward us, where the seating area was. When they neared, I played my part.

"Excuse me," I asked with my friendliest smile. At least this was a part easy for me to play. If Char had wanted me to be some badass, I'd have struggled far more.

Rachel, the older sister, paused and looked at me. Her expression remained guarded for a moment as her gaze moved over me, slowly, taking in all the details.

Which even I knew we'd nailed. I wore a trendy name brand dress, had a purse on the table worth five grand, and had forced my feet into heels that had cost nearly a thousand. Between that and flawless makeup—even I could do that much on my own—I looked exactly like they did.

Rich.

Rachel smiled back, telling me I'd passed. "Yes?"

"Did you just come from yoga?" When her gaze sharpened, I let out a soft laugh. "I just moved here and I'm *dying* to get back to my yoga practice, but I just can't find the right place. You look like you probably know the best places to go to, so I was hoping you could give me some help."

After a short pause, Rachel's smile returned. She pulled a seat out across from me and sat in it, her sister following suit. "How can I say no to a fellow practitioner in need? My name is Rachel, and this is my sister, Dilaura."

"I'm Emily," I offered up, the fake name sliding from my lips with ease. Using fake names wasn't new to me, so they were one of the few lies I could tell without problems. "And this is my brother, Trent."

Char flashed that dazzling smile he had, the one that could melt even me. Even if I knew it was fake, that it meant nothing, it still could make my heart beat faster.

Especially because he never looked at *me* like that.

"It's nice to see girls who take good care of themselves," he said. "We came from California, and girls there are something else. I was afraid I'd miss out on seeing bodies like that anymore. Thank you for proving me wrong."

Wow. If I heard a line like that, I hated to admit that it would probably have worked for me. I'd have fallen for it, especially because Char had this way of looking at a person, at smiling at them as though they were the only things that existed in the entire world.

And this burning feeling in the pit of my stomach started, growing with each word he said, each flirty look.

Was this jealousy?

When Char reached over and took Rachel's hand in his, turning it over to peer at her nails, the touch so casual, his thumb stroking against her soft skin, I swallowed hard.

Yep, that's jealousy.

Char

Rachel and Dilaura were the sort of women who made me want to curl my lip in disgust. Between the clothing they wore, the way they judged every person who walked into the shop, they carried every red flag I knew of.

Of course, they were also the type that were so easy to fool. They fell for tricks happily, because they were so sure they were wonderful that they adored being told so.

Which was why it took only a few minutes to have both women eating out of my hand.

"You two don't look anything alike," Rachel said as she looked between Kenz and me.

Which was fair. No one would think we shared blood, after all.

"Step-siblings," I said. "My mom married her dad. It gave me an adorable little sister to look after."

"You are such a good brother," Rachel said. "I wish I had a brother like you."

"Do you have any brothers?" I asked.

Her smile fell. "Not any really, not anymore. I had an older brother but he died a while ago. Even my dad died, actually. I have another brother, but he wasn't raised with us, and he doesn't come around much."

A part of me that should have shamed me immediately latched onto that detail. I was great at pinpointing a person's weaknesses, at seeing what they wanted, what they needed and how to convince them that I could give that to them. It meant as soon as I heard that yearning in her voice, the quiet words, I knew this was a girl looking for a male influence in her life.

Which worked fine for me. I could offer that to her, and she'd give me anything I wanted for just the chance.

"I'm sorry to hear that." I set my hand on top of hers, offering her a smile that promised support and affection—just what she craved.

"How can you be so nice?" she asked.

"What can I say? I just can't stand to see a pretty girl sad."

Kenz stood, her chair scraping the ground against the floor. "I'm going to get another tea," she said.

Rachel gave her sister a sharp, telling look, and Dilaura rose as well. "I want a scone, too." She left, following Kenz and leaving Rachel and I alone.

Rachel really is good at manipulating those around her, isn't she? She didn't seem to do it as purposely as I did, but that didn't change her talent for it.

"I think I'd like to see you again," Rachel said.

"I'd like that, too."

She smiled shyly, though I easily saw through that little trick. She thought that by looking cute and innocent, she'd get away with more. It was a stark difference from Kenz, who constantly looked innocent and cute when trying hard to be taken seriously.

"Let me see your phone. I'll put my number in." I held my hand out to her.

She didn't so much as hesitate before handing it over to me. I opened her contacts and put in my number, taking the chance to take a quick glance at her recent calls. I memorized the number listed under *"mother,"* then gave it back.

"Make sure you call me," I told her.

"I will, absolutely." She stood, then glanced around for her sister. "We should get going, though. My mom's a worrier, and if we don't get back soon, she'll end up sending someone looking."

"No problem at all." I rose as well, then stuck my hand out for a handshake.

She set her hand in mine, and I pulled her closer. I pressed a kiss to her cheek, rewarded by her pulling in a startled breath. Her being uneasy was perfect, and I used that moment to slip the tiny tracker into her purse. Even if she found it later, it looked like a small pebble, something she'd not think twice about.

Rachel pulled back, a flush on her cheeks. She said her goodbyes before collecting her sister from where the other girl spoke with Kenz.

Kenz came back over to me, a new tea in her hand. She didn't look at me, and I got the sense she was upset.

Why, though?

Despite my ability to read people, somehow Kenz could confuse me. Maybe that was because I wasn't sure what to do or think around her, because she threw my skills off.

"You ready to go?" I asked.

She nodded, but still avoided my gaze.

I don't like this one bit.

As it turned out, things didn't get any better as the day went on. I drove us back to the house, but Kenz immediately turned to cleaning pretty much the moment we stepped foot inside.

I might be an idiot some of the time, but Hayden would have recognized that as a bad sign. Cleaning calmed her, so what exactly had worked her up?

Had Dilaura said something to her? Had she been upset about not being able to plant a tracker on the other woman? Sure, we'd asked her to if she could, but that didn't mean I'd be mad that she didn't.

"It's fine," I told her as she wiped a rag on the kitchen countertop despite the fact it didn't have a single crumb or spot on it. "I planted a tracker. It wasn't like I actually expected you to do it."

Her hand stopped, the stillness telling me I *might* have picked the wrong thing to say there.

"Well, I'm glad you think so little of me," she snapped. "But since you didn't ask, I *did* plant it."

"Really? How?"

"She saw me playing with the pebble and asked about it. I told her it was a rock that I'd gotten from this amazing psychic in LA for good luck, that I always carry it and it works. She asked if she could have it, so I said yes."

And wow, did I not expect that. Planting a tracker was hard enough, but to get a target to not only ask for it, but to convince them that it was important was a hell of a good job. If Rachel switched bags, my tracker became useless. If Dilaura carried hers around, though, it would benefit us far more.

"So then what's your problem?" I asked. "If it isn't about the tracker, why are you so mad?"

"I'm not mad."

"Right, this is just your usual charming personality." I injected every bit of sarcasm I could into my words. Maybe it wasn't fair to be so hard on her, but something inside me really disliked the way she shut me out, the wall she'd erected around herself.

She turned and the look on her face was so ferocious, I found myself stepping backward. "*My* charming personality? That's what you want to say right now?"

"I have no idea what you're talking about. If you want to have a conversation, try opening your mouth and actually saying what you want."

She pressed her lips together in a thin line then shook her head. "What's the point?"

"The point is that *this* being pissed without talking to me sure doesn't do a thing. What, is it your time of the month again or something?" As soon as the words escaped me, I knew — *too far*. Still, my mouth ran away from me when it came to Kenz, and that fact pissed me off even more. Why was it that I had perfect control over my words, over my actions, over my expressions in any other situation but the second I saw Kenz, that all went to hell. She undid all that practice, turning me into some tongue-tied idiot.

Annoying.

"Well, then why don't you go talk to *Rachel*?"

I frowned, her words throwing me off. That sure as hell sounded like jealousy, but that didn't make a bit of sense. "What are you talking about?"

"Nothing." She turned her back on me and continued to scrub the counter as if it had done something to personally offend her.

I know I did, but she seems willing to take it out on the counter.

I caught her arm and turned her around, trapping her between my body and the countertop. "Clearly, it isn't nothing, so out with it."

She huffed, then turned her gaze from mine, staring off into space. "I just hate to see you working like that."

"Why? You've seen me pretend plenty of times. It's just part of the job."

"I guess I didn't realize how much it would bother me to see you flirting with girls."

"Are you jealous?" I set a finger beneath her chin and tipped her face up toward mine. "That's *almost* adorable, you know? You don't like to see me flirting with women? Are you getting possessive?" I knew I was being a dick, but something about Kenz always made me want to do that. It made me want to tease her, to bother her, to be myself in a way I couldn't with anyone else.

She finally looked me right back in the eyes, but it wasn't playfulness I found there. It was hurt, as though I'd somehow wounded her deeply. "I don't care that you flirt to get jobs done—I just wish you'd treat me like that just once, like I mattered, too. You can seem to be so nice to other people, give them your best, but for me? For me you can't seem to do it. I've accepted that—not like I have much of a choice about it—but I don't like having the fact shoved in my face all the time."

Her words froze me in place, and that gave her the chance to knock my arm out of the way and leave the kitchen, her steps quick but just shy of running.

I stood there, the hurt look in her eyes sticking with me. I recalled how I'd spoken to Rachel, that hated mask I was forced to wear, and the idea that Kenz wanted that too, it hurt.

I'd thought I'd found someone who liked *me*, who I didn't have to hide from, but maybe I'd been wrong?

Chapter Five

Kenz

"So the residence is here?" I asked as I tapped on the monitor, looking at it over Hayden's shoulder.

"Seems that way. Both the trackers go back there at night, and when Tor staked it out, he spotted Pauline leaving and coming back. Her schedule looks pretty regular."

"So what's the plan, then?"

"Now that we know where she is, Vance is setting up a meeting. We'll show her the evidence of what Lorien has done, show her that backing him is a bad idea."

"Can I go?"

Hayden froze, the way he always did when I knew he was about to turn me down. "That's not a good idea. Pauline is a serious threat. If she doesn't agree with us, if she sides with Lorien, I don't want you in the middle of her territory."

"I'm not useless, you know," I argued.

He turned then cupped my cheek in his large, warm palm. "I know you're not useless, Kenz. I just won't be able to focus on the meeting if I'm worried about you, if I'm thinking about you. It'll go much better if you stay out of the way and safe."

I sighed, my shoulders slumping as he sidelined me yet again. "But that is *my* world. She's the sort of person I grew up with. You know a lot about security, but we're talking about the Mafia here. You don't think I might be useful in that case?"

Hayden slipped his hand to the nape of my neck and tugged softly, pulling me into his lap. "I'm not asking you to stay behind because I don't think you can handle yourself. I'm asking you to stay behind because I can't handle you being there. Please, just this once, listen to me?"

His words melted my resolve. It was hard to argue with him when he looked so earnest, when he asked so nicely. I knew it wasn't about me so much as being about him. In his expression, I saw his fear, at what could happen to me, at him possibly failing me.

It was why I understood, so I nodded. "Okay. Am I going to stay alone?"

"Of course not. I'll have Char stay with you. Vance is needed for the meeting, and Tor will cover us. It makes the most sense for Char to stay here with you."

The mention of Char's name made me flinch before I could stop myself. Since the night before, when I'd snapped at him, we hadn't so much as looked directly at one another. I couldn't even blame him, not entirely.

After a night of tossing and turning, I knew my words hadn't been fair. Still, even if I understood that, I still couldn't stop that hurt inside me. I felt unimportant to him, as though working hard to make others happy was worth it, but I wasn't worth putting in that same effort for.

Even still, I wasn't sure how to approach him, how to make things better.

It felt disingenuous for me to just apologize, not when I felt so raw, but I didn't like where things were, either.

"Did you have a fight with him?" Hayden asked.

I blew out a slow breath, then shrugged. "Not exactly a fight."

"I'm the last person who'll scold you for losing your temper with Char. He's a difficult man to deal with." Hayden rubbed his hand over my back, the touch sweet and comforting. "He's different since you've come here, though."

"Oh yeah? He seems as unpleasant as ever."

"Oh, he *is*," Hayden said with a chuckle. "But that's the thing. Before you, he never talked more than he needed to. He was to the point, direct, never bothered to even insult people. He didn't seem to care enough to put in that effort. That's different now, though."

"So I'm the lucky one who he likes to insult?"

Hayden ran his fingers through my hair, brushing it from my face. "You don't get it, do you? You're the first person he's let close enough to see that part of him, the part he hides, the part he doesn't think others will approve of."

"That sounds like bullshit that people tell young girls, how a boy is only mean to the ones he likes. I'm supposed to put up with it because it's just how he shows his affection?" I huffed softly, annoyed that I was supposed to not only understand but somehow be thankful for his bad behavior.

Hayden wrapped his arms around me, pulling me tighter against him. It reminded me just how close we were, how intimate our position. I'd been so distracted by our talk of Char that I'd somehow failed to notice before.

Now, it was hard to ignore.

"I'm not saying that at all. I'm just saying that it's worth realizing that he doesn't have the greatest way with people, that he's used to hiding his real personality, and that instead of judging him by what he isn't, you should maybe take a little time and judge him by what he *is*."

I hated that he wasn't entirely wrong. The points he made were fair, after all.

It had me letting out a sigh and crossing my arms in a pout. Getting scolded was *never* fun, but when I deserved it?

It was even worse.

*　*　*　*

Hayden

It felt like it had been a while since I'd worn a suit, and somehow, it chafed more than before. I didn't think I'd gained any weight, yet I seemed very aware of where the tie sat at the front of my throat.

My mind went back to when I'd left the house, to how Kenz had reached up and straightened the black tie. *Maybe that's why.* I didn't think I'd ever had that happen before, and something about her sweet face as she'd looked up at me had me ready to blow off the meeting entirely for a little more time with her.

Except, this meeting was far too important to ignore, so instead of what I wanted, I'd behaved like a responsible adult and headed out with Vance. Tor had already left, scoping the place out ahead of time.

Char and Kenz remained at the house, out of the way and safe. Vance had managed the meeting, Lorien's mother evidently a fan of Vance's work. His connections to the rich and famous proved themselves useful, and this time had been no exception.

We planned to meet at a restaurant, a safety precaution for all involved. We hadn't told her why we wanted to meet, instead using the cover of Vance wanting to discuss a piece of his that she owned. Figuring out that she'd bought it a few years back had been easy once we'd started looking into her.

The rest of the information we needed was on the tablet in the bag that hung across Vance's chest, our proof of everything Lorien was up to, of all the things he'd done.

Any smart leader would recognize his instability, that he would drag them all down with him if she let him. I had to hope that was enough for her to cut ties.

The smell of spices inside the restaurant was far more subtle than I would have expected. It was delicate, like a caress rather than a slap. The place was upscale, and it didn't have a single large room like most places I attended. Instead, every room was its own space, which was likely why it was so often booked for private meetings.

Vance gave his name, and the hostess escorted us back with a professional smile. She didn't seem startled by my appearance, though I'd suspect anyone who could work long at a place like this saw enough for little to faze them.

We went through the long hallway, and I had no doubts that Tor was nearby. Even I would struggle to pick him out of whatever spot he hid in, but he'd watched the meeting location enough to know the entire layout. While he made me uneasy at times — our jobs being stark opposites — I trusted him to do what he did well. There was no one else I'd rather have watching my back.

The hostess opened the door to the room, gesturing for us to enter. Inside, the woman seated at the large table, a cup of tea in her hand, was hardly what I'd expected. I'd learned a lot about Nem since finding out who Kenz really was, so I'd somehow thought all female mob bosses would be like her.

The sort of person who could give a person nightmares with a single look.

Pauline, however, didn't fit that mold. She wasn't some frail old woman, but neither did she seem capable of the things a woman in her position had to do.

She looked up at Vance, first, and smiled. Her gaze moved to me, studying me carefully, before dismissing me. Then again, acting like a bodyguard wasn't hard for me — I actually was one.

"You didn't really need security, did you?" she asked, a playful teasing to her tone.

"People in my position can never be too careful," Vance said, using that playboy charm that he turned on with ease. "Thank you for meeting me."

"How could I refuse? I've followed your career for years — hearing you wanted to talk to me was a bit of a dream come true. What was it my daughters said? That I was fan-girling?" She laughed, the sound unworried.

Vance took a seat, and I sat to his left, both of us across the table from Pauline. The room was quiet, and the lack of noise from adjoining rooms said the soundproofing was good.

It made me wonder why they needed soundproofing *that* good. A person should always worry if a room was made so screams couldn't get out.

A server came in and delivered two more teacups, placing one before Vance and the other in front of me. She said nothing as she poured from the teapot at the center.

"I went ahead and preordered a tea service. I hope you like tea?"

Vance nodded and lifted the delicate cup to smell it, his motions surprisingly smooth. It was one of the times I was reminded of what a different life he'd lived. He'd grown up around people who went to things like tea service regularly.

"It smells wonderful," Vance said. "I don't think I've had good tea in a while. I miss the months I spent in China, because they had these wonderful tea ceremonies my mother would take me to when I was little."

Pauline lit up. "It's so nice to find a kindred spirit. I used to bring my daughters here, but when they got to their teenage years, they stopped wanting to come. I also preordered a selection of pastries and desserts. I didn't know what you liked, so I had them pick out the bestselling ones."

I peered down at my tea, then glanced around for sugar.

"I take it your bodyguard isn't as used to places like this?" Pauline asked.

"I just like sweeter things," I muttered.

She laughed then picked up a small white jar with a lid and stood, bringing it over to me. She took the lid off, then used a tiny spoon inside to scoop some of the sugar and pour it into my glass. After one look at my face, she poured another two spoonfuls in with a chuckle.

"Thanks," I said begrudgingly, then took a sip of the now tolerable liquid.

"My husband never cared for unsweetened tea either," she explained. "I tried for years to get him to accept it, but he never did. Eventually, I gave up and they started putting a jar of sugar in here for me in case he came by. In fact, I should be thanking you, because that was the first time I've gotten to add sugar for a man since my husband passed away. It was a fond memory."

I stared at Pauline for a moment, her expression a mixture of sorrow and joy, as though recalling something precious but also aware that she would never have whatever it was back. Losing people hurt— I knew that better than most. It was one reason I worked as hard as I did at my job, to protect others, to keep people from suffering that terrible feeling.

Pauline shook her head, as though waking herself. "I am very happy to get to meet with you, to get to talk to you, but I have to admit I don't think I'll be able to part with the painting of yours I own. It was a gift, you see, from my late husband. He knew how much I adored your work, and he bought it for our anniversary. Sadly, he bought it months before that date, and he passed away before the date arrived. I can't imagine ever letting it go." She offered a shy smile. "I could have told you that before, but I didn't want to miss out on meeting you."

Vance said nothing at first, and I wondered where his mind had gone. He seemed startled, frozen in place, staring at Pauline. After a moment, he blinked slowly, and let out an uneasy laugh. "Sorry," he said. "I guess I haven't really heard someone say my work mattered to them like that in a while. I'm not used to it anymore."

"I noticed you haven't put out any work in a long time. It was one reason I was so grateful to get a piece of my own. They're hard to come by." Despite her pointing out his absence, she didn't push, didn't ask him why.

Vance nodded, then rolled his shoulder, his expression shifting slightly. It showed he was back on track. "To be honest, I wasn't entirely truthful either."

And just like that, Pauline showed exactly why she was boss. She sat up straighter, her eyes losing that softness from before, sharpening like a predator waking. "Oh really? I am curious why you are here, then." Each word she said was like a dare.

Vance didn't wilt, though. He took out his tablet, hit the button on the side to turn on the screen, then set it on the table between us. There sat Lorien's face—a picture from an article about the staff at the university.

Pauline's mouth tightened. "I don't like games. Either say what you wish to say or leave. I don't take threats lightly."

"This isn't a threat," I said.

She turned her gaze to me. "So you aren't a bodyguard, then? Usually they don't speak."

"Oh, I am a bodyguard," I said with a half-smile. "I'm just not working at the moment. That is your son." I tapped the edge of the tablet. "Grisham Oreando, his other name being Lorien Hatchett."

"If you know that much, you are quite foolish to be here. No one who understands his position—or mine—

would make such a mistake unless they had a death wish."

The truth was...I did have a death wish. At least, I thought I did. Sometimes, when I thought of Kenz, I wondered...

That didn't matter at the moment, though, so I kept my mind on the point at hand.

"Do you know what he's been up to lately?"

"What Lorien does has nothing to do with me. He is barely connected to me or my work. He lives his own life as he pleases."

"Isn't he the next male heir?" Vance asked.

"Yes, he is, but as he hasn't officially taken over, he doesn't currently lead or work with us. If you're trying to use him against me, rest assured that won't work."

"This isn't a threat, Mrs. Hatchett," I said. "We aren't here to threaten or trick you."

"And I'm supposed to believe you when you lied to get me here?"

"Would you have come otherwise?" Vance asked.

The two stared at each other before breaking the standoff with a soft chuckle that eased some of the tension.

"If you are not here to threaten me, then explain what it is you want."

"We're just trying to share some information so we can potentially help one another."

"And how is it you think you can help me? From where I sit, there is a rich artist and a bodyguard before me. What use do you think either of you could be to me?"

I reached across the table and swiped the tablet to the side, bringing up another page. "Lorien has been working for a while, and he's managed to cause a lot of trouble for a lot of people." The screen showed an article about the death of a prominent politician who had perished in a car bombing. I slid my finger across the screen again, showing one article after another. Among them, of course, was the hotel bombing that had set us all on this course.

Her expression didn't change, not outwardly, and she said nothing as she stared at the carnage her son had caused. This was risky, since the truth was that she was a criminal.

Would she care?

Even if she didn't, the heat he could bring down on her might be enough, but things would be *far* easier if she had at least somewhat of a conscience.

"I am aware of his activities," Pauline said, her voice still strong though an undercurrent in it said she might not be happy about it.

"They haven't stopped. If anything, they've gotten worse over the years. It's like he's looking for a bigger thrill each time," I said.

She released a sigh, then tore her gaze from the picture of the rubble at the hotel, the firetrucks and ambulances that had sat outside of it. It was like she couldn't bear to look at it for long.

She swallowed loudly, then looked across the table at me. "It's you, isn't it?" When I didn't answer, she continued. "Lorien has mentioned a group of people after him. That must be you, right?"

I saw no good reason to lie to her. "Yeah. That bombing there—" I tapped on the tablet again to force her to confront it. "We were caught up in this. He wasn't after any of us, but he ruined all our lives."

"And instead of trying to make the best you could out of what you had left, you decided to throw away the rest of your life to chase him?"

"The rest of what we had?" Vance lifted his hand, an anger in his voice. "You told me how much you appreciated my work. Do you know why I haven't worked in five years? Think *carefully* about when that bombing was."

Pauline glanced again at the tablet, gaze searching the screen. When she found what she was likely after — the date — she had the decency to at least pale.

Vance pulled his glove off, then removed the prosthetic — something he rarely did. Then again, what better way to prove his point? "What life is left? He took everything from me, and I'm not the only one. So if you're wondering why I would devote my years to making him pay for that, you only need to look at what's left of my hand, then look at the painting you find so precious. It should become clear."

Before she could respond, the door opened. I clicked the button on the side of the tablet again, darkening the screen, hiding the gory truth on it as a server walked in with a large platter of brightly colored treats.

She set it on the table, between us, but left quickly as though she could feel the tension in the air.

It left the three of us there, alone, with the truth that none of us liked.

But would it be enough?

That I didn't know.

Chapter Six

Kenz

The house felt surprisingly empty with Tor, Hayden and Vance gone. I'd lived alone the last year — had lived mostly on my own for a while before that — yet I'd somehow gotten so used to these men that when they were gone, the house seemed too big, too quiet.

A knock on my door had me smiling. Had Char finally forgiven me? I called for him to come in, and when the handle twisted, when the door opened, my stomach fluttered.

He had that dazzling smile on, the one I'd wanted to see so badly. He held two cups in his hands, both with whipped cream and chocolate shavings piled high over the rim. "I thought you might want some hot cocoa."

His tone took me off guard, so different from the man I was used to that I hardly recognized it — or him. However, when he handed me one of the cups, I couldn't stop myself from taking it.

He sat on the corner of my bed, facing me, a smile across his perfect lips. "Don't worry — it's the sugar-free stuff you like. Go on, have some. Nothing like heat and sweet to make a hard night go by faster."

I blinked slowly, struggling to catch up with what was happening. After a moment, I took a sip of the drink, trying to go along with this. It was what I'd wanted, right?

However, I could barely taste it, something bitter on my tongue that had nothing to do with the hot cocoa.

"Do you think they're okay?" I asked.

"Oh, I'm sure they are. They're smart and tough, after all. I thought you'd be worried, so I figured maybe a drink and a show if you can't relax. I can even run you a bath."

"A bath?" It was like the very meaning of words had gone right out of my head, like I couldn't understand them anymore.

"Yeah. A nice hot bath can ease the mind. If you wanted, I could get in there with you." He lifted one of his dark eyebrows, his red bangs falling into his face. He looked like some pop idol, his gaze compelling and charming and just the right amount of mischievous.

And it made it hard for me to understand him at all. Or myself. I'd wanted him to treat me nicer, but now that he was?

It didn't feel good at all.

Instead of facing why, I got off the bed in a hop. "You know what this needs? A little cinnamon. Hold on."

A noise from behind me as I escaped said he'd called out for me, but I had no idea what he'd said. I didn't want to hear it.

My heart pounded, but not in excitement. Instead, it was like I kept eating something rotten, something I hated but couldn't stop putting into my mouth.

This was the exact man he'd shown to Rachel, the same cunning sweetness, the same sugary words, the same care and comfort that I'd wanted so badly. So why was it that it felt so bitter when I experienced it?

I went to the kitchen and set my cup on the counter, struggling to slow my breathing and settle my stomach.

"Are you okay?" His voice made me twist in a rush, and standing at the entry to the kitchen was Char—or rather the fake him.

That's when it really hit me.

What Hayden had said, what Char had told me before. He'd played this part even with his wife, showing her only the person he thought she wanted. He'd turned into the version he thought others could accept, hiding the real him away because he didn't think anyone ever wanted to see it.

I remembered how he said no one would adopt him, how they always sent him back because he wasn't the ideal child.

I did that, too. I'd proven him right with my careless words, had made him feel like he needed to hide the real him.

"I'm sorry," I whispered.

He smiled, the edges of it perfect even if I knew it was a mask. "You don't need to be sorry about anything."

I shook my head, my eyes burning. The way he looked at me, the way I'd wanted him to for so long, it wasn't what I'd hoped for. Instead of making me feel cherished, it felt like a big shove away from him, like he'd used it as an electrical fence to keep me from getting near the real man.

"Don't do this. I was wrong, okay?"

His smile dimmed just the smallest amount. "But you were hurt by the way I was before. I might not be the best man, but I don't want to cause you pain."

Which really drove home what my words had done. I wanted to explain to him how I felt, but the words wouldn't come. I really wasn't sure what else to say, how to explain it.

It brought me back to the things I'd somehow forgotten in the face of my own jealousy. The half-smirk he gave me, the one that I saw that few others ever did. The subtle way he did things for me without ever actually bringing them up, without saying a thing or making a show of it. His words weren't sweet, perhaps, but they were honest. The things he said might be sharp, but they'd never been used viciously, never to hurt me.

And instead of recognizing those things, instead of seeing him for what he was, I'd ignored that all and only asked him to pretend to be someone else.

I didn't know *how* to fix this, but the sight of that smiling face of his only broke my heart all the more. I couldn't face it anymore, couldn't bear to see it, so I turned my back on him.

A heartbeat later, a heavy, warm weight pressed against my back, trapping me between the counter and it. Hot breath teased my ear. "You don't like who I really am but you don't want the mask, either? What the fuck is it you want from me?"

"I'm sorry," I repeated.

A sting in my ear said he'd nipped my lobe. "I'm not asking you to be sorry. Fuck, kitten, I just want to not hurt you, to do what's best for you. I spent a long time behind a mask, and if that's the person you want? I can wear it for you, for as long as it makes you happy."

I shook my head. I didn't want that, especially not when he put it that way. I'd only thought about myself, about what would be fun to have, not about the reality, not about him at all. Suddenly, the idea of not hearing that snarky, sarcastic voice of his sounded totally unacceptable.

He rested his forehead against the nape of my neck, sighing heavily. "You really are a problem, you know that? Just as fickle as the kitten I call you. Never happy with what you've got, always trying to get something else. *Fine*, I'll be myself, but when you get tired of that, just tell me. I'm used to my mask—I'll wear it for you." He didn't wait for my response—and didn't that sound just like the man I knew? He grasped my hips, then turned me, setting my ass on the kitchen counter. His eyes almost glowed, obscured by his red hair that had fallen in front of his face.

Finally. The man I loved, the difficult, stubborn and sarcastic man who didn't know how to say something sweet if his life depended on it. And seeing him like that, a wicked glint in those dark eyes of his, made me smile.

"You're smiling?" He chuckled as though I hadn't fully grasped the situation. "Oh, kitten, I don't think you'll be smiling all that long."

And just like that, I wondered if there couldn't have been just a little middle ground between the asshole he really was and the sweet man who didn't want to push me to my limit and past.

Char

The lingering doubts hadn't entirely gone, but I'd still chosen to let that false personality slide away. The tortured look in Kenz's eyes, the way she'd backed away from me — those were the exact things I'd wanted to prevent.

Still, fear gripped me. I'd been rejected my entire life for who I was. I'd been too difficult, too stubborn, too much for people. Even back when I'd been a kid, people hadn't been willing to accept me. I'd been shuffled from house to house, from foster family to foster family, watching as others got homes but I didn't.

I'd learned the only way to get along in the world was to become who I had to be, who people really wanted. I'd learned that the world found my true personality unacceptable.

However, I stood here at the edge of a rope bridge suspended over a massive chasm. I could stay there, on the solid ground I knew, or I could risk everything and venture onto the bridge.

One look at Kenz gave me the courage to take that first step onto unsteady ground.

I caught her chin and leaned in, taking her lips in a kiss that I didn't ease into at all. Easing in, coaxing, those things were from that fake version of me. The real me was demanding and rough, it enjoyed seeing that hesitation in her eyes, the uncertainty.

However, she kissed me back just as eagerly, accepting even this part of me without reservation. I moved forward, her thighs parting around my hips so I fit in that heavenly space between. She tilted her head and licked against my lips, like a shy little request for me to part, and maybe I was feeling generous because

I did so. She slipped her tongue into my mouth, teasing me with tentative little strokes.

Those drove me crazy, especially when she wrapped her arms around my shoulders and pulled me closer. How many times had I been pushed away in my life, yet here Kenz was, accepting me entirely, wanting more.

It was a heady feeling, and before I knew what I was doing, what I planned, I wrapped her legs around my waist and slid her off the counter. Her ass fit perfectly in my hands, and I didn't stop myself from squeezing as I carried her.

She held on tight to me, not pulling away, just trusting me to carry her, not seeming to care where I took her. That level of trust made me never want to break it, never want to lose this with her.

I took her to the living room — the bedrooms were *way* too far away and I lacked the patience to traverse the steps.

I wanted Kenz *now*.

So I dropped down onto the couch, keeping her in my lap. It lifted her up so her face was above mine, her knees pressing into the cushions on the side of me.

"You're in those little shorts again," I whispered to her as I ran my palms over her hips and the outsides of her thighs. "Those things drive me crazy. Every time I see you in them, I think about how wet and tight your pussy is and how easy they make it to get into you."

Her cheeks turned that pretty pink that made my cock twitch in response. Her embarrassed really was a thing of beauty. I wanted to push her more, to see how that shame covered her, to draw it out of her and get her to accept everything I wanted to give her.

I moved the fingers of one hand up her inner thigh, then slipped past her shorts as I had before. How was it that her cunt could already feel so familiar? It was tight and wet and so hot that I felt as though it could burn me. She tightened around my fingers as I pushed two into her, her body accepting them.

She rose slightly, as if to get away, but I gripped her hip with my free hand to hold her still.

"Take it, kitten," I told her, not looking away, giving her nowhere to hide or lessen this connection between us. Staring into her pretty brown eyes as I delved my fingers into her felt oddly intimate, like we were in a moment between just the two of us. Often sex was frantic, passionate and rough, and somehow locking gazes as I filled her fed a part of me that craved connection.

When my hand pressed against her mound, when I couldn't sink any more into her, I groaned at the sensation. "Good girl. Do you think about what it'd feel like for me to really fill you? For me to spread that pretty cunt of yours with my cock?"

She took her bottom lip between her perfect white teeth and nodded.

I wanted to kiss her, to leave bite marks and hickies all over her skin, but I refused to break the eye contact. I wanted her looking right at me as she came, to not let her escape this closeness.

"I can't believe how lewd you are," I said. "For a virgin, you sure heat up nicely. If I didn't know any better, I'd think you were a hedonist who'd done this plenty of times." I withdrew my fingers, then plunged them back into her, fucking her slow and deep and hard while ensuring the heel of my palm rubbed against her clit.

Instead of trying to get away, Kenz had surrendered to me, to the moment. Now she lifted her hips and sank back down, almost looking as if she rode my cock instead of my fingers.

Talk about a nice sight.

She dragged her tongue along her full bottom lip, a spark of hesitation in her eyes before passion washed it away. She set one hand on my arm, gripping tightly, then brought her other down to the waist of my pants. A flick of her fingers had the button undone, then she tugged at the fabric like a kid trying to get into a toy.

The action made me laugh, and that only made her flush harder. Even though embarrassed, she didn't stop her actions.

Funny that it was adorable yet sexy at the same time. I'd never thought anything could be both. I'd usually gone for sexy women, for flashy ones, but somehow seeing Kenz struggle to get my cock free was better than any of them.

I took the hand not fucking her and helped her with my pants, lifting my ass slightly to lower my slacks and boxers enough to free my cock. The air only cooled it for a moment before she wrapped her small hand around my shaft.

It made me groan, the way she gripped me. It wasn't a talented or skillful touch, but as it turned out, that didn't matter in the least. What got me was that look in her eyes, the passion and need in her movements. It made me want to come immediately, to coat her in my seed again like a claim, to prove she was mine.

I grasped her hip again and shifted my hand so it rested against my thigh. "I want you to ride my fingers, kitten. Fuck yourself on them for me, won't you? Stroke my cock at the same time and imagine that's what you're bouncing on, that you're taking me deep into you. Picture it, kitten, because it's only a matter of time until it happens."

She paused, her body tense. Then again, I was putting her on the spot, demanding something that pushed her out of her comfort zone. It had me waiting, a delicious anxiety as I had to see if she would do it or if she'd let her nerves get the best of her.

However, she proved yet again how strong she was when she shifted to the side, moving her legs so one knee remained on the cushion outside and the other between my legs, straddling my thigh. I kept my fingers still, the back of my hand anchored against the top of my leg, my middle and pointer up. They glistened from her wetness, and I couldn't deny the filthy thrill of the sight.

Kenz rose to her knees, shifting as she positioned herself above my waiting fingers, her hand still grasping my arm for balance. The sight of her lowering onto my fingers, taking them into her herself, was impossibly hot.

It was one thing to fuck her on my own, to plunge into her, but it was a whole different thing for her to fuck herself, to use me to make herself feel good. She sank down, her cunt squeezing around me, a soft whine leaving her.

And *fuck* did it test my resolve. Staying still was damn hard when she looked like that, especially when she grasped my cock again. Her little hand stroked me slowly, her grip not tight enough, as though afraid of hurting me.

It was damned cute.

"Tighter," I groaned out, wanting more.

Kenz nodded and dropped her gaze. I let her do it because she stared down at my cock, and as it turned out, I rather liked that, too. She lifted her hips then sank back down, her rhythm rough as she found a speed and angle she liked. She matched it to the way she stroked my cock, tightening her grip.

I watched, enthralled by her movements, by the sight of how pretty she looked there in my lap. She evened out her motions, riding my fingers like a pro in no time. She not only rose and fell, but rolled her hips, seeking the places inside her that felt the best. I could tell each time she found one, too, because she shuddered.

She was wonderfully sensitive and so honest that she didn't hide a thing from me.

A tightness in my balls said I wouldn't last much longer. The little panting breaths she let out, the tightness of her pussy, the stroking of her hand on my cock were all more than I could hope to resist.

I thought back to when I'd met her, to when I'd seen her at her job then later at the house. I sure as fuck hadn't thought about her like this, wouldn't have expected to ever be here, to want her this bad or feel so lost to her.

This felt so different. All the sex before, I'd had to hold myself back, had to play my part. I'd never let myself just feel, just experience it because I'd had to keep a part of my brain focused on keeping that mask in place.

That realization, the ability to just let go and be myself, to not care what came out of my mouth, what I did, not think about whether it fit with who I showed the other person, it created a depth to this that I'd had no idea could exist between two people.

Her cunt twitched, clenching in quick waves as she rode me faster, her hand matching the pace. She was close, but fuck, so was I.

"Come for me, kitten," I said.

Even though I wanted to keep looking at her face, she seemed to have reached her limit. She leaned forward, resting her forehead on my shoulder, a thin whimper leaving her as she strove for her release. She came hard, even her thighs clenching around my leg as though every part of her went rigid.

The rhythmic tightening of her pussy made me fantasize about pulling her over again and sinking deep into her, even as she rode out her orgasm, enjoying the way she'd struggle against the overwhelming feeling. That got me the short rest of the way to my own release and I came, my head dropping back against the cushions of the couch as I struggled to slow my rapid breathing.

Meanwhile, Kenz leaned against me, her body lax and trusting, her cunt still tightening around my fingers, each time causing a shiver to run through her worn-out body.

I pulled my fingers from her, even when she whined at the feeling. Kenz lifted her head again, a drowsy, drugged expression on her sweet features.

My heart clenched, a feeling I couldn't identify or fully understand growing inside me as I looked back at her. It didn't feel like just love, which to me had always been one-sided. That had always been about me doing what I had to, about giving and giving and never asking for anything.

Instead, this thing with Kenz felt reciprocal. It felt like a back and forth, a give and take, and a fear I'd never experienced before came over me.

I didn't know if I could survive losing this.

Chapter Seven

Vance

While Hayden appeared uncomfortable, this was far from the first time I'd scarfed down tea and treats as though nothing were wrong while ignoring the huge issues in the room.

It was a skill honed by the rich, one I'd picked up even as a baby. It meant that despite Pauline thinking and staring at us, I could sip the tea and enjoy the sweet desserts spread across the table.

I should bring Kenz here sometime. I imagined she'd rather like it here, and, given her upbringing, she could easily tolerate the atmosphere. In fact, the thought of dressing her up again sounded damn nice.

At least, until I recalled how uncertain our future remained. Maybe I'd just ensure she had a reservation, so that when the inevitable came to pass, it would leave her with something. It reminded me of Pauline's story, how her husband had left her a gift even after he was gone, and the happiness in her expression at that memory.

Pauline released a long sigh and in that sound, I heard her answer.

"I'm sorry, but I can't help you," she said. The worst part was that she actually sounded sorry. "You're putting me in an impossible position, asking me to choose between strangers and my own flesh and blood."

"It's not about choosing—it's about seeing that he's a problem. His actions can end up bringing trouble to you, to your family."

"I'm aware, but in my position, protecting family is the most important thing. Nothing matters more than family, after all, and I have already lost so much of it. You can't expect me to turn my back on what little I have left."

I thought about my own family, about all the problems between us. I'd learned that blood didn't matter all that much in the end, that people did what was best for themselves. They used blood and last names as stones to climb atop, to better their positions, to build themselves a platform and occasionally as weapons against those in their way.

However, Pauline spoke as though it actually mattered to her.

"Sometimes a family member isn't worth it," I said softly.

"No parent would think that."

"Then you don't know many families. I say this as someone all but disowned by my own family, all because they didn't feel that I fit in with them. Sometimes a family member is just a diseased limb that has to be cut off for the whole to survive."

She shook her head. "That is a sad sentiment, and one I can't share. If you keep doing that, you'll end up with no limbs. Sometimes, you have to treat the wound instead of just considering it a lost cause. Lorien isn't a monster, not in his heart. I know him, remember him as a young child just looking for beauty in a world that was cold and lonely. He grew up knowing he didn't belong where he was but also knowing the place he belonged had cast him out. If I keep working with him, if I give him the love and acceptance that he didn't get before, he'll come around."

I struggled with her response. A part of me wanted that for myself, the dedication of a mother willing to risk so much for the benefit of her child. However, it also didn't help that it was the exact opposite of what I needed at the moment.

"Mrs. Hatchett," I started to say, but her sharp look cut the words short.

"I understand your reasoning. Trust me, I do not take betrayal or harm to me or mine easily. I don't let that slide, so I won't blame you for it. However, your feelings are not my problem or my responsibility to factor into my own choices. I'm sorry that you've suffered, but I will not choose you over my own son. Lorien is my priority, and I will do whatever I have to to protect him. He is the future of this family, and I can't allow things like pity to stop me from doing what must be done."

She rose, the action elegant and regal, fully fitting her position as matriarch of a crime family. "Despite how this has gone, I am grateful to have met you, Mr. Moore, and I hope that you are able to let go of the anger you harbor, because I do wish for you to have a good life."

I said nothing back, frustration eating away at me when she nodded politely and left the room.

"Damn it," Hayden muttered, shaking his head, clearly as bothered as I was about this.

"We knew this was possible," I said even if I didn't feel that.

"What now?"

I blew out a breath, then shrugged. "Now, I guess we pocket some of these desserts because I'm pretty sure Kenz would love them."

Hayden said nothing at first, then chuckled when it seemed he couldn't resist it anymore. "What, you can't afford to buy some?"

"Hey, I haven't worked in a long time, remember? Besides, some petty part of me likes the idea that Pauline there had to pay for it."

A server brought a lovely white box and packed up the multitude of sweets that had gone untouched, Pauline having picked up the check before she left.

Our trip back to the house was quiet and uneventful, probably because we both thought about how much it sucked going back empty-handed. We'd wanted to get further, for this to have made a difference, but instead, we were no better off.

Hell, if anything, we potentially opened ourselves up to additional risks by dragging Pauline directly into the mess. Still, I had to believe that it was worth the risk, because we had to do something.

On the porch stood Tor, his back against the doorframe as he waited. I hadn't caught a glimpse of the man, but the fact he beat us back suggested he'd been close enough to keep an eye on it all.

We left the car and I held the box, tied with a piece of twine that created a handle.

Tor lifted his eyebrow as we approached, and I shook my head in answer. "No go."

He sighed but nodded, as if to tell me it wasn't a surprise. Unfortunately, that didn't make me feel any better. Having him not shocked that we failed didn't make me feel less like a loser.

Worse, the uneasy feeling inside me had just kept growing as all our options failed. The paths we had to take, our choices, they all seemed to be closing down right before our eyes. It felt like running through a hallway in a horror movie and finding all the exits slamming shut in my face.

Except it wasn't my life on the line—it was Kenz's and that mattered to me.

A hand came to rest on my back in a pat that knocked me forward a step. I glanced over my shoulder to find Hayden giving me that fatherly, 'don't be so hard on yourself' look that I wished I'd ever seen from my actual father.

I offered him a forced smile then turned away, having no desire to continue this little therapy session. I opened the door, a sense of relief hitting me.

This place was home in a way nowhere else had ever really been, and no matter how rough the day had been, I found myself able to breathe more easily when I go here. It made me want to find Kenz, to see that smile of hers, to hear her voice.

Maybe it wasn't fair to expect her to lift my spirits like this, but she was the only thing that could do that for me anymore.

When I stepped into the living room, I froze.

The sun was just starting to set, to lower to the horizon, so I'd thought Kenz would either be in her room painting or playing around in the backyard with the flowers. Which was why when I found her on the couch, my brain stuttered to a stop.

Well, it wasn't *just* that she was there. It was more the state she was dressed — or rather undressed.

She wore a top but no shorts or underwear, stretched out on the couch on her side, with Char behind her.

Both had their eyes closed, looking like they'd passed out after having some fun.

My cock swelled at the scene, at how Kenz could manage to look almost innocent but so filthy at the same time. I rubbed my hand over my mouth, forcing myself to stay rooted in place.

Sure, my brain went straight into the mud, thinking about inspecting every inch of her body with my lips, with my tongue, finding every trace of Char that he'd left on her. I wanted to tease her, to steal that relaxation she'd found, to exhaust her all over again.

Before I could do anything about it, before I could act on it, Hayden cleared his throat loudly.

Killjoy.

Kenz's eyes opened, and she blinked slowly as she peered around as though trying to figure out where she was and what had happened. She stared over at us, a sleepy contentment on her face.

She shifted to sit up, Char grumbling and wrapping an arm around her to tug her against him again. That must have woken her up the rest of the way, because her eyes widened until she looked like a comic book character. She shoved at Char's arm, not giving up until he released her.

Tor wandered closer while Kenz rushed, trying to hide herself, looking all around. Char, meanwhile, didn't seem the least bit bothered, even though his pants were still undone and the head of his hard cock showed through the waistband of his boxers.

Instead, he chuckled at Kenz's frantic motions, resting his head on his hand, not bothering to get up or help in the least.

"You're back early," Kenz rushed out.

"Not really," I answered and made a show of looking at my wristwatch. "In fact, I think we're about an hour later than expected. Were you distracted by something?"

She narrowed her eyes in a glare that made me glad she didn't have a weapon on her.

Tor bent down behind the couch, then held his hand out when he rose again. Her shorts dangled on his outstretched fingers.

She snatched the shorts away, but frowned when she looked at them.

"They look a bit dirty," I said. "Are you sure you really want to put those on? Seems they got covered in something that's since dried. Can't imagine that's comfortable."

If her cheeks could have burst into flames, I was pretty sure they would have right then. Instead, she took one deep breath then rose, holding the dirty shorts over her crotch to block our view.

Char smirked and tilted his head, clearly enjoying his own personal show since he was behind her still.

She twisted, keeping us in front of her, as she backed away. She tripped on the steps a few times, but eventually, made her way to the top and took off.

Once she was out of sight, Hayden let out a groan that suggested holding himself back hadn't been any easier than it had been for me.

"Welcome home," Char said, a self-satisfied grin on his face.

"That girl is going to be the death of me," Hayden muttered and took off toward the kitchen, shaking his head. "I'm too damned old to deal with this. Think about my heart, for fuck's sake." Even when he left the room, the low rumble of his continued complaints floated back to us, telling me he hadn't been able to wipe the memory from his mind.

Tor snorted and shook his head, then took off toward the steps, turning toward his room at the top of them.

"Well, I've come home to worse sights," I said with a laugh. "Though I could have done without the glimpse of your dick."

"Jealous?" Char asked.

"A bit. Now cover up—you've already had your fun so you don't need to be waving that around like a fishing lure while we talk."

He tucked himself back into his boxers, then winced as he buttoned the slacks. His expression said he wanted me to feel bad for him, but that wasn't going to happen.

I wasn't about to pity the asshole for a hard-on. In fact, the idea of him being uncomfortable while we all talked struck me as fair turnabout.

After seeing Kenz looking so sweet and well-used, I had a feeling we'd *all* be grinning and bearing it until we got some alone time later tonight.

Misery loves company, after all.

* * * *

Tor

By the time Kenz showed back up, she'd showered and seemed to shore up her courage. She'd changed, too, which was a damn good thing.

I couldn't stop myself from recalling how tempting she'd looked earlier, how much I'd wanted to touch her, to ignore the stresses of life and set them aside for the pleasures of her body.

However, now wasn't the time for such things. It meant that after I finished cooking something for dinner—a simple meal of spaghetti and a meat sauce since we didn't have much in the kitchen—we had to focus on what had happened with Pauline and where we went from that.

We sat in the backyard, probably so no one looked toward the living room and recalled what we'd walked in on. Kenz was already on the swing out back, wearing a long-sleeve shirt and a pair of pajama pants like armor to erase how little she'd worn before.

Good luck with that. She could have worn a tarp and it wouldn't have dimmed my memory at all.

I balanced three large bowls of food in my arms, with Hayden holding another two behind me. I used a foot to open the slider, then went out to the patio area.

I handed one of the bowls to Char, then the other to Kenz. She didn't meet my gaze but mumbled out a soft thank you. I nodded, even if she didn't see it, then took a seat on the patio, my legs crossed.

Hayden sat in a chair he'd pulled over after handing Vance the last bowl of food.

Kenz had her legs crossed in front of her, leaving the swinging to the men on either side of her. She poked at the noodles, but made no move to actually put any of them into her mouth.

"Eat," Hayden said.

"I'm not that hungry," she answered.

"Food is important. You learn pretty quick to eat even when you don't feel like it or you won't have the energy when you really need it. It's like only filling up your gas tank when it's already on empty—don't wait until you need it or you'll end up stuck on the side of the road."

Kenz looked up at him, a smile tugging at the corners of her lips. "You do realize that is the most old-man way you could have described that?"

Hayden snorted. "You're such a brat."

At least that broke some of the discomfort, and Kenz went ahead and took a bite of the spaghetti. She appeared pleased, which warmed me. Cooking only felt worth it if someone enjoyed it, after it.

"I'm sorry," she said after another long pause. When no one responded, she pressed on. "What you walked in on—that was probably weird, right? I mean, it had to be uncomfortable."

"You're the only one who seemed uncomfortable," Vance said with a chuckle.

She gave him a harsh side-eye. When he smiled instead of appearing chastised, she sighed. "I'm serious. Look, as you know, I don't have what you'd call a lot of experience with dating or dealing with men. I do know that people don't normally do this with four different people, though."

"Last I checked, isn't your sister sleeping with four men?" Char pointed out.

"Yeah, but that was different. They were always together. The Quad are almost one person in four different bodies. You guys are different. You're together right now because you have a shared goal. That doesn't mean you want to do...whatever this is."

I allowed a smile to spread across my lips, unable to help it in the face of how she tripped over her own words. We were essentially discussing the fact that we'd all been with her in some way, and now she struggled with that. She wasn't sure that was okay, wondering if it was fair to us, if it said something negative about her.

I understood those sorts of questions. As a man who'd spent his life doing something seen as immoral by most people, I knew well the toll such questions took on a person, and I wasn't even someone who normally thought that deeply.

For a girl like Kenz, someone who wanted so badly to be accepted, to be seen as good, her wondering if her actions made her bad would wear heavily.

Hayden set his bowl on the small side table beside his chair, then leaned forward, putting all his focus on Kenz. It sure reminded me of an interrogation, even if I doubted he'd meant it that way. "Are you saying this because you don't like it or because you're worried we don't?"

"Does it matter?"

"Of course it does. If *you* don't want to pursue something with all of us, well, that's one thing. It's your choice, after all, and none of us will push you or force you into it."

"I might," Char muttered, rewarded with me moving my leg and kicking him hard in his shin.

He reached down and rubbed the spot, then moved his lips as though he were still arguing but silently.

Hayden shook his head but went on, ignoring Char's little comment and my retaliation. "So if you don't want this, if you don't like it or it makes you unhappy, that's fine. We'll back off. However, if this is just you worrying that we're unhappy or jealous or that something like this is wrong, well, that's a whole different matter."

Kenz shifted in her seat, as though that might help her mind catch up with our conversation. She ran her finger along the edge of the bowl, her gaze locked on the food. Was she working through her thoughts until she could make sense of them?

It felt like an eternity later when she finally spoke. "I don't dislike it," she said softly.

Well, there's one hurdle.

I wasn't sure how I'd react if she'd said she didn't enjoy her time with us, if she felt forced or manipulated into any of it. Her admitting that she at least didn't hate it, well, that was something, right?

"I'm sensing a 'but'," Vance said. "No one starts a statement off like that unless they plan on saying a 'but' afterward."

"*But,* it doesn't seem right. I didn't exactly grow up with a normal family, but I sure know it wasn't a mom and four men. How does that even work? Nem makes it work, sure, but she's *Nem*. If she decided that night was day I wouldn't be shocked when the sun rose at midnight. So her managing it doesn't mean that I could. What happens when one of you gets jealous? When you decide that this doesn't work? What happens when I end up losing you all?"

Fear drenched every word. No matter what she said, what excuse she came up with, it all held the same undercurrent. The girl was terrified, and it came out with this pulling back.

I set my bowl down and slid closer to the swing, then placed my hand on her knee, squeezing once to reassure her. I offered her a slight smile to press the point.

She gave me a smile back, though hers held gratitude. Yet again, I fell harder for her somehow, even though I wondered how that was possible.

"If I had a problem with how things are, I wouldn't have set a hand on you." Char shrugged as if it were obvious. "If this whole thing with all of us bothered me, I wouldn't just ignore it. I'd say something and I wouldn't have put myself in the position. As I recall it, I literally pushed your head down on Tor's cock—not only did it not bother me, but I enjoyed it."

Hayden choked at that, the action making me laugh softly. How could he be the oldest and still get thrown so hard when anything like that was said?

Still, Vance picked the conversation up next. "I don't care about stuff like that. Women aren't tissues that get dirty and used up, for fuck's sake. I don't give a damn if you sleep with them—I only care about the time we spend together, and that time is important to me." He looked away after he finished speaking as if his words embarrassed him.

"You really don't mind?"

"Not one bit," Vance said easily. "In fact, maybe it makes me a pervert, but I can't deny I got hard seeing you all wrapped up with Char on the couch like that. That's a pretty good sign that I don't mind it a bit."

I glanced at Hayden to see if he was still breathing, but thankfully he'd stopped eating and drinking to prevent any more mishaps. Not that it didn't change his expression, one that implied he didn't think Vance and Char were helping in the *least*.

Kenz peered down at me, her lips pursed, uncertainty coloring her features.

I took my phone from my pocket, opening the texting app with a press of my finger. I typed a message and sent it out in a group text, my motions quick from practice.

I'm not an idiot. I'm far from a perfect man, so thinking I could do everything for you, that I could be everything you need, that's foolish. If you'd asked me a year ago if I'd trust these three with what mattered most to me, I'd have called you an idiot. Now, though? I've got no problem with the arrangement as-is.

Even typing it out forced me to acknowledge the truth of it, to recognize just how much not only Kenz but Hayden, Char and Vance had permeated my entire life. Where I'd lived in the shadows on my own before, content to watch things from a distance, to never be a part of anyone or anything, that no longer fulfilled me. It was as though they'd given me a glimpse of something more, and now nothing short of that could satisfy me.

It both reassured and saddened me that we were so limited in our future. I was glad that I didn't have to worry about losing it, about having to return to those shadows on my own after experiencing something better. However, I couldn't deny the pain at knowing I couldn't have this long term.

Kenz read over my words, taking long enough that I suspected she read it multiple times. The others did the same, the pause in the conversation normal for me since I was used to people needing to read, which slowed the back and forth.

When she finally finished, she lifted her gaze from her screen to my eyes, her expression so sweet that I couldn't stop myself from reaching out and stroking over the soft skin of her bottom lip. It reminded me of how it had felt to slide past those lips, how she had wrapped them around my cock.

I pressed my thumb deeper, enjoying the wet heat of her mouth, and the way her pupils widened made it clear she recalled the same thing. In fact, she moved her tongue, wrapping it around me, then sucked gently in what I doubted she realized was nearly as provocative a move as it was.

"That's enough, kids," Hayden said.

Char snickered softly. "That's right. Leave room for Jesus."

"Forget Jesus. Leave room for me," Vance interrupted.

"I swear, you all make me feel like I'm the chaperon on a field trip of hormonally charged teenagers." Hayden rubbed his face hard, but even that didn't change the slight smile he wore, a sign that he didn't mind it nearly as much as he put on.

"You didn't say what you thought," Kenz said, her voice quiet and nervous.

Hayden dropped his hands, and his expression softened when he looked over at her. If that wasn't the face of a man hopelessly smitten, I didn't know what was.

"I didn't realize I needed to," he said.

That had Kenz dropping her gaze with a frown, clearly taking his words as a rejection.

I shot him a dirty look, cursing again at just how useless Hayden was with women. How was it he could be so talented when it came to protecting people, to securing locations and escape routes and predicting behavior to keep others alive no matter what, but he couldn't manage to read or talk to women at all?

Hayden winced. At least he figured out his mistake quickly. Did that mean he was learning?

A man can hope.

"I don't mean it like that," he rushed out. "I'm saying that even I've got eyes, that I've known you're interested in them, too. It's never been a problem for me. I'm with Char on this—if I didn't like that, I'd have spoken up from the start."

"You really are terrible with women," Char said and shook his head.

"We should start hosting lessons," Vance agreed. "If he keeps that up, we're all going to end up cock-blocked because of his mouth. I refuse to end up going to bed with a hard-on because Grandpa there can't manage to string a useful sentence together."

Kenz turned her gaze over us all, then burst into laughter so quickly it made me jump. It was as though the tension that had run through her broke all at once, like she suddenly let it go. Hell, it sounded very much like she needed that, and the feeling of us all just having some fun was something we *all* needed.

After the stress of Lorien, of everything, the ability to eat some good food and just relax was far too rare a thing.

It made me hesitant to say anything about Pauline, to admit to our failure, and I noticed that Kenz hadn't said a word about it.

I glanced Hayden's way and he offered a quick, almost imperceivable shake of his head. Seemed that he agreed.

We'd have to discuss Pauline, but we'd earned at least a little time to take it easy, hadn't we?

I knew better than most that our problems would still be there later, waiting.

Chapter Eight

Kenz

I took the bowl after Tor had rinsed it and I placed it into the dishwasher. "This is nice," I said.

Tor lifted his eyebrow as he rinsed the next bowl.

"I do a lot of chores, but they're always on my own. I didn't learn to do chores with my mom, didn't cook in a kitchen with her teaching me, so doing stuff like this was always just me. It's nice to do it with others. It feels...homey, I guess."

He smiled and nodded in response, as though to tell me he agreed. Then again, he'd been on his own most of the time as well, so I'd bet he truly did understand what I meant.

"What if I just keep you company while you do chores?" Vance asked before hopping up to sit on the kitchen counter beside the dishwasher.

"That sounds like you being lazy."

"Oh, I could help if you really wanted me to."

"Why is it that those words sound more like a threat than a real offer of help?"

He smiled wider but didn't respond, telling me I'd probably interpreted it right. I could imagine him breaking every plate I handed him and managing to streak the floor when mopping it, leaving it worse than it had started. I recalled parents complaining about how their kids' help only made chores harder and take longer and I had a feeling Vance would be *exactly* that sort of help.

So why did that amuse me so much?

Hayden came back into the kitchen after taking the trash out to the cans, and Char entered behind him, the glasses from outside stacked and held in his arms.

The question that had spun in my head since they'd gotten back refused to be ignored anymore. I'd let it go, at first because I'd been mortified to be found half naked, and later because the nice dinner and conversation had been too wonderful for me to want to bring up anything tricky.

And it really wasn't tricky, was it? The fact that they hadn't said anything made me suspect it was bad news. I had a feeling if they'd gotten Pauline to agree to their terms, they'd have said it the moment they'd walked in—whether I had pants on or not.

"So I'm taking it the meeting didn't go well?" I broached the topic slowly as I placed the last dishes into the washer, then closed it and hit the Start button on the front. I turned back to face the others as the machine started up.

The men exchanged looks that said I'd gotten it exactly right.

And, as usual, Hayden was the brave one who actually spoke up. "She didn't go for it."

"What did she say?"

"The expected—that she wouldn't pick anyone over her own son, that she knew he'd done some terrible things but believed that he could be better."

"Is there any chance that she might change her mind?"

Vance shook his head, tapping his heel against the cabinet door as he remained seated on the counter. "I don't think so. Loyalty and family mean everything to her, and I don't think it would matter what Lorien did—she'd still pick him over strangers. I wasn't sure I'd ever see a mother who actually had that whole unconditional loving-your-kids thing, and I sure didn't think that if I did, it'd be a mob boss. I think we could bug her every single day and she wouldn't change her mind. We're going to need a new plan."

I pressed my lips together, hating having to hear it all second-hand. "I want to go see her."

"No fucking chance," Char said so fast that he probably guessed what I was going to say rather than hearing me actually say it. "You're going nowhere near her."

"But I understand her better than you could. I grew up in her world. Hell, her world *is* my world. I know how she's feeling, what she wants to protect, what she's afraid of."

"None of that matters if what we want is for her to betray her own son," Hayden pressed, his voice gentle as though trying to soften the blow to me. "I'm sorry, Kenz, but I don't think any amount of understanding or background is going to get her to change her mind on that."

I drew my hands into fists, feeling as though I stood on the outside of a fence, forced to watch people I cared for on the other side, in danger, and with no way to intervene or help. I hated this feeling of impotence. "Please, let me help. I just want to do something."

Hayden sighed, then stepped closer, but his expression remained a big fat no. "I know you do, Kenz, but it isn't safe."

"It wasn't safe for you to go, either. In fact, it was even less safe for you. If Lorien had realized about the meeting, he could have set a trap."

"We had Tor watching for that."

"So why can't Tor do that for me, too?"

"Because putting us in danger is one thing—that's a calculated risk we're okay with," Vance said. "But if she were to take you, none of the rest of this would even matter."

And we were *right* back here again, with them expecting me to just accept their lives as being worthless, just things they'd toss away without a second thought.

"I know I can't do much," I choked out. "That I can't fight or track people or infiltrate somewhere. I realize that I'm not much use in a lot of things, but I *can* do this. I've lived my whole life in that world and I understand it. Please, I don't want to sit back and watch something happen to you when I could have done something to help. I'll listen to you, do whatever you tell me to, but please, let me help."

Even before the last word left my mouth, I had my answer. It was etched in the expression of each of the men, a rejection that they refused to address or reconsider. Basically, it became clear that no matter what I said, how much I begged, what I did, they wouldn't let me anywhere near this.

"I'm going to lie down," I said, exhausted by doing this again, by having this same old conversation.

At least this time none of them stopped me. They didn't try to hold me there, to make me understand. It was like they'd accepted my anger, my hurt. They might not like it, but they wouldn't change their answer.

I closed the door to my room, the silence getting to me. I thought about Hayden and Vance sitting across from Pauline, a part of my brain replacing my own mother's face instead. I'd grown up seeing my mother do the job Pauline did, had since then watched Nem taking over the role.

I wouldn't sit here and wait to see the men I loved die because they were too busy protecting me to see what needed to happen.

If they didn't want me to help—well too fucking bad.

I was Mackenzie Williams and the women of my family weren't known for following orders.

* * * *

Hayden

Guilt sucked. No matter what I did, I couldn't shake it. I'd reviewed papers from my company, I'd exercised, I'd showered, but none of it helped. A whole night had passed but I didn't have any better idea of how to deal with it than I had before the sun had risen.

Each time I closed my eyes, I saw Kenz's hurt expression.

I wanted to turn around and tell her okay, to give her what she wanted if it took away that sorrow.

Except…I couldn't. Doing it would only make things worse. It would give me a nice night but risk her life.

I couldn't do that just so I got to play the part of the good guy.

A night of no sleep had put me on edge, since I'd tossed and turned all eight hours.

Still, I couldn't just ignore her. We had to keep moving forward, which had me at her door by nine the next morning. I knocked, then waited.

The lack of an answer made my heart race. It took me back to what felt like a previous life, when she'd slipped our grasp and left the house to turn herself over to Lorien.

A sinking feeling in my stomach had me knocking again—louder. I paired it by calling her name, knowing my voice wasn't nearly as calm as I wanted it to be.

Again, nothing.

I gripped the handle, finding it locked. I could have gone to my own room, gotten the spare keys, but that felt like it would take far too long. Instead, a universal boot-shaped key sounded great to me.

One size fits all.

I took a step back, lifted my foot and kicked hard, aiming for just to the side of the handle. The flimsy, hollow door cracked beneath my worry and fear.

I rushed inside, finding exactly what I'd feared.

An empty room, a bed that hadn't been slept in, and Kenz's phone and glucose reader on the dresser along with a note.

I'm sorry to do this again, but I can't just stand by and do nothing. Please, trust me, because I can do this.

Kenz.

I stared at the words, terrified they were the last things she'd ever say to us.

Chapter Nine

Kenz

I knew I wasn't great at infiltration, but I'd learned enough from Colton in the past to at least hop a fence when needed and check for cameras. It also had let me tiptoe through the men's house and lift the keys to Vance's fancy sports car.

Those meager skills had brought me safely to the backdoor of the large, sprawling estate. It reminded me so much of places I'd been before — especially the house in the mountains that my father had put me in before the wedding. Really, that was the worst of the places to remember. The huge, empty rooms, the tree line that felt as though it crushed me.

I swallowed down those feelings so I could focus on now, on what I needed to do. Getting in and over the fence was the easy part. Sneaking into the actual house was different. However, it seemed to me that security wasn't as tight as I might have expected.

I hadn't spotted any patrols, and even the cameras seemed poorly placed and easy to avoid. It struck me as something between confidence and arrogance, as though Pauline didn't believe anyone would strike against her so didn't concern herself with extreme measures.

The house was three stories from what I could tell, probably with an attic space as well. Colton's words rang in my ears from old conversations, when he'd said that security measures were always laxer on the upper floors. People got far too confident in their safety and forgot how agile humans could be.

Of course, Colton scaling a three-story building was a big difference from me doing the same. Suddenly all the times I'd skipped the gym came back to haunt me.

A sound from inside made me jump, and I rushed to the side, ducking behind a large shrubbery that sat to the left of the door just a moment before it opened.

A man in a black shirt and a pair of sweatpants stepped out of the house, another younger man, beside him. "She's got a meeting tomorrow," the older man said as he pulled a vape pen from his pocket.

"Are you going?" the younger asked.

"Not this time. It should be pretty quiet, and she's been wanting me to stick closer to the girls for some reason."

"Some reason? Is there a problem?" The men walked down the stairs and to a small table and chairs a bit farther away. The door remained open.

Lazy, stupid security. If Hayden had been here, no doubt he'd given those two a piece of his mind about proper procedures when dealing with a client's home. However, their stupidity was my gain, so I slipped into the darkness of the house while the useless bodyguards smoked outside.

The interior of the house was spacious and lit only by nightlights that allowed for a general glow through the living space. I kept my steps soft but quick, going for the stairs. Mansions were mostly set up the same, and living spaces were always on the upper floors. I also thought back to the map that Hayden had gone over, where Tor had listed the rooms and who stayed in them.

Pauline's room is to the left, at the end of the hallway. I went to the left, light along the baseboards of the walls just enough so I didn't trip over anything. Brighter light showed at the bottom of the door, soft music escaping as well. That suggested that even now, at three in the morning, she was awake.

So this was it. I grasped the handle and twisted it slowly, trying to avoid any creaking that could give me away. I needed her to *see* me before making a move, or I might just get a bullet for my efforts.

I slipped into the room to find the woman whose picture I had seen on Hayden's screen, just dressed down. Instead of wearing makeup and lovely clothing, she wore a basic rose-colored nightgown and her hair was tied up in a bun at the back of her head. A pair of reading glasses perched on her aristocratic nose, her gaze on the book. "I don't need anything, thank you." She spoke without moving her eyes from the pages of what she read.

I shut the door behind me, then kept my hands out to show I had no weapons. "Even a conversation?"

Pauline finally looked up, but didn't so much as flinch. Instead, she arched one of her gray eyebrows, a famous motherly 'just what do you think you're doing?' expression.

It had been a long time since I'd seen a face like that, and boy did it feel oddly nostalgic.

"If you're here to hurt me, I suggest you think very carefully about the consequences."

Despite those words being the ones coming out of her mouth, what I heard was, *'make good choices.'*

"I'm not here to hurt you." I lifted my hands to once again prove I had no weapons, nothing to do harm to her with.

She closed her book quietly, then set it on the small table beside her chair. Even still, she didn't rise.

Then again, she likely knew that standing wouldn't help her position and doing so would only risk escalating the issue.

"So why are you here?"

I swallowed hard and forced out the truth, something I rarely had said over the past year. "My name is Mackenzie Williams."

Pauline said nothing at first, dragging her gaze up and down my form in a slow perusal. "So you're the one at the heart of so many problems? At least you're pretty, I suppose." She sighed, then gestured for the seat across from her. "If you're going to be here, you might as well sit down."

I did as she said, partly because I saw no reason not to. The chair was lovely, the cushion soft and feeling broken in, not stiff as though never used.

"My youngest daughter would sit in here and read with me some evenings. It's been a long time since we did that, though. I'm happy to see her growing into her own person, but I do miss the time we spent together when she was little. I understand your mother passed away?"

"Yeah, my mom was murdered when I was eight. I don't remember a lot about her."

"You poor child," she said, an honest sorrow in her voice. Perhaps it was her outfit, how dressed down she was, but she didn't seem nearly as unapproachable as she had in the pictures I'd seen. "And you recently lost your father as well, did you not?"

"About a year ago."

"So you're all alone now?"

I almost said yes, because for a long time I'd felt alone. For so long I'd thought I had nothing more than chains on me, but my view had shifted over the time with my men, because they'd reminded me what family felt like. "No, not alone." Her expression let me continue. "I'm not alone at all. I have my sister, I have the men who are like my brothers, I have a man who has stepped in like my father and now I have men who I love as well. I might have lost both my parents, but I'm less alone now than I ever was before."

Pauline didn't answer right away, and when I lifted my gaze to hers again, she had her head tilted as she studied me. "You have a lovely smile when you talk about these things. Perhaps this is an unwelcome or inappropriate statement, but I think you'll make a lovely addition to our family. I'm not sure I could ask for a better daughter-in-law."

Her words almost made me smile. Sure, I didn't *want* that future, but at the same time, hearing someone welcome me into their family not due to my name but rather because of my personality? I'd craved that for so many years.

I chose my words carefully. "I appreciate that sentiment, but I don't want that and I won't accept it. I don't want to be with Lorien and that won't ever change."

"He isn't the bad man people think. I realize he doesn't always do things that make him appear kind or trustworthy, but that's only because he was raised in a difficult situation. He was raised by my sister to hide his true parentage, but he wasn't truly accepted there, and he was a very smart child. He knew he was unwanted there, that he didn't belong, and it warped him. It forced him to find beauty where he could. I truly believe that with the right people around him, he could get better."

"That story is similar to my sister's," I admitted softly. "My mother was pregnant with my sister when she married my father. He knew that Nem wasn't his, and he always treated her differently. In fact, when he had my mother killed, he attempted to kill her as well. She was raised the same as Lorien in a lot of ways."

"And from what I've heard of your sister, I would think you'd understand why he is the way he is. They seem to have reacted in a similar way—by hardening, by keeping others away, by recognizing that they could rely on no one but themselves. You trust your sister despite that—why can't you trust Lorien in the same way?"

"Because my sister didn't turn her anger against innocents. I won't pretend she's a good person. She'll do whatever she has to to protect those around her, but she doesn't enjoy hurting people just to cause them pain. She doesn't see that as beautiful or as art. Instead, the terrible things she does are *because* she still loves people, because she cherishes them."

"Lorien cares as well. Perhaps it's harder to see, more difficult to identify, but it's there. Can you explain all that he's done for you in any other way? He's never fought with me about anything. He's always done what he wants to do no matter what my feelings are, but for *you*, he has stood his ground."

"That's not the same as love and you know it. I saw your face when you talked about your daughter reading with you. It doesn't matter what other people say about you—you love her, right?"

"Of course I do."

"Would you hurt her to keep her with you? Would you ignore her feelings and threaten the things she cares about to get your way?"

Pauline didn't need to answer—her face did it for her.

"That's the difference. He doesn't care about what I want, what would make me happy. He sees me as something he wants to have, something he thinks will fix him, and you see me as the same. I lived my life knowing that I'd be given away to whoever my father wanted, that it was my duty to do that, but I was wrong. I watched what that does to people. It destroys them. Lorien doesn't want me—he wants what he thinks having me will do for him. It might not be power for him, but he thinks I'm going to fix him, that with me, he'll see the world differently, that he'll feel differently, and I can't do that." I tried so hard to explain it, to get her to hear me.

She wasn't heartless—it was clear in her expression, in her words. However, seeing something was wrong and being willing to do something about it were two very different things.

And when she sighed, I knew her answer. "I'm sorry. I really wish I could resolve this in a way that would give you what you want, but at the end of the day you're asking me to prioritize you over my son. You're asking me to place your wants and happiness over my own son's life. Can you not see that is an unreasonable expectation? That you place me in an impossible position?"

A crushing weight settled on my shoulders as doubt crept into my mind. I'd come here thinking that because I understood her, that because I'd lived my whole life around people like her, I could make her understand. I'd thought that I'd be able to convince her, that I could speak her language and get her to agree.

However, it wasn't just a mob boss I spoke to right now. That fact made me pause as I thought back to my mother, to Nem, to the gentle smile as Pauline had thought about her daughter.

I was talking to a woman first and foremost.

"What about your daughters?" I asked.

"What about them?"

"You're pushing for Lorien because you want him to take over, right?"

"Yes. You're well aware of how important strong leadership is. I won't be around forever, and I have to ensure this family does not fall into chaos. That should have been my oldest son, but he didn't survive, so it falls to Lorien."

"But why?" At her look, which implied she didn't understand, I pressed. "Why do you need him to take over? I've *met* your daughters. Don't look at me like that—I wasn't going to come here without a little more information. My point is that they're both strong, capable women. Why do you need your son to take over?"

"Because it's always been the sons who take over."

"But you've led this family since your husband passed away, and from what I've heard, you've done an amazing job."

"It isn't uncommon for a woman to run things for short periods of time, until the next-in-line comes of age. I've simply kept the family going until Lorien was prepared to take over."

"Stop putting yourself down. You haven't just kept the family afloat, you've held it together. You've weathered all the problems, grown your power and position and assured your family a strong future. Your daughters can do the same because they've seen *you* do it. My sister is proof of that. Our family has never been stronger, never in a better place than since she's taken over."

A line appeared on Pauline's forehead, her eyebrows drawn toward one another. It surprised me that this seemed like the first time she'd truly considered such a thing.

Then again, before Nem, would I have considered it either? After growing up seeing women only used to prop up men, would I truly have been able to envision a woman taking over, to think about a man relenting to her wishes?

Probably not.

"You've said yourself that your sister is different, though. She is an enigma. Who is to say that what she's done can be done by anyone else?"

I looked straight at Pauline, praying she truly heard me this time, that she listened, that she accepted it. "Your daughters *deserve* the chance to try, don't you think? Lorien's warped—you know it. I've seen no evidence that your family matters to him at all. The rumors are that he was behind the death of your husband and other son, after all."

"There's no proof of that," she rushed out.

"Maybe not, but you're too smart not to know the truth. In your heart, you know whether or not Lorien is capable of it, whether or not he did it. Do you really think Lorien can lead the family? That he has what it takes to put the needs of your family first as you have?"

"With you…" Her words trailed off, an uncertainty there.

"I can't change him. That's not how it works. He's willing to run over and remove anyone who doesn't serve him, so if you place him in that position, do you really think your family will survive? Do you think he'll protect your daughters?"

She looked down at her hands, and I could almost see the way she thought about the wrinkles there, the spots that had come with age. Things like that could convince a person, could force them to recognize how quickly time passed and make them come to terms with a reality that they'd never wanted to see.

"So what do you want me to do? How is it that you think me betraying Lorien is going to help anything?"

"I'm not asking you to betray him. I'm asking you to let him face his own consequences. I'm only asking that you don't hand him *your* power so he can force it on others. Let him stand on his own. Let me deal with him and face him on his own. If I lose, then I lose."

"And if that leads to his death? If what I do results in the death of my own son? Then what?"

I pressed my lips together as I thought back to how many things I'd gone through, what I'd witnessed, and the truth spilled from my lips, my voice quiet and soft. "I've seen people come to power and fall. I've watched other families succeed and fail and do terrible things for power, and you know what I've seen at the core of so much of it? People willing to sacrifice their women. They sell their girls to other families to buy fleeting peace, they tell their wives to smile and stay quiet and play the part and they train their daughters from day one to be useful while their sons run amok and do as they please. All I'm asking is that you don't sell out your daughters for the sake of a man. Don't trade their lives and their futures to pay for his mistakes."

And there it was, the truth that I'd buried inside me, the wound I'd carried from a lifetime of seeing myself as nothing but a product, something to be traded and used for the benefit of those around me.

I couldn't change my past, couldn't change what had happened, but I could damn well open my mouth and try to ensure it didn't happen to someone else.

And now? All I could do was hope that Pauline listened.

* * * *

Vance

I'm going to put that girl over my knee and spank her until she cries. No, more than that! I won't stop until she's actually sorry!

Even as I thought that, I knew it was a bluff. Just seeing her face safe and sound would be enough for me to forgive her. All I wanted was her back, to make sure she hadn't gotten hurt, to kiss her until she was breathless and understood just how much she'd terrified me.

It wasn't the first time she'd done something like this, but it was so much worse than before. This time, she knew better than to take anything we could use to track her, which left us with no chance of finding her.

Not that I didn't know where she'd gone. It wasn't hard to guess exactly what her plan was.

She went to Pauline.

Which meant she'd headed straight into enemy territory, alone and unarmed. And we had no choice but to wait, because any show of force would only endanger her more.

The roar of the engine to my car was a sound that I could never forget. I was off the couch and headed toward the door before it even fully registered in my head.

I refused to feel relieved yet, though, not until I actually saw her, until I knew she was okay.

Hayden was at the door when I reached it, and he yanked it open, rushing out before me. Char was on my heels, and Tor was already outside.

My car came to a stop in the driveway, the tint keeping me from seeing inside. The door opened, and my knees nearly gave out the moment I saw the familiar brown hair, when she stood on her own.

She's alive.

I grasped the side of the house to keep myself upright, just the sight of her stealing all the energy from my body. *Fuck*, I felt like a girl about to faint.

It made me realize just how much I needed her, how integral she'd become to my entire life. What if she hadn't come back? What if something had happened and I'd never gotten the chance to see her again?

Would my revenge even matter in that case?

Only to avenge her…

Hayden pulled her against his chest, hugging her tight before checking her for injuries. Tor and Char stood off to the sides, watching over, and at least Kenz had the decency to look regretful.

I swallowed hard but stayed in place as they all walked up to the porch, where Kenz offered me a look that implied she knew damn well she was in trouble.

"Vance," she said, her voice enough to break what little restraint I had. Suddenly, that sound strengthened my legs enough for me to let go of the wall and grab her by the arm. If I'd been thinking straight, I didn't think I'd *ever* have touched her so roughly.

I wasn't, by nature, a rough man. I much preferred teasing women, making them melt from gentle caresses and my eager tongue, but Kenz had shattered that. I pulled her to me and took her mouth in a kiss so demanding I had no doubts it would feel like an attack.

However, it was the only way I could express the depths of what I felt—the fear, the bottomless worry, and how damned relieved I felt at having her back.

Kenz didn't fight it—in fact, she responded in kind, giving back the same passion, the same desire.

A throat cleared, waking me up. "Let's take this inside," Hayden said. "I think we have some things to talk about."

Kenz broke the kiss, her cheeks blazing, her gaze darting away from mine.

Right. We have to talk about what happened.

We managed to get inside, to all sit down in the kitchen, at the table. Hayden—ever the family dad—brought bottles of water and set them on the table for each of us.

Kenz took hers, opened it, then drank some all while not speaking.

And we gave her that time to sort through her thoughts. Pushing her wouldn't make this any easier, wouldn't get her to open up any faster. I'd learned that Kenz did things at her own speed, and fighting her on that only made it all the more difficult.

Finally, she put the lid back on and took a deep breath. I prepared myself for bad news.

"She agreed."

That wasn't what I'd expected. Sure, her coming back meant that Pauline at least hadn't trapped her, hadn't given her over to Lorien, but never in my wildest dreams did I expect her to actually succeed.

"What does that mean exactly?" Char asked.

"She's agreed to withdraw all official support for Lorien. Her contacts, her people, none of them will help him. He's got his own talents, of course, but he won't have her backing. She'll send out official word this morning and by noon, any support or help he got from her or her family will be gone. He'll be on his own."

I blinked slowly, stunned to silence as I tried to make sense of that. This whole time, Lorien had been a risk partly due to his family. It had given him reach and backing, like having a snarling wolf pack standing behind him. It meant all our steps had to contend with that danger.

Now, however, that was gone. Kenz had single-handedly stood against those wolves and come out the winner.

"Fuck," Hayden whispered, the word taking everyone by surprise since we all turned to look toward him. "Sorry," he muttered. "I just really didn't think she'd budge, not after talking to her. I can't believe you got her to do that…"

Kenz sighed softly, her expression not showing much pleasure. Then again, he didn't say he was proud. He basically said he was shocked, and given Kenz's general lack of self-confidence, that was probably not the best way to phrase it.

At least Hayden caught on, because he did that stammering thing that meant he figured out he'd said something wrong even if he wasn't sure what. Sadly, he often had no idea still how to fix it. "I just mean I didn't think *anyone* could make her change her mind. I was so damned worried about you going off like that without us, that hearing you managed it, it's surprising."

She offered up a half-smile, the sort of look meant to reassure him. "Like I said — I lived with people like her. You all know my real life, how I grew up, but I feel like you really don't understand what it means. Pauline is not a big deal to me. In fact, if my mother had survived, I'm pretty sure they would have been best friends. I understand that world, know how to navigate it, how to negotiate with people in it. You really should stop seeing me as some poor lost kitten who hasn't experienced anything. I know I was sheltered in a lot of ways growing up, that the Quad always tried to keep me from anything terrible, but that doesn't mean I didn't see it. You should trust that I can handle this, that I can help."

As much as I wanted to argue with her over that, it was hard to do so after she'd done what we couldn't. She'd risked herself, her freedom, her very life to walk up to Pauline and confront her. Even alone, without us, without knowing how it would go, Kenz had stood there and convinced Pauline to do what we had not.

It was impossible not to be impressed by her, not see her in a different light. Instead of a lost kitten, instead of someone who needed protection and shelter, I caught a glimpse of the fully grown woman she really was.

And my blood heated at that. Sure, she excited me when I saw her as innocent and sweet, but watching her in all her power was one hell of a turn-on as well.

"You have a nasty habit of running off, you know," Char said, his tone saying he didn't give a damn if she'd succeeded — he wouldn't let her off that easily.

"You wouldn't have let me go if I hadn't."

"Damn right we wouldn't have," Char snapped. As soon as the words left him, he stopped himself, took a deep breath, let it out slowly, then spoke again in a calmer voice. "But clearly we would have been wrong. You can handle yourself and you've proven that."

She lifted her head higher, a relieved smile pulling across her pink lips. "Does that mean I'm not in trouble?"

"Oh, I wouldn't go *that* far," I said.

She turned her gaze to me, her eyebrows pulling toward each other. "But you just said…"

I glanced to the side, toward Char, who offered me a smirk as though to tell me I'd figured out *exactly* what he thought.

And I agreed.

"Oh, we're proud of you all right." I rose from my seat, then crossed over to where Kenz sat. I leaned against the table, to her side, and stared down at her.

She looked up at me, and *damn* was that a pretty sight. Pink tinged her cheeks, and her dark eyes were opened wide. She'd parted her lips to breathe more easily, and all of it made her look so innocent.

"You've proven yourself capable, right? That's what you wanted, to prove you were a grown woman. Well, that means there's no reason to hold back anymore, is there?" I traced her cheek with a finger of my left hand, refusing to look away, to miss a single second of her pretty face, especially after the fear I'd suffered before.

She swallowed but didn't pull away, didn't try to escape. Her only reaction was an eager nod.

The table groaned slightly, which pulled my gaze to the other side of Kenz. Hayden leaned against the table just like I did, on her other side, trapping her there. Likewise, Char and Tor had also risen and come to stand behind her.

It made her look even smaller than she normally did, more fragile, like prey between four starving beasts.

"You do understand what he's saying, don't you?" Hayden asked softly, his voice coaxing and sweet, as though he wanted to ensure she had the ability to truly think through it. "I don't want you to agree to something you'll regret just because you didn't know what we're asking for."

Part of me expected Kenz to wilt at that. She was still rather innocent, after all. Even after what we'd done so far, she was still a virgin. She still hadn't gone all the way, not yet, and here we were basically saying that her first real time would be with *four* men. Even if she agreed, I couldn't imagine her doing it with much less than a shy nod.

However, that wasn't what happened. Instead, she stood, still trapped between us. The position made her appear less tiny, but not by a whole lot. Still, she pulled her shoulders back, straightening her posture, moving her gaze from one of us to the next as if wanting to ensure we *all* heard her loud and clear.

"I know exactly what Vance meant, what you mean, and I'm saying yes. I want to have sex with all four of you—please."

And just like that, she'd proven yet again that no matter how she looked, no matter how small and fragile, no matter how innocent, no matter how many times we assured ourselves that she needed our protection, she was more than a match for each of us.

Which meant, for the first time, I had no intention of holding back.

If she wanted the four of us…well, I'd give her all she could handle and more.

Chapter Ten

Kenz

My back hit the mattress of my bed when Vance tossed me down. That action shook my brain enough to wake me from the moment, to make me look around at the four men who I'd just asked to have sex with me.

You really are jumping in with both feet, aren't you?

Leave it to me to not ease into anything, to not think about this logically. I'd never had actual sex with anyone yet here I was, ready for a roll with *four* men? It was like never having hiked then deciding my first time out would be to take on Mt. Kilimanjaro.

Yet, I'd never been the type to go slow, not when I wanted something, and I really wanted this.

"You having second thoughts?" Hayden asked before crawling onto the bed, resting to my left and cupping my cheek in his warm, comforting hand.

"Yes," I admitted.

He hesitated, as though he might pull away, but I caught his wrist to keep his hand on me. "I'm not saying I want to stop. I'm saying that only an idiot wouldn't have second thoughts. I want this, though. I trust you — all of you."

Hayden smiled, rubbing my cheek with his thumb. "Okay, Kenz. If you change your mind, though, you speak up. We'll slow down, we'll change things, we'll stop all together if you want."

"Don't tell her that," Char snapped, drawing my attention to him.

He stood at the foot of the bed, his lips drawn into a smirk, the sort of look that made me rub my thighs together. This side of him, the one I'd thought I hated, had changed so much. Now I saw it as special, as the real him that others didn't get to see.

This was *my* Char, the truth of him that he kept hidden deep down from every other person. He protected it, terrified that no one else would accept it, yet he let me in. He let me see it, trusted me to accept it.

This side was snarky, it enjoyed teasing and toying with me, but I trusted it — and him — entirely.

It made me stick my tongue out at him in response to his comment.

He undid the top button of his shirt, each of his actions slow and methodical while the corner of his mouth tipped up. "You're feisty, huh? I wonder just hold long you'll hold on to that after we start to fuck you, hmm?"

And just like that, I was pretty damn sure I wouldn't last long against them.

My expression must have amused Char, because he chuckled as he went on unbuttoning his shirt. That somehow felt more threatening than if he'd spoken to me. His silence promised something far lewder.

Beside him, Vance grabbed the hem of his shirt and pulled the fabric up and over his head. He took it off in one swoop, tossing it aside as though it no longer mattered. It allowed me to see his bare, pale chest, and again I found myself stunned by the sight.

How could he be so perfect? How could anyone appear so flawless? He removed his gloves, next, one at a time, then glanced at the prosthetic on his hand. He didn't move at first, as though unsure what to do about it.

"You can take it off," I whispered.

He lifted his gaze from his hand to me. "You sure? It's not pretty."

"I don't care about pretty. I care about *you*. If you want to leave it on, if it makes you feel better, you can do that. Just don't leave it on for my benefit. I don't care."

He nodded, then dropped his gaze again as he slid the silicone off, setting the prosthetic on the dresser along with the gloves. The funny thing was that despite the mangled hand, I still found him flawless. That didn't change my view of him in the least. I wanted him every bit as much as I had before I'd ever known about his injury.

He swallowed hard, then gave me an adorably shy smile, relief clear in his expression.

He put one knee on the bed, then bent forward, placing his right hand against the bed for balance before leaning over and taking my lips in a kiss that said everything he hadn't.

I parted my lips, inviting him deeper, offering up everything I had to him. He had more than enough experience to show me all the things I'd missed out on, everything I wanted that I hadn't yet tasted. I couldn't ask for better guides through this than these men, after all.

My attention remained locked on Vance and his teasing lips, so distracted that I almost missed as someone undid the hook of my slacks. Hands grasped the waist of them and tugged them down my legs, pausing only long enough to pull off my shoes and socks. I had no idea who did it and honestly?

I didn't give a damn. It didn't matter to me, didn't change a thing, so long as they didn't stop.

Lips touched me, right at the waist of my panties, leaving a string of kisses along the sensitive skin there. I almost thought it was Hayden until a sting made me lift my hips — *Clearly, Char.*

His breath heated my skin when he chuckled before he took the lace between his teeth, pulled it, then allowed it to snap back. I gasped at the sharp pain, more so because after the initial shock of it, it lessened to a delicious burn. That was so much like him, wasn't it? A bit uncomfortable, a bit scary, but in the end, something I enjoyed.

He grasped the panties and worked them down my legs, the cool air brushing over my pussy when he spread my legs afterward. The position exposed me fully in front of the men.

And while I hadn't thought myself to be someone that nervous normally, especially about my body, it turned out that letting the men I loved see me in such details stirred up all my worries.

As quickly as they rose, however, Hayden washed them away by running his hand up my side, pushing up my shirt as he went, so his fingers stroked across my bare skin. He traced the band of my bra, over my ribs, taking extra time over the scar that rested there from when I'd almost died.

He leaned in and offered a gentle kiss to that place, a reverent touch that was so much deeper than lust or need. Instead, it showed a connection between us, something that bound us more than just our bodies.

Hayden moved his kisses along the band, then up the inner edge of one of the cups. He was *so* close to the place that yearned for his touch, where my nipple pebbled behind the thin lace of the bra. I arched up, something between a plea and an offer.

Vance broke the kiss, freeing my lips and letting me breathe more easily. He ran thumb across my bottom lip with a smirk. "You still haven't learned to breathe through your nose? You really are going to be fun to train."

The word 'train' would normally annoy me, but when he said it in *that* voice? I was all for becoming the best of students in any lesson he wanted to give me.

Char ran his hands up my thighs as he spread them wider, my hips nearly aching from the stretch. If I'd thought I was exposed before, it was *nothing* compared to this. The position left nothing unseen, nothing hidden or private. I glanced down my body to find Char there, his shirt gone, his pants unbuttoned but still on, and the most devastating smile that I had ever seen painted across his lips.

It wasn't his fake one, this one far too threatening to be his mask. It made me shudder hard, wondering just how I could be expected to survive whatever these men had planned. I'd been the one to agree, the one desperate for this, yet he could make me wonder if it'd been such a good idea.

I'd never been a reckless person, someone more likely to think carefully about my actions, to do as expected from others, to bend to the rules at the end of the day. These men made me feel as though that wasn't important, though. They made me think that nothing mattered but them, but this moment, but having this with them.

I knew how fast life stole away the things that mattered, had experienced the crushing loss when the universe took those closest to me, and I wouldn't let them slip away—not without savoring every last memory and moment with them.

The bed shifted, causing me to look up and find Tor crawling onto the mattress near the headboard. He'd stripped down to nothing, not bothering to leave his pants on as the others had.

The fact drew a grin from me—especially because I had to admit—his body impressed me. It was different from the others, leaner but no less strong, his skin a darker color, his golden eyes bright and catching the light.

He caught my arm and tugged softly so I sat up and rolled toward him, now kneeling on the bed before him.

The intensity and need in his gaze unnerved me, until he gave me a gentle smile as though to reassure me. That quiet way he had drawn me closer, made me lean in to brush my lips to his, wanting to feel him against me.

He gave me the kiss I needed, but it didn't last long. Instead, he leaned against the headboard and shifted me, my back to him. His long, agile fingers easily undid the fasteners of my bra, the band loosening. He pulled the shirt from me, over my head, then did the same with the bra. It left me entirely naked, and meant I felt *every* inch of him when he tugged me back by the hips and fitted me against his chest.

His heart beat hard enough that I felt it where we were pressed together, and his hard cock nestled against my lower back. He reached forward — his arms long enough to wrap around me — and he grasped my inner thighs, near my knees, then spread my legs open.

He kissed the side of my neck, the touch like a burn, as though he'd branded me. I tilted my head, giving him all the access he wanted.

"Mine," he whispered, his voice soft and possessive and just as dangerous as the man himself. That one word, that one declaration stole my thoughts away, so all I could do was nod in agreement.

Yes, I wanted to be his. I wanted him not to fight this, for none of them to fight this, for them not to reject me or push me away anymore.

Something brushed against my thighs, further up than Tor's grasp, causing me to snap my eyes open.

Vance rested there, between my legs, a smirk on his lips as he moved his hands up to the juncture of my thighs. I shivered, instinct making me try to snap my legs closed, but Tor's hands kept me from hiding.

Vance laughed softly and leaned in and lapped at my drenched cunt, the feeling of his tongue on me already familiar and welcome. In fact, it seemed as though he'd already taught my body about this, because I reacted instantly.

My body heated more, straining toward relief, prepared as if it already knew where he would take it.

"Good girl," Char said, that compelling voice of his reaching out to me like the darkest of whispers. He sat on the corner of the bed, his pants gone now — I had no idea when he'd done that—and his hand wrapped around his cock as he watched.

His gaze was just as hot as his voice, as the sight of him stroking his dick. "You need to let Vance there get you off so you're ready. You see, you wanted this, you wanted us to fuck you, right? That'll be far easier on you if you're relaxed. So just lie back and let him work, let him make you come, because the sooner you do, the sooner you'll get your first cock of the night."

First cock of the night.

Never had I expected to hear those words, and despite the embarrassment of something so blunt, they served their intended purpose. His statement, combined with Vance's lips, with the subtle rocking of Tor's hips that ground his cock against my back—it all tossed me over that edge.

My eyes slid closed as I came hard, everything going dark, like a channel changing on a television, something that shorted the world out around me. My hands flew out wildly, one going to Vance's head, the other gripping someone to my side—I was too far gone to even know who it was.

I rode out that orgasm, each rise and fall crushing and overwhelming and shattering to my sense of self. It was like my body wasn't even my own anymore, as though I wasn't the person I'd always been.

When the orgasm subsided, when I was nothing but a quivering mess, a hand on my cheek forced my eyes open.

Hayden smiled at me, making me realize they'd shifted. I was still against Tor, but Vance had moved and Hayden now knelt between my thighs, his palm against my cheek, his expression gentle. "You still sure?"

I nuzzled against his palm then nodded, the answer easy for me. I couldn't possibly back out, not now, not when I had what I wanted so badly so close.

He smiled warmly. "Brave girl. You sure outlasted us, huh? Been turning you down all this time, trying to keep my head on straight, and here we are anyway. I've taken on the most dangerous criminals, but I was brought to my knees by one little girl." He leaned in and brushed his lips against mine as he moved his fingers to my pussy, sinking two of them into me. "And I wouldn't have it any other way."

Hayden

I pulled back from my kiss with Kenz and stared down at her body, unable to believe I was here, touching her like this. Sure, we'd agreed, and I'd come to terms with it—mostly—but it still didn't feel quite real.

Kenz was so far above what I deserved. She was stunning, young, strong, powerful and I was a man in that past-his-prime group where I could still recall my glory days because they were just barely past.

Tor had released Kenz's thigh and reached his hand out. I frowned for a moment until I saw what he held out to me. I took the foil wrapper, thankful *someone* had thought this through.

Not that I'd planned to have sex with her without a condom, but it had been so long since I'd had to think about it that it never occurred to me to pick any up.

Kenz's expression was still dazed from her orgasm, but the color on her cheeks deepened from a light pink to a deeper color, as though the condom made this real.

"I wouldn't risk you," I said softly. "So we'll take all the precautions we need."

"You know, you totally ruin the moment," Char muttered to my side. "This is supposed to be sexy, but you always manage to sound like an old man."

"Shut up," I snapped. "I'm just not a vulgar brat like you."

He laughed, a sure sign that our bickering wasn't a result of either of us being actually upset. In fact, it broke some of the tension and helped me relax.

By pointing out the obvious—that I was older, that I hadn't done this in a while, that Kenz *was* so much younger—it helped me accept it and stop worrying.

Kenz knew who and what I was, and she still wanted me. Who was I to decide I wasn't good enough for her?

I ripped the foil open, then rolled the condom over my shaft, my gaze locked on Kenz's pussy. After one more deep breath, I shifted forward, getting closer, one hand around my cock and the other grasping her hip. Even through the condom, the heat of her cunt seared me when I pressed against her, when I fit my cock into the softness of her pussy, not pushing hard enough to enter her, just enjoying the sensation of this, the long, teasing moments of expectation before I finally had her fully.

I lifted my gaze to hers, staring into her dark eyes, reassured to find no fear resting in the depths. Nerves? Sure, but that was to be expected. The trust got to me, though. Even now, even when she didn't have enough experience to know what to expect, she gave herself over to us fully. She believed in us, that we wouldn't hurt her. It humbled me, and I swore that I'd never betray that trust.

I'd never risk that trust, never let anything harm her, never give her a reason not to look at me like this.

I didn't lean heavily against her, wanting to watch my cock disappear into her gripping heat. It would embarrass her, but that was too bad. The need was too great to resist.

I shifted my hips forward and her tight cunt squeezed the head of my cock so much that I let out a loud groan. *Damn it.* I wanted to seem cool, to be in control, but this girl stole that from me so easily.

I was a mess around her all the time, unable to control or sort out my thoughts. She was just too much for me to stay calm and collected around.

I released the base of my cock and instead grasped her other hip. Because of the way Tor held her legs, I had my arms wrapped outside of them, holding her hips and ass so if Tor didn't have a hold of her, she could have set her feet on my shoulders.

It not only gave me one hell of a view, but it also gave me complete control over her — over the depth of my cock, over moving her as I pleased.

Tor released her legs and instead cupped her breasts, leaving the rest to me.

Kenz shifted her hips, though I couldn't tell if she was trying to get more or less. I held her firmly so she could get neither on her own, then plunged another inch of my cock into her. I advanced and retreated in small movements, spurred on by the noises that escaped her sweet pink lips.

She whimpered, her hands going to my wrists, her blunt nails biting in as she tried to gain some control of the situation, of herself.

Tor nipped her earlobe, his lips moving in a way that suggested he whispered to her, and the way her pussy tightened each time he paused made me suspect whatever those words were did it for her.

"Breathe, Kenz," I forced myself to say, shoving the words through my gritted teeth. Talking at all felt far too difficult given the way she wrapped around me, but I couldn't stop myself from saying it. "Almost there."

She nodded, her eyes closed tight. *Brave girl*. I didn't think, if I were in her position, I could have said yes to something like this. I couldn't have given myself over to four men like us, been willing to put myself in such a vulnerable position. No doubt that girl was stronger and braver than she gave herself credit for.

I tightened my hands once more, pulled back the tiniest bit, then plunged the rest of the way into her, sheathing my full cock inside her. Kenz arched her back, her body looking like a sacrifice.

And the sight of her cunt spread around my cock was *magical*. My body pressed tight against her, not a centimeter of my cock outside her, claiming her as deep as possible.

Vance moved over on the bed, beside Kenz, and caught her chin. He turned her face toward him, grasped his cock in his other hand, then rubbed the head against her soft lips. "Open up for me, sweetheart."

Kenz didn't bother to even open her eyes before parting her lips.

And here I was, at my age, learning new things about myself. I never would have figured that seeing another man's dick sliding into the mouth of the woman I loved would do a thing for me.

Or maybe it was better to say I didn't think it'd do anything good for me. If I ever considered it, I might have thought I'd want to punch the man at most. It was why a sudden rush of pleasure took me so by surprise.

As it turned out, I found it a huge turn-on. Kenz's cheeks hollowed out, her lips stretched around Vance's cock, but even still, she didn't release her grasp on my wrists. Instead, she trusted Vance not to go too deep, just gave him the ability to use her mouth as he pleased.

Normally, lasting longer would have been a point of pride for me. I'd have wanted to prove I could please a woman—especially the first time—and struggled against my own release. However, this was her first time, and she had a *long* night ahead of her.

So I stared at the way Vance's cock filled her small mouth before I pulled back and plunged hard into her, taking her deep, allowing myself to enjoy the tightness of her pussy. I chased my own release, though chasing it didn't take much effort since I'd wanted this for so long. I recalled the way she'd gotten herself off before, thought about all the times I'd caught fleeting glimpses of her, all the times I'd wanted *this* so badly.

It was impossible to resist, so I buried myself as deep as I could just as Tor moved one of his hands down her body, to her pussy, where he rubbed her little clit. She came again just as I did, her vise-like grip milking my cock as I spilled into the condom.

I panted hard, my breath rough and uneven, my gaze locked on the shivering, gorgeous woman trapped between us.

Even if I'd wanted to deny it or run away from it before, it was all the more obvious now.

I loved this woman with everything I had, and for the first time, I really wanted the chance at a future.

Tor

Kenz's body was a special kind of torture. I'd spent time in some of the worst places in the world. I'd had to track targets in war-torn foreign countries, had spent nights in filthy little hovels in crime-infested neighborhoods, yet none of those were as challenging as the sensation of Kenz's body against my cock.

I wanted to sink into her, to get more stimulation, but instead I had to endure as I watched her come apart on Hayden's cock. The sight was something else—something so passionate and miraculous it could cause a non-believer to believe in something larger than themselves. Hell, it made a believer out of me, and I'd lived my life with no faith of any sort.

I'd happily devote my life to worshiping at the altar of her body. It sounded like a damn good way to spend my remaining years.

Hayden grasped the base of his cock to hold the condom as he pulled out of her, Kenz shifting as he did so. He groaned, then tugged the condom off, tied the base and tossed it into the wastebasket near the wall.

My fingers remained on her pussy, though I'd stopped rubbing her clit, giving her a moment to catch her breath, to come down from the latest release. Even so, she still had Vance's cock in her mouth, though he'd remained shallow. Her throat moved as she swallowed, her jaw shifting, suggesting she moved her tongue against him.

I moved my hand forward slightly, following her wet folds until I could press my middle finger into her pussy, finding it twitching and swollen and drenched. She moaned, the sound muffled by Vance's dick.

It reminded me of how it had felt when she'd blown me before, how tight and hot her mouth had been, how it had felt to spill onto her tongue. My cock jerked in response, desperate to plunge somewhere tight and warm.

Kenz moved, though she didn't stop pleasuring Vance. She rose slightly, rubbing back against my cock, her desire clear.

I looked over at Char, who only smirked in response. The bastard was enjoying this show *far* too much. He really was a pervert, wasn't he?

Maybe no one here has a right to call anyone else a pervert.

He offered a single nod, telling me I could go next. It made sense—Char seemed content to wait until last and Vance was enjoying Kenz's eager mouth.

Kenz rose slightly, the action placing her more in my lap rather than sitting on the bed in front of me. It let my cock move from between our bodies to resting along her hot folds.

"Isn't she eager?" Char said with a laugh. "One round and she's already like this? She really *is* perfect for us, isn't she?"

Something touched my cock, making me jump, until I glanced down to find Hayden there. *This is the last thing I'd have expected.* He'd torn open another condom, and he rolled it down the length of my cock. He did it slowly, and the sensation of his large hand against me felt far better than it had any right to.

Maybe it was one of those times where, especially in the moment, when I'd ended up this far gone, a hand was a hand. Anything stroking against my shaft at this point would feel amazing.

Once he had the condom all the way on, I groaned as he stroked down my length once more, then grasped the base. He used his other hand to hold Kenz's hip, steering her higher, her weight on her knees but her body still pressed back against my chest.

"Look at that, taking care of the kids," Char mocked, though no one could miss the fast his hand moved faster on his cock, a sure sign that no matter what came out of his mouth, he enjoyed this.

"Why don't you just call me Daddy and get on with it?" Hayden responded, as though trying to go toe-to-toe with the mouthy redhead.

Stupid. Few people, if any, could face Char when it came to his smart mouth. Trying would only frustrate someone all the more.

Sure enough, Char responded without missing a beat. "Okay, *Daddy*, why don't you stop keeping our kitten there waiting any longer?"

Hayden sighed, but still did as Char said. The warmth of Kenz's cunt mixed with the feeling of Hayden's strong, large hand on my cock, blurring the line between right and wrong.

Kenz shifted down, and nothing had ever felt quite so good as her gripping tightness on my length. She whined, but Vance set his hand on the back of her head to hold her still.

"Focus on me, sweetheart," Vance said. "The rest'll take care of itself."

I kissed her throat, then whispered into her ear, knowing my voice was so quiet it would only carry to her. "You feel good. Hot. Wet. Tight."

She shivered but gave in, so I moved my hands to her hips, my fingers brushing where Hayden's were for a moment. I didn't expect her to ride me — with as much going on as there was right now, even an experienced person would have trouble with that. With her in this position, it gave me the chance to control the depth and speed, to pull her down and thrust my hips up at the same time.

So I did just that, tugging her down as I lifted my hips to fill her entirely. My cock delved as deep as possible into her, filling her, and she tightened so much around me I wondered if she'd come again.

By this point, I'd expect that those would mix together, one after another, impossible to tell when one ended and the next started. Her body was nothing but a mess of sensation and hormones and pleasure — and damn it, I liked her like that.

Hayden shifted back, stretching out on the bed, and despite him lowering himself enough that I couldn't see him anymore, I sure figured out what he was up to when I felt a mouth and tongue against Kenz — and given the small amount of space, they also brushed my cock.

I groaned at the sensation, but it only spurred me on to position Kenz slightly up, giving me room to thrust up and into her. She didn't have to move — in fact, I held her tightly so she couldn't, pinning her against my chest. I rolled my hips, fucking into her deeply, taking her the way I'd craved for so long.

I had to be careful always, restrained. I knew what my skills could do, what I was capable of, that I had a part of me that took life without concern or regret, which meant I always held myself tightly. Now, however, I released that hold.

I let myself take her exactly as I wanted to, my lips moving as I whispered to her, having no idea what I was saying until the words left me. "I love you," I admitted softly. "You are the only good thing I have in my life." I hadn't talked this much in...

I wasn't sure I ever had. Each word taxed my vocal chords and my voice had started to crack, my throat burning. Still, I didn't regret a single one of them. They were important, and I wanted her to hear them from my lips.

Not from a screen, not written on a board. I needed her to hear them in my voice—broken as it was—because they were the only words I'd ever spoken that *mattered.*

"I need you." This time, my voice completely gave way, the last word scratching out and almost impossible to hear.

Kenz pulled again, and this time, Vance released her. She slid her lips off his cock, then twisted enough to see me. Even still, it wasn't the most comfortable position, but her sweet gaze sought mine. "Don't hurt yourself," she whispered, her breathless voice coming out similar to mine, the words interrupted slightly by each time I thrust into her.

Her gaze dropped to my lips, and I knew exactly what she wanted.

Anything she wants, I want to give her.

I caught her chin with one hand, then leaned enough to give her the kiss she craved. I used it to tell her the things I struggled with any other time, the words that my throat wouldn't let me get out. A saltiness lingered on her tongue, a leftover from Vance's cock, no doubt, and I hungrily captured each taste I found. Something that may have seemed impossible before, something I didn't think I could possibly enjoy, now had me thrusting up and into her wildly.

I licked into her heated mouth as I plunged my cock into her, the familiar tightening in my lower back telling me I neared my end. I moved one of my hands to her lower stomach, keeping her pinned against me, as I took her hard and deep.

I came in a hard rush, my frantic kiss turning slower and sweeter as the energy seeped away from me. Hell, if we had been alone, I was pretty sure I would have happily wrapped my arms around her and drifted off right there on the spot.

I offered one last lick to the inside of her mouth before pulling back and looking at her flushed, lust-drunk face.

She was a light, something bright and sweet and kind. They were things I'd never had in my life, and now that I'd experienced them, I knew I'd never be able to let them go.

A life without her warmth would never be enough again.

Chapter Eleven

Vance

My cock was wet from Kenz's saliva and the cool air of the room chilled it. I'd manage not to come, to hold off despite how wonderfully Kenz had sucked on me, how she'd toyed with the head of my cock with her tongue, how amazing she'd looked getting fucked by Tor at the same that Hayden had licked her.

Basically? It had tested all my resolve not to spill right into her hot, eager mouth. I'd even nearly convinced myself that I could make it work, that I could get it up again for another round if I needed to. I had the same self-talk every addict did when they wanted to try to convince themselves of something they knew wasn't true.

So I'd managed to hold off, to resist, and I had no idea how much longer I could do that.

I glanced toward Char, and he only nodded at Kenz. *Good.* I didn't think I could hold back if I had to wait for him, too.

I caught Kenz behind the neck with my good hand and pulled her forward, toward me, taking her mouth in a deep kiss. It moved her out of Tor's lap, and when she might have tumbled, I caught her easily. I tugged her against me, feeling how weak she seemed, how none of her muscles appeared willing to work, which was fine with me. I had no issue doing all the work in this.

I broke the kiss, then twisted her around. I placed her knees near the side of the bed and pushed between her shoulders until her chest pressed against the mattress. It arched her back and left her open to me where I stood behind her.

She whimpered when I ran my fingers up through her folds. Even still, she didn't jerk away, didn't try to escape.

Good girl.

"You look tired," I told her. "But you're only halfway through."

"Assuming we each take only one turn," Char added in.

Kenz's pussy tightened at that, and I could feel the reaction even though I hadn't pressed my fingers into her at all. It made me chuckle, so I didn't even scold Char for the threat.

I knew better than to believe him. He might joke about that, but he knew damn well that our girl was strong to just make it through one round each with us her first time out. No way would he expect her to do anything more than that.

He was an asshole, but he wasn't *that* much of one.

"Well, since you're already well-used, I guess I don't have to worry about getting you ready, do I?"

Kenz shuddered but didn't so much as lift her head in response. Why did that turn me on even more? The absolute and total surrender of her to me — to us?

I tore open the condom Hayden had handed me, then rolled it over my aching cock. Going later had an advantage, which was a lessened need for prep. I didn't have to hold back, to ease her into anything. I could take her rough and hard from the start, which sounded amazing to me.

I ran the head of my dick through her folds, gathering the wetness on the condom, enjoying the way she whimpered against the blanket on the bed at each touch. When I ground my cock against her clit, that was the first real reaction I'd gotten from her.

I laughed softly. "Is your clit a bit sore, sweetheart? Poor girl, you've sure been fucked thoroughly. Okay, I'll leave it be and give you what you really want." I grasped her hip with my good hand and used my right hand to aim my cock, then sank into her with a single hard thrust.

She took me easily, despite the rhythmic tightening of her cunt that went to show how sensitive she was after having been teased and toyed with for so long. It made me want to spread her out some time and keep her on that edge for hours, then force orgasm after orgasm out of her all night long. She'd look so pretty, covered in sweat, pleading and begging for a break.

However, that was a fantasy for a different time, and the clutching grip of her cunt was more than enough for me.

And judging from the lovely noises she made, it was enough for her, too.

I went to grasp her waist with my bad hand but froze just before I made contact, that old fear rising. In the end, I was a coward and leaned over her instead of touching her with my mangled hand. I slammed into her, caging her in with my body, trapping her beneath me and my need.

Kenz had already frayed my control with her blow job, which meant I'd teetered on that edge for a while. No doubt her pussy would take me over that edge fast.

Still, I savored each second of it, the way her body gave so well beneath me, the way she gripped my wrist when I set my good hand over her on the bed for my balance. She was everything I could have wanted.

I'd feared meaningful connections for so long, so used to letting others down that I'd convinced myself one-night stands were all I needed. She'd shattered that delusion so easily, though. She'd torn it to pieces around me, forcing me to come to terms with how empty my life had been, how shallow.

I set my bad hand on the bed to her other side, needing the leverage to take her as I wanted to, to thrust as wildly as I needed into her.

I jerked slightly when something touched my right hand, the action causing me to pause my thrusts and look down. Kenz had wrapped her hand around my wrist, then turned her face toward my damaged hand.

I recalled the few times where people had seen my hand — typically in medical settings — and they'd always shied away from it. Even professionals had treated me as though that hand were bad, always reaching and handing things toward my other hand.

Kenz didn't do that, though. Instead, she pressed her lips to the damaged skin, to the area I usually tried hard not to even look at. Her touch didn't feel like pity, but rather like washing filth from a wound, as though her affection could cleanse the doubt and hatred I'd always had toward the injury.

She nuzzled my hand, wrapping around it as though nothing else mattered, her actions startling me for a heartbeat before the needs of my cock overcame it.

No, that wasn't exactly right. It didn't overcome it, rather added to it. The acceptance she had, the way she didn't reject me, didn't avoid even the parts of myself I couldn't accept, it made it impossible to resist. I took her harder, the slap of my skin against her ass a testament to how badly I needed her.

She cried out but didn't stop lavishing attention to my hand, and it drove me right past the ability to hold back. I slammed deep into her and shuddered hard as I came, a deep groan escaping me, feeling as though we'd forged some unbreakable connection.

I'd taken her, come while held deep inside her, and she'd accepted every bit of me without reservation.

I pressed my lips against her back, the salt of her sweat clinging to my lips as proof of just how we'd worn her out, how we'd exhausted her. Her pussy tightened again, the stimulation too much, so I withdrew my softening cock before offering another kiss to her back.

How could I have thought I didn't need anyone? That I could live happily on a string of one-night stands? Those were like sips from a stagnant pond that I'd convinced myself was all I needed and Kenz was my first drink of fresh water.

She'd opened my eyes to what else I could have, and now anything short of it wouldn't be enough for me.

Char

The sight of Kenz took me back in a strange way. I'd had sex since the death of my wife, had indulged in other women, but it had always felt as personal as scratching an itch. I hadn't thought about my wife during those times, hadn't seen her face, hadn't even felt any guilt over it.

This time was different.

Seeing Kenz breathless and needy and lost to pleasure made me think about my wife, to recall the last time we'd slept together, the morning before she'd died. It had been sweet and gentle and caring — the way I'd always taken her.

It had fulfilled me in a way, because I'd known she'd enjoyed it, but I'd known the entire time that I was not much different than a sex toy for her. She didn't see me that way, of course, but it was how I acted. I planned everything I did carefully for her enjoyment, to appeal to her, to be the perfect man for her. The only pleasure I'd found was in fulfilling that role, in offering her that fantasy, in making her happy.

But had it ever made me happy?

That was why, when I watched as Vance pulled out of Kenz, as she slumped to her side, panting and exhausted, I knew I couldn't do that anymore, not with her.

For the first time since writing off my true personality as a kid, when I'd concluded that no one would ever accept me as I was, I didn't want to hide anymore. I wanted Kenz to see *me*, to feel *me*, to not hide a bit of myself from her — the twisted, sarcastic, often unpleasant man I really was.

So I grabbed another condom and sheathed my cock in it, then crawled over Kenz. I rolled her farther, from her side and onto her back, then in one smooth, quick motion, filled her with one steady thrust.

Her hands flew up, wrapping around me. Her lips touched my shoulder, but it wasn't the kiss I expected. Instead, a sudden sting said she'd bitten down on me. It made me laugh, but I didn't pull her away.

No, if she wanted to mark me, I'd happily let her. I planned to leave my own marks on her in return, after all.

When she did let go, though, I disentangled her arms so she lay flat on the bed. It allowed me to see the multitude of red marks and bites that dotted her normally flawless skin, and damn that was a nice sight.

"I wanted to go last," I told her, "because you'd be so sensitive by now. What can I say? I guess I have a bit of a sadistic streak when it comes to you, and I think when you get this teary-eyed look, it makes me want to fuck you harder." I grabbed her legs and hoisted them up, hooking her knees over my arms and lifting her ass off the bed. It let me take her the way I needed, leaving her spread out on the bed, making her look somehow both innocent and lewd.

And instead of giving her what she wanted, as I'd done so much of my life, I did as I wanted, instead, showing her every ugly part of my personality, offering it all up to her.

"And let me tell you, I plan on getting you in to a doctor to start you on birth control. I wanted to fill this sweet little pussy of yours up with our cum, to slide into you after we've each taken a turn, to watch it drip out of you, to gather it up on my fingers and feed it back into you." My words excited me, as though they manifested those desires into the real world, but that wasn't the best part.

No, the best part of it was Kenz's reaction, the way she tightened around me and moaned, her eyes closed. She didn't fight me, didn't tell me no, didn't try to change me. She didn't tell me I was wrong, that I was wrong.

Instead, she accepted it all. She took my words in and they excited her. She took my rough thrusts and lifted her hips for more. No matter how ugly a part of me was, she didn't reject a bit of it.

Which had me swinging my hips forward, and had I not had a hold of her legs, she'd have slid on the bed from the roughness of my thrusts. I chased my own release, moving my gaze over her as I memorized every detail.

She was perfect, not because she was so pretty, not because of her past or her money or her name. No, she was perfect because she was everything I could have wanted. She was the safe place that I'd never had, the home I'd craved but thought impossible for me to find.

Even though I wanted to let this last long, to hold off, I couldn't stop my release from shuddering through me. It made me breathless and tired but the sight of Kenz there was something worth savoring.

I'd never expected to find a place where I belonged, didn't think such a place existed. I'd been prepared to hide my true self forever, to fit in only because I pretended to be whatever I thought others would want.

Yet somehow, this girl had created that safety for me, had made the only place in the whole universe where I could let go of the masks I'd worn, where I could just be myself. She'd become that place for me, and even if I had no idea how to do it, or if it was possible, I'd find a way to repay her for that.

Kenz

My body had moved beyond exhaustion and felt as though I were floating in nothingness. Even the effort to open my eyes seemed like far more than I currently had.

Something wet touched me, and I jerked in surprise. *Not again.* As much as I loved these guys, there was absolutely no way I could make it through any more.

"I'm just cleaning you up," came a deep, comforting voice. *Hayden.* Always taking care of me, wasn't he? His words helped me identify the sensation as a washcloth wiping me off. He gently cleared off the sweat, even removing the wetness from my inner thighs. I would have been embarrassed if I had the energy for that emotion.

As it was, I could deal with that tomorrow. Right now, I enjoyed the pampering.

Once he seemed content that he'd done the job well, something soft and warm enveloped me. Sleep came to me in small waves, as though I bobbed on the surface of awareness, dipping down from time to time before rising again.

Fingers ran through my hair and hands rubbed over my arms, my back, the touches comforting and gentle and coaxing.

Words floated through that darkness, but I struggled to make sense of them, to catch them all. I had no hope of actually retaining or responding to them. It didn't matter what they said, though. That wasn't important.

It was the tone that got to me, the way they made me feel warmer than the blanket around me, safer than the best security system could. I was pretty sure that if I could just stay like this, with these men, that I could face anything else that came my way.

This was the only thing I really wanted.

Chapter Twelve

Lorien

I held my hand in a tight fist, something between anger and disbelief raging through me.

I'd received word from a contact of mine, but I wrote their claims off as unreliable. It made no sense and thus couldn't be the truth. Even so, when I'd gotten a text from my mother, a worry grew and gnawed inside me.

I walked up the stairs in her home, the place making my skin crawl. This wasn't my home, had never been my home. My siblings had grown up here, but I'd always been a stranger. I had come to visit as a child with the people who pretended to be my parents, had seen this place from the position of an outsider.

My mother had wanted me to live here, just as her daughters did. She'd wanted to bring her children all together, but the idea never sat well with me. This house represented everything stolen from me, a birthright they'd denied me. Even after I took over, when I ran everything, I would never live here.

In fact, a part of me couldn't wait for the day when I got to watch as someone bulldozed this place to the ground, when they knocked it down to rubble. Maybe I'd turn it into a parking lot just to add insult to injury.

At the top of the stairs, I paused in front of my mother's office. She hadn't taken the one where her husband had worked from, leaving that like some shrine to him. Hell, I'd bet she expected me to move into there.

At least, I would have thought so.

After what my contact had told me, however, I wasn't so sure anymore.

I knocked on the door, and my mother called for me to enter. Her office appeared as it always did, the same as it had for all the years since she'd used it. My mother sat at the desk, but she didn't rise and leave it. She didn't come around to the couch as she normally did, to sit beside me to talk.

Which did not bode well.

Instead, she gestured at the chair across the desk from her. One bodyguard remained in the room, near the corner beside her, standing there like a guardian statue. *Another bad sign.*

"You wanted to see me?" I asked.

"Yes. I'm sure by now you have heard some rumors today."

I nodded as I sat where she'd indicated. "Yeah. I heard you sent word out about how I was removed from the power structure of the family. I told the person they must have made a mistake. I don't know what this is about, but I'd suggest you come down hard on whoever caused this mess, because it doesn't look good for stability."

"They weren't wrong," my mother said as she folded her hands on the desk. "I sent out word today that you no longer speak for our family and hold no official position. I removed you from all bank accounts, all properties and any holding connected with our family or business. I have ensured that anyone in a position of power will no longer take orders from you. In short? I have removed you from any authority or official position within the Hatchett family."

Her words had me pulling in a sharp breath, unable to quite come to terms with what she'd said.

She'd basically disowned me? Cut me out of the family?

I inhaled slowly, then released it in a steady stream, trying to relax. I used the same method to calm myself as just before pulling the trigger during a dangerous job.

Afterward, I kept my voice steady to reply. "I thought you wanted me to take over. You've told me over and over again that is what you want. How is that possible if you do this?"

"I've changed my vision for the future of this family. You've had many chances to come into the fold, to fall in line, but you have continued to do things as you wish without concern or thought about the family as a whole. I had hoped that this would change, that you would see reason, but you have failed to do so."

"So you just throw me away? Like you did when I was born?" The same old pain that had sat with me at night, when as a child I'd known I'd been unwanted, dug its sharp claws into me and made it difficult to draw breath. "You got rid of me back then, too, found me too inconvenient to deal with."

Her eyes softened for a split second, as though I'd landed a critical blow. However, as quickly as it happened, she pulled her shoulders back. "I never threw you away. I protected you in the only way I could, by ensuring you had the space and time to grow up. Believe it or not, I am doing the same now."

"The hell you are. You're taking away the only power and protection I have. How is that helping me?"

"Because I fear some of your behavior has happened because you know you have my power to fall back on. You take that for granted, never thinking things through, never dealing with the consequences of your actions. You're an adult, Lorien, and it's time for you to stand on your own feet."

I fisted my hands and cranked my molars together for a moment. "What do you want from me? People don't do anything unless they expect to manipulate someone into doing what they want. So, Mother, what is it you want me to do to put things right?"

She sighed softly and shook her head. "You don't get it. Even now, you don't understand. You see the world as nothing but something you can control, and people as things you can use or manipulate. I didn't do this to make you change, to force you into anything. I simply took a good look at my options, at the reality of the situation, and realized that by ignoring your behavior, I wasn't helping anyone. I wasn't helping you to grow and become better, and I wasn't helping my other children, either."

"So what? You'll put one of them in charge?" I laughed at the stupidity of that idea.

However, she didn't laugh or deny it.

"Are you serious?" I asked. "They're spoiled brats. They've never been taught to lead, and they're far too weak for such a position. By handing the family to them, you're all but ensuring that it fails."

"They deserve the right to try." My mother's voice made it clear that she would not change her mind, that she wouldn't hear anything I heard.

I hadn't lost often in my life, but this felt like a loss. I'd never wanted to lead this family, but I'd relied on the power it gave me. I'd formulated my plans around the assurance of having that assistance. Without it…so much of my future fell apart.

If I didn't have that backing, how could I force Hayden and the others' hands into giving me Kenz? How could I ensure that I got what I wanted? What I deserved?

I had my own money, I had a reputation and skills, but power was different from that.

I looked across the desk at the woman who had birthed me. So many times I thought I might feel love, that I might feel some connection to her. It hadn't come, but a part of me thought with time, it might. However, staring at her now, that emptiness grew like a black hole, so heavy it collapsed in on its own weight and pulled everything else in.

The fact we shared DNA didn't matter in the least — she was here, throwing me away *again*. Choosing other children over me, content to betray me in exchange for the benefit of another child. Yet again I was nothing to her or to this family.

And before I knew what I was doing, I sailed over the desk at her. I wrapped my hands around her thin throat, surprised again by how frail she felt. For a woman who held as much power as she did, who had landed a blow to me like she had, it amazed me that she could be this physically weak.

I expected her to grab my wrists, to tug at them uselessly. That was what women did, fighting back in the dumbest of ways. She wouldn't be able to remove my hands like that, of course, and if I got just a little more leverage, I might even snap her neck before I had to worry about strangling her. No doubt her bodyguard rushed forward as well, but if I had just a *little* more space and time, I'd end her.

A sharp pain in my wrist forced me to loosen my grasp, my hand refusing to obey my commands. I yanked backward to find a silver letter opener jammed into my wrist, blood escaping so fast that I knew something important had gotten cut.

My mother stumbled backward just as the bodyguard reached us, tugging her farther away, placing himself between us. At the same time, the door burst open and more security rushed in, telling me they'd waited outside.

I glanced at them, my lip lifted in a silent snarl. "So you expected this, huh?"

She didn't reach up to touch the darkening skin of her neck, as though the injury didn't matter to her. "I thought you might behave rashly, and I'm not so foolish as you seem to think. Do not underestimate me."

"I should give you that same advice. So what now? You have your muscle kill me? Get rid of me like you probably wanted to do the moment you found out you'd had another son? You could have saved us all a lot of pain if you'd done that." I thought my words would wound her, but she showed no reaction to it.

I had no idea if she was actually that strong or just pretending to save face.

Either way, she stood tall and stepped beside her bodyguard, as though she wanted to face me directly rather than hiding behind anyone. "No. Let me make myself *perfectly* clear, however. Your father was tough, but he was nothing compared to me. Any strength you think you have, you got it from *me*. So before you even think about standing against me, about moving against me or anything I care about, know that every bit of viciousness you hold came from me. I suggest you do not test that."

She turned her gaze to one of the security beside me. "Take him and deliver him to his house. No harm is to come to him. However, should he be spotted within a mile of this estate, or near either of my daughters, I authorize a lethal response."

With that, the men on either side of me grasped my arms, and as much as I wanted to fight them, I knew better. Getting myself killed here would serve me no purpose. Besides, my hand still hurt, and I feared my left hand wouldn't ever work quite right again. Resisting now wouldn't help me at all, and this all wouldn't stop me.

All it did was change my plans slightly.

Step one—get Kenz.

Step two—kill the men who dared keep her from me.

Step three—kill every person who stood in my way, starting with my turncoat of a mother.

I'd done everything I had thus far for beauty, for art, and I couldn't think of a more beautiful color right now than red.

I'd paint the fucking world with it now.

* * * *

Char

The ringing of a phone in the other room made me groan. After the long night and the longer—and more enjoyable—morning, everyone had ended up falling asleep for a few hours.

However, the incessant ringing of my phone forced me to open my eyes.

I found a body a lot larger than Kenz in front of me.

Tor? I blinked slowly as I woke, sitting up to acknowledge that, yeah, I'd fallen asleep behind Tor and even had my arm tossed over like he was the weirdest body pillow.

I woke up with a man and I wasn't even drunk.

Instead of trying to make sense of that—there wasn't much to make sense of, really—I rolled and put my feet on the floor. Kenz was on the other side of Tor, with Vance at the end. The only person not there was Hayden.

Which, all things considered, didn't surprise me. Hell, I'd bet he was either cooking or had run out to pick up food so he could feed everyone after the long night. In fact, I could almost see him talking about needing to regain the calories we'd lost with all our action.

I pulled myself from the bed, not bothering to dress. What was the point? After everything we'd done last night—or early this morning—modesty had lost all meaning.

Kenz grumbled softly at the noise, then cuddled in closer to Vance. A smile tugged at my lips at the sight before I picked up the phone from the dresser, finding out it was Kenz's.

I hit the Answer button as I left the room, closing the door behind me so as not to wake the others.

"Hello?"

The voice that responded belonged to a woman who spoke as though used to giving orders. "Who is this?" *Talk about suspicious.* "I called Mackenzie's phone."

"She's sleeping. She was up late last night. This is her friend, Char."

She made a soft sound, as though the fact checked out. "This is Pauline Hatchett."

I paused, unsure what to say back to that. Talk about an unexpected call…

Thankfully, Pauline continued. "I'm sorry to contact you on such short notice, but I felt you should be aware."

"Aware of what?"

"I informed Lorien of what Mackenzie and I spoke about last night, and the conversation did not go well."

"That's not surprising. No one hears they're being cut out of the family and reacts well."

"True. However, he reacted even worse than I'd expected. He attacked me before being thrown out of the estate and told if he returns, he'll pay with his life."

That didn't bode well. He was crazy, of course, and his past behavior proved that he was willing to do just about anything to get what he wanted. However, attacking one's own mother felt like even a step further, like something I really hadn't thought even him capable of.

Then again, hadn't I learned that familial ties weren't nearly as strong as people liked to believe?

"I'm sorry that happened," I said honestly.

"I neither need nor want your pity." When she said that, I had to admit, I liked her a hell of a lot more. Something about strong women always forced me to respect them. "The reason I contacted Mackenzie was to warn her. His behavior is more erratic than I would have expected, and because of it, I'm unsure what he might do. I want her to be more cautious right now, because Lorien is capable of nearly anything. I've ensured my own children are safe, but I don't want to hear that Mackenzie met a sad end at Lorien's hands." She also sighed softly, then went on, "Also, I want to make sure she knows that I did as I said, so anything he does wouldn't come back on me."

I snorted at that, at the reality of her call. Sure, it sounded like she actually gave a damn, but I also understood the rest. She didn't want Kenz's family coming after her if the worst came to pass.

Which, from what I knew about Nem, was probably a pretty fair understanding.

"Thank you for letting us know," I told her. "I'll tell Kenz, and we'll be careful."

"Good." She paused but didn't hang up. It gave off the sense that she had more to say but struggled to come out with it. Finally, she spoke, her voice soft. "Please watch out for her. Lorien is my fault, and I don't want to see her hurt because of him — because of me." With that, she ended the call.

I turned and stared back at the closed door, thinking about Kenz asleep in there, about how far we'd come and yet how many questions remained. We'd separated the wolf from the pack, but by doing it, we'd cut his leash as well.

Anything that might have held him back, that restrained his choices, was gone.

It meant the old game was over and the new one had just started. And unfortunately, this new game lacked any rules.

It was kill or be killed, and for the first time, I gave a damn about that.

* * * *

Hayden

I tried to hold back the yawn but I just couldn't stop myself. The best I managed was covering my mouth and trying not to make it quite so obvious.

It was a reminder of my age. Back in my twenties, I'd been able to pull all-nighters with no problem at all. I could stay out on a mission or drink and party and the next day get everything I needed done with just a bit of coffee.

Now, though? If I got less than six hours, I damn well felt it the next day, and given I got maybe two hours of shut eye last night, I was dragging.

Kenz, however, rebounded nicely.

Her skin had a pretty flush to it, and her smile had brightened significantly. At first, I'd thought it was more about me, that after what we'd done last night, after how I'd seen her, that she just looked different to me.

However, after seeing her interact with others, I'd started to suspect it was more than that.

And, hell, maybe it was self-centered or egotistical, but I wanted to think the change was due to me — to *us*. I liked the idea that finally giving in, finally accepting our connection had somehow helped her. I'd heard people say that a woman in love became prettier, and even though I didn't think she could get any prettier, I couldn't deny the change.

We were at her school because she had a class she couldn't get out of. I hadn't wanted to bring her here, not with what Pauline had said, but we couldn't really hold Kenz back forever.

According to Char, he'd looked into it, and it seemed, like we'd expected, the withdrawal of Pauline's protections had put a target on his back. In fact, he hadn't shown back up to work, since Tor had stopped in and found a note on his office door from the university stating that *'Grisham Oreando has taken a sudden leave of absence.'*

He probably realized he couldn't show up here anymore, that the carefully created barriers he'd had were gone and anyone who might have known who he really was no longer had a reason to avoid targeting him.

I could only hope that Pauline was wrong, that he might have recognized Kenz as the least of his problems, now. If we caught a break — which would be nice — he might write Kenz off as no longer important.

And seeing Kenz here, back in class, made me want to smile. It made me want this to go away.

I could ignore Lorien, at least for now, if it meant giving Kenz back her life, that she could return to her school, to the art that she loved. I wanted that for her, to see her get the things she deserved in her life.

The class was a life drawing one, and the model was a man who stood in the center, nude. I'd already had to fight my initial desire to toss Kenz over my shoulder and carry her out of the room.

I'd never thought myself to be a jealous man, yet the idea of the girl I loved staring at some stranger naked seemed to hit all my buttons when it came to anger. Why I didn't care if she was with Char, Vance or Tor but I cared about the hard body in front of us, I didn't know and didn't feel the need to examine too much.

Just put a towel on at least!

I shook my head, then forced my gaze to Kenz and her work rather than the naked man in the center of the room. She moved her pencil over the large canvas quickly, the lines light. I rarely watched her draw, since that was more Vance's area of expertise, but I had to admit, there was something compelling about it.

She had such focus, as though the rest of the world disappeared around her when she worked. I'd bet, after everything she'd gone through, all she'd suffered with, that such a moment of peace was not only welcome but needed. She took her lip between her teeth as her gaze darted between the canvas as the model, as she added light line after light line, changing things as she went.

What she drew came to life before my eyes, and I found myself stunned by her talent. The ability to create something so life-like was an amazing talent, really, and I wasn't sure I'd ever fully recognized it as such before.

It made me want to ensure she got to continue with it, to follow her dream, to keep at something that was clearly so important to her.

In fact, I allowed myself to fantasize for a moment, to think about a future where she had her own art studio at our place, where she got to work during whatever hours she wanted, where we could go to her shows when she had exhibits.

Normally such distraction would be bad, but at the college here, with Tor and Char both around as well, a few moments of harmless fantasizing was probably okay.

The class wrapped up after about two hours, when the model *finally* put his robe on and headed through a door at the front of the class, toward what was likely a changing room.

Kenz put her tools away, carefully packing her pencils and sliding the box into the messenger bag that she slung over her shoulder. She took the large canvas and carried it over to a table full of open slots, each one with a number at the bottom. She carefully slid the picture into one of the slots while other students did the same, telling me it was storage for the pieces worked on in the classroom.

Which meant she'd work on it more later?

She walked over to me, her gaze not quite meeting mine. She'd done that since she'd woken up, as if she wasn't quite sure how to interact with me after what we'd done.

Which I understood. I'd probably feel just as uncomfortable if she wasn't already being awkward. Somehow, that took some of the stress off me. I didn't have to worry because she did enough of it for both of us.

"You look mad," she said, her voice soft as though nervous.

I tried to smile and reassure her. "I'm not mad."

She *finally* looked up and into my eyes. "Really? Because you've been glaring since class started. I'm pretty sure you made a lot of students nervous."

I nearly reached up to feel my own face, as if I could make sure she was telling the truth, but then a glance up when the model strolled back in—dressed but somehow still looking just as handsome—made it clear she was probably right.

As much as I'd have loved to skip over the embarrassment of admitting anything, after a few more students rushing out after glancing at me, I probably needed to address it.

"Does the model really *need* to be entirely nude?" Even as I said it, I crossed my arms in what could only be called a pout.

She tilted her head as she looked up at me, the expression on her face so adorable it was unfair. "Are you jealous?"

"No." I huffed at my stupid answer, then added on, softly, "Maybe."

Kenz smirked, the look helping neither my attitude nor embarrassment at all. However, she wasn't the type to just make an expression like that. Instead, she stepped closer and wrapped her arms around me, the action showing none of the fear those other students had when they'd looked at me.

It reminded me that although Kenz probably had good reason to be wary, she wasn't, not around me. It forced me to stop crossing my arms and wrap my arms around her as well.

And damn...she felt good in my arms like this. Her body fit perfectly against me, her curves giving, and she just melted right against me. She wasn't stiff, didn't resist in the least. It felt like a balm against my jealousy, as though she eased that negative feeling away entirely.

My phone vibrated, so I turned my wrist to see the message stream across the face of my watch.

Is now really the time?

Tor's text made me snort, so I twisted my arm to allow Kenz to see it as well. Her cheeks flushed and she stepped back quickly, as though caught. "I can't get away with anything around you all, can I?"

I caught her chin before she could quite escape, then tugged her forward and kissed her softly, giving myself that small concession because lord knew I wanted a hell of a lot more than that.

As fast as it started, I broke it, then nodded toward the door. "Are you ready to go?"

Kenz nodded, those cheeks of hers flaming as she tugged softly at the strap of her bag. "Yeah. I just need to drop off a paper to a teacher."

"What paper?"

"Art history. I missed that class a few times and the professor said a paper would get me caught up. He said he'd be here today for me to drop it off. That'll be the last thing I have to do for that class."

Again, I found myself impressed by Kenz's work ethic. With Vance's influence, she could have slacked off and likely skirted by with a passing grade. She'd gone through so much stress, so much change, yet she still gave every class her all. She worked hard to do everything asked of her, to never fall behind or just float through life.

So I nodded and held my hand toward the door. "Where is his office?"

"His office is on the ground floor. He uses a cane, so they give him one closer to the parking garage so he can get there easier. I suggest you stay outside because he isn't all that nice," Kenz said with a laugh. "Also, he tends to spit when he talks."

Her wording made me chuckle as we got into the elevator. "You're always taking care of those around you, aren't you?"

"Well, I have to deal with him—you don't. There's no good reason for you to suffer too, is there?" She flashed me a bright smile that made my heart speed.

My phone rang, so I pulled it from my pocket, saw Char was the one calling and answered.

"Is everything okay?"

Char responded with the same sarcasm he always had. "You worry too much. It's bad for your heart and a man your age needs to worry about your heart."

"I'm hanging up if that's all you have to say," I warned.

"I just wanted to tell you that we've had no sign of Lorien. I think we're in the clear. There's no way he'd be dumb enough to come here, anyway. He's got bigger problems."

"Good. Keep an eye out, though. Kenz has to drop off a paper to her art history professor, then we'll head to the car. I want you in the car and Tor providing support."

"We aren't your employees. Did you forget that again?"

Why was it that talking to him always gave me a bit of a headache? Even though I'd gotten to the point that I knew he'd do as I said, he never let me get away with issuing an order without him snarking back at me.

Kenz leaned in closer, a mischievous grin on her face that I had a feeling she'd learned from Char himself. "Well, if you don't want to be in the car, I guess that means Hayden and I get to go somewhere on our own."

The suggestion in her voice about knocked me on my ass. Kenz was sweet — not seductive — but there was no way to ignore the sensual theme of her idea.

"You need to stop learning from me," Char muttered. "Fine. I'll bring the car around like a good boy and be waiting out front. You had better plan to reward me, though."

I snorted at Char's quick agreement — Kenz was no doubt the only person who could get him to listen to anything — before I hung up.

"You handle him well." I slid the phone into my pocket.

"He's easy to deal with when you understand him."

The elevator door opened on the bottom floor, this area of the school having fewer people around. I'd memorized the layout of the school, of the different buildings, so I knew them rather well. This area mostly had storage and a few offices, such as for the art history professor. The parking garage opened right to this floor, which made it perfect with its wide hallways and direct access without stairs for a man who struggled to walk far or navigate stairs.

"You never give yourself enough credit," I said as we went down the long hallway, my focus tuned to our surroundings even as we spoke.

She glanced at the side toward me for a moment, reminding me that I'd picked up the conversation a tad bit late. It was a risk of my profession, since I split my attention between the client and the environment. It meant occasionally I filed away our conversation and picked it up a few moments too late, forcing the other person to catch back up.

However, Kenz was quick enough to manage it well. "I don't know about that," she hedged.

"It's true. You always think the things you are talented with are unimportant or don't matter or anyone can do, then you focus your attention on the things you struggle with. I've known Char a while, and I can assure you, *no one* handles him the way you do. You need to have more confidence in yourself."

She didn't respond at first, but I hadn't really expected her to. I knew better than that. She worried too much, didn't see her own worth that was so obvious to everyone else.

We had time, though.

When was the last time I thought such a thing?

It almost took me by surprise how casually I thought about things like that now, how much I considered a future, just accepting it. With Lorien backing off, with things settling down, could I actually have such a thing?

I glanced at Kenz, trying to keep it subtle, wondering how on Earth I'd managed to luck out so much?

"Here it is." Kenz came to a stop in front of a door with a silver plate on the front, the professor's name and department etched into it. She knocked on the door softly, and the voice of an elderly man called back out.

Yeah, he sounds like someone who would spit when he talks…

Kenz walked into the room, and through the door I caught a sight of an older man who could have played the nearly senile professor in any movie. His back was to the door, his hands reaching for a book off a tall shelf. It reassured me that the professor was in fact in there.

The door shut behind Kenz, and I turned my back to it, standing watch outside, keeping track of the empty hallway.

No sound escaped the rooms, but I'd found the doors in this school to be rather thick. Then again, while their focus and prestige was mostly in the fine arts, they did have both music and theater courses. Good soundproofing was no doubt a benefit for such things.

A part of me felt antsy, but I reminded myself that I couldn't expect to interfere with her schooling. Our actions had caused her enough strife, making her life much harder than it needed to be. The least I could do was sit through her meetings and classes she tried to catch back up.

My phone vibrated, and I sighed when I spotted the caller. I had no idea what Char wanted, but knowing him, he probably had to get the last word from our last argument.

"What?" I answered.

"Do you have eyes on Kenz?" His tone put me on alert. He wasn't the type to make jokes about something this important.

"She's in the office with the professor."

"I called into the office to ask about that professor's office hours. He isn't scheduled in until Monday."

Part of me came up with other ideas, that the professor had come in just to meet with her, but my body reacted before I could voice any of them. I gripped the handle of the door and twisted it, but nothing happened. *Locked.*

It wasn't the first door I kicked down — I doubted it would be the last.

I moved back and slammed my boot against the door, but unlike those in the house, this one refused to give. I called Kenz's name, but no answer came back, heightening the fear that plagued me.

I moved backward, then ran at the door, using the wider hallway to my advantage for momentum. Pain shot through my shoulder when I struck the door, but between hurling my bodyweight at it and the previous kick, it gave up the good fight, the doorjamb giving way so it opened.

And inside the room, my heart stopped. The window was open to the outside, a man was dead on the floor — the man I had thought was the professor — and there was no sign of Kenz.

"Lorien has her," I whispered into the phone.

Never had I felt fear like this.

Chapter Thirteen

Kenz

Looking at the back of the professor, something strange struck me. I couldn't put it into words. Couldn't identify the growing unease, but something in my head grew fuzzy, like trying to remember a dream that just kept slipping away.

I shut the door behind me then reached into my bag for the paper. This professor was old as dirt and hated dealing with anything digital, so I knew he offered better grades when things were printed out.

"I brought the paper, Mr. Allen," I said, raising my voice because he was hard of hearing.

My attention was down on my bag as I sorted through it to pull out the stapled pack of pages. When I lifted my gaze, that unease made sense.

The man who turned from the bookcase was *not* Professor Allen. He was the right height, right weight, had the same receding hairline, but he was not the man I'd expected at all.

I went to call out for Hayden, but something wrapped around my mouth to muffle the sound.

"Be a good girl and behave yourself," whispered a voice I'd never forget.

Lorien.

I lifted my foot to stop down on his, my body reacting the way it had been trained to do, but a jerk from Lorien's hand upset my balance and stopped me. His voice in my ear stopped me as he reached his other hand out, showing a gun that he held. "Hayden is standing on the other side of this door, right? Do you really think it would be difficult for me to unload a single shot at head level there? It would go through that door, through Hayden, and it would do you no good. I don't mind killing him — it would make things easier on me — but believe it or not, I'm *still* trying to get you to see that I'm not the monster you think I am. So the choice is yours. Will you come with me, or will you have Hayden's blood on your hands?"

He twisted us and aimed the gun at the door — right where I was sure Hayden was — and removed his hand from my mouth.

I went to speak, but instead of the scream I knew Hayden would have wanted, I whispered, "I'll go."

The press of Lorien's lips to my head made my stomach turn, but I fought against that. "Good choice. Come on, let's go." He turned the lock slowly so the mechanism made no noise. He moved his hand to my forearm and tugged me toward the desk.

I looked toward the other man, who smirked as though pleased with the outcome. He was older, similar in many ways to the professor, but not an exact copy. It explained why he'd kept his back to me at first. "When do I get the rest of my money?" he asked.

"You get your reward now." Lorien released me, then moved so fast that I had to cover my mouth to remain silent. He swung his hand out in a wide arc, the silver of a blade in his grip flashing through the room. The way it sliced through the other man's throat as though there was no resistance at all went to show just how sharp it had to be.

The man grasped his throat, but with a wound that deep, he wouldn't survive. The only sound that left him was a desperate gurgling. The man collapsed to his knees, then to his front, but Lorien didn't wait to watch.

Instead, he slipped the blade back into his pocket, his actions so fast that the weapon didn't seem to have blood on it, then opened the window smoothly. He grasped my wrist once more and pulled me through the window, away from the room, from safety, and to the unknown.

Once outside, Lorien moved so fast that I started to pant almost immediately. I'd had to run before, but I didn't think it had *ever* been like this. We moved through the courtyard, and the way Lorien turned, the focus he had, told me he knew *exactly* where he was headed.

Fear beat at me, a part of me wanted to resist, but another part was terrified of what might happen if I did. Lorien was dangerous. He'd just murdered someone before my eyes. What would he do if I fought with him? Who might pay the price?

I tripped, my foot catching on a root, and nearly pitched forward to the ground. I expected Lorien to just yank me harder, to drag me if he had to, which was why it startled me when he skidded to a stop to catch me before I slammed into the ground.

"Sorry," he said softly, the word almost oddly sweet. "We have to move fast, though. Just stay with me a little longer. Don't worry — I won't let anything happen to you."

I didn't even have the chance to respond before he tugged my hand again, pulling me along with him, ducking into a door I didn't recognize. Despite all the time I'd spent at this college, it seemed my knowledge was nothing compared to his. I kept losing my way, unsure where we'd ended up.

He took my bag from me, moving the strap up and over my head. "Sorry, but I have no doubts they can track things in here. We'll leave it here. I'll get your more paints, more brushes — anything you need." He tossed the bag down as though it were unimportant, then moved his hands over my chest.

I swatted out of instinct, terrified to somehow confuse this touch with the ones I'd grown used to, that I adored.

He caught my wrist and bent down slightly, trapping me with his eyes. "I'm not feeling you up, Kenz. I'm looking for other tracking items."

I believed him, but somehow that almost made this worse. The way he touched me, so carefully, felt like he gave a damn about me. I'd gotten that sense before, that he had some twisted obsession with me that included his own version of care, that implied he wanted me safe and happy.

Yet his own view of the world warped it, because at the end of the day, he cared more about himself than me.

Even still, I couldn't fight him when he pulled my jacket off, tossing it to the floor. He knelt before me, then tugged my shoes off. "Can't be too careful," he muttered before pulling something off the shelf beside me.

A dress?

He peered up at my face, his expression serious. "I'm going to turn my back and you need to change. Everything off, even your underwear and any jewelry."

"I don't want this," I whispered to him.

He rose to his feet, then cupped my cheek. "You're just afraid, but you'll see that I'm right. Now, if you don't do as I'm asking, I'll do it for you. I don't think you'll like that very much, so be a good girl and do as you're told. The longer we take here, the better the chance that someone finds us, and I can assure you that I will not lose you, no matter what it takes." He didn't have to flash a weapon at that—I got the meaning from his words alone.

He must have seen my agreement in my eyes, because he nodded as if assured of my cooperation, then turned his back to me. My hands shook as I stripped down, my blood thundering through my veins, my head fuzzy and difficult to sort through.

Once I'd removed everything, a wave of vulnerability hit me. Standing completely naked in the same room as Lorien felt worse than when I'd been in the cage at that auction. I quickly pulled the dress on, the fact that it fit almost sickening to me. Just how much had he studied me? The dress had a tie just below the bust that fastened in the back, and it had long sleeves and the bottom hem reached the floor. It was the softest gray cotton, and had extra fabric at the back, where the neckline was.

Lorien turned back toward me, his eyes softening as if seeing me in this was somehow special to him. He reached out, and I couldn't stop myself from flinching away at his outstretched hand.

He sighed. "I'm not going to hurt you," he repeated, then grabbed a pair of shoes from the shelf and leaned down. He put my bare feet into them, then laced them quickly so they fit snugly on my feet. He rose and grasped the extra fabric of the dress, pulling it up to show it was a hood.

The last thing he did was slide behind me, then tie the dress so it fit snugly right beneath my chest. Thankfully, the bust of the dress had a built-in shelf-bra, since he'd insisted I remove all my underwear.

He grasped my hand again, then looked once more at me. "Keep the hood on and your head down. We'll go to the private parking just down that hallway, then we'll be home free. If we do this right, we'll be gone and everyone will be safe. So behave just a little longer, and this will all be over."

I found myself nodding because I knew he expected that response.

He squeezed my hand as though to reassure me, then opened the door to the hallway, peering out for a moment before heading out. He moved quickly as he had before, but this time I saw no one around. The hallway led toward a large double door, and Lorien struck it hard enough it opened despite how heavy it was.

I'd never been to this parking structure, and my glance around said why. It held cars worth a lot more than what students or normal staff could afford. This had to be for the upper-level administration or important alumni, given the sports cars and imports.

Lorien didn't explain anything as he pulled me to the left, stopping in front of a motorcycle. Two helmets sat on the ground beside the large, black bike. He picked up the first one, then pulled off my hood before putting the helmet on me. He said nothing as he hooked the strap beneath my chin, then put his own helmet on.

He slung his leg over the bike and held his hand out to me. I stared at that offered hand, wanting to argue, to pull away, to bolt. The other times he'd grabbed me, pulling me along, but this time? This time I had to move first, to give in, and my body refused.

"Don't do it, Kenz." His voice didn't come out muffled, and instead felt as though he whispered into my ear. *Right, there's a mic set up connecting the helmets.* His voice got me to obey, though, the memory of his gun on his hip getting me to move.

I still had no idea if Hayden had realized I was gone or not yet. Was he freaking out right now? Was he searching for me? As much as I wanted him to find me, the idea terrified me.

What if Hayden ran out through that hallway right now? What if he tried to stop Lorien and got hurt instead? What if he took a bullet all because of me?

I took Lorien's hand and got on the bike behind him. The dress pulled tight and went up to my shins to make room to straddle the seat. Lorien grasped both my hands and wrapped them around his waist, which pressed me against his broad back. My heart thundered, but it wasn't from excitement.

"Hold on tight," he said through the sound system. The words barely finished escaping him before the bike roared to life and lunged forward, forcing me to cling tighter, afraid of falling off.

Tor

It was strange how the world slowed down when things really went to hell. I'd learned it during missions in the past, when I'd had to react to changes almost instantaneously, when I had to take in information then decide how to respond based on what I knew.

The moment I'd gotten the alert from Hayden and Char, when I'd realized that Kenz had disappeared, I'd slipped into that same mode. My brain sorted through the layout of the building as my hands moved over my phone, bringing up the tracker on Kenz's glucose reader.

It showed in a room near the south side of the campus. Not moving implied she'd left the reader behind. I knew Hayden would head to that spot, but she wouldn't be there anymore.

I closed my eyes, picturing the entire campus like an overlay in my brain. A hallway connected to that room. To the right, it headed out toward a clearing that had street access. To the left? A dead end.

No, wait. I furrowed my brows as I used my memory to recall the details when I'd searched the actual campus.

I'd often found that official layouts weren't always correct. Businesses liked to keep certain things to themselves—usually anything that housed things private or valuable. There was no good reason to let potential thieves know where they could find the things worth stealing, after all.

To the left, down that hallway, had been...

A private parking garage. I recalled the fancy cars, the exact sort of thing they might not want to let others know about. I took off in that direction, my feet moving faster than I'd known possible. I'd chased targets plenty of times, had pushed myself to my limits to finish a job, but this put all those times to shame. I had something so much more important than just a success this time.

I hopped a fence that sat just outside the parking garage, just as the roar of a motorcycle struck my ears. The sound wasn't uncommon on its own, but because I was so attuned to anything around me, to any hint, it caught my attention.

Through the small open space between the outside of the parking garage to the inside, I spotted the bike moving inside. It had a man on the front and a small woman on the back. She didn't wear the same clothing Kenz had, but that didn't mean anything. The body shape was right—for both of them.

It has to be her.

I grabbed my pistol as I rushed toward the one exit of the parking garage, but what was I going to do? I couldn't shoot Lorien, not while he drove. That bike going down at that speed would do more harm than good. In fact, a crash like that could kill Kenz.

My gaze moved to the gate, the only entrance and exit from the garage to the street. It had a single red arm that blocked the path for vehicles, but still allowed others to enter and exit by foot. With cars as expensive as those inside, they must have a remote they gave to open it from either side.

I lifted my gun, aiming for where the arm connected, for the engine that must move it from inside. I fired shot after shot just as the arm started to lift.

I wasn't a man who'd ever prayed to a higher power, who'd ever seen a purpose in that. I'd learned to rely on myself, which meant succeed or fail, rise or fall, was all up to me. I'd never seen a reason to trust anything larger than myself, content to fail if I was going to fail.

Yet in that moment, as the bar shuddered, I prayed as hard as I could that if there was something bigger than me, something looking over me, that it helped me just this once. I sure as hell didn't deserve it, but it wasn't for me.

Please, help me save Kenz.

Kenz

A loud bang rose above the roar of the engine. No, not just one but a few. The red barrier before us had started to lift, but it shuddered, paused, then fell back to the closed position.

"Shit," Lorien snapped, the word echoing in my helmet before I flung forward, against Lorien's back as the bike decelerated rapidly. I tightened my grip more, then turned my head to the left.

I spotted Tor there, his gun out, aiming at the gate. *So that's how it happened.*

"Hold tight," Lorien said as he tipped the bike to the side, taking it up and onto the walking path beside the barrier. The curb there was tall, making the bike jump up, and I'd have easily fallen if I didn't have a death grip on him.

To the other side, I spotted Hayden, a ways off, running in our direction, Char beside him.

Be a good girl. The order echoed in my head, how I'd so easily gone along with the wishes of others because it seemed easier, because I didn't know I had any other choice.

The bike bounced around as he drove it over the path, past the now broken gate. If he hit the road ahead of us, he'd gun it and we'd be gone. Now was my only chance, when he had to keep the speed down.

So when he neared the grass, just before the road, I took one last deep breath. *Now or never.*

I let go of him and dove to the side, thankful that at least I had a helmet on. Brain damage was the last thing I wanted or needed.

Pain hit me as I hit the ground. While I landed on the grass, the momentum was enough for me to roll all the way to the hard asphalt of the road.

"Kenz!" Lorien's voice came so loud through the helmet that it made me wince. However, stopping or changing directions on a bike that large wasn't easy to do. Just ahead, he stopped it, twisting to the side at the same time, so the back tired skidded and he looked back toward me.

I couldn't see his face due to the helmet, but I didn't need to. I could feel his gaze on me, the anger and frustration like a slap to my face.

A foot moved before my line of sight, and I glanced up to find Tor between Lorien and me. He had his gun up and pulled the trigger, no hesitation in the movement. It went to show how comfortable he was with removing obstacles when needed.

"This isn't over, Kenz," Lorien said. "I won't lose you, so you should really come to terms with it. You'll only get yourself or someone else hurt if you keep fighting it. The next time we meet? It will be the last time." He revved the engine, then took off again, the bike lurching forward as he escaped.

Tor didn't fire again—probably because a stray bullet could do far too much damage, and he understood that better than most. Instead, he turned toward me and dropped down as he holstered his pistol.

Maybe the fall had done more damage than I'd thought, or maybe I'd exhausted myself from all that running, or maybe the relief had gotten the best of me now that I saw Tor's face because everything went dark, with Lorien's threat—and promise—echoing in my head as though he still whispered it to me.

Still, the only thing I could think was that it was worth any amount of pain to be here with Tor and the others. I'd jump off any motorcycle if it meant Tor would hold me just like this.

Chapter Fourteen

Char

I held a few strands of Kenz's hair, running my fingers along the ends. The hair was dark with slight waves in it, and it never failed to amaze me how soft it could be. Perhaps it was all the years of coloring that had sapped that velvet feeling from my own.

I shook my head at the stupid thoughts. This wasn't about her hair, but that was so much easier to focus on rather than anything real.

Like the bandages on her arms, like the bruises she had, like the fact she could have died, that she nearly got abducted.

And now she slept there, in the bed in her room, and I couldn't shake the memory of her diving off that bike. She'd struck the ground and rolled, my heart in my throat as I watched, unable to do a damn thing.

We'd called over a doctor I knew who was willing to examine people without leaving a paper trail, and he'd said no serious issues seemed likely. If she had any problems later, to bring her to the hospital, but for now, it appeared to only be scrapes and bruises, mostly to her arms when she'd rolled and her thigh where she'd hit the ground.

It would have been far worse if she hadn't worn that helmet.

As much as I hated Lorien, I supposed I had to be grateful for that much.

She furrowed her brows and shifted on the bed, as if in pain.

"Shh," I whispered, then ran my hand over her head and through her hair. The touch eased her, because she settled back into a deep sleep.

"Still asleep?" Hayden asked as he came into the room, his voice low. He took a seat in the chair beside me.

"Yeah. She was exhausted already before this all happened. I bet she'll be down until morning."

"That's probably for the best." Hayden rubbed his hands over his face, suddenly looking every day of his age. Then again, the sight of her diving off that bike could age anyone.

"Did you figure out who the man in the office was?" I asked.

"Yeah. No one important—just a lowlife looking for quick cash. There were no connections back to Lorien, nothing to use against him. I bet he killed that man to leave no one who could identify him." Hayden sighed softly.

Kenz shifted once more, so I looked over at Hayden and gestured toward the door.

He nodded and followed me out of the room. While the idea of leaving Kenz alone didn't sit well, she needed her sleep, and I didn't want to risk waking her up.

We headed down the stairs, then to the living room. Tor and Vance were already there, neither of them appearing any happier than I felt.

I plopped down on the couch and ran my fingers through my hair. "You know, it's funny. If we'd gotten this close to Lorien a month ago, I'd have been fucking elated."

Vance nodded. "I know what you mean. He's against a wall, we have something he wants more than anything. We've got the high ground finally. This is *exactly* what we wanted."

"And it feels horrible," Hayden muttered then let out an empty laugh. "Isn't that the old saying to be careful what you wish for? It's never as great when you actually get it, I guess."

Tor nodded along, seemingly on the same exact page as the rest of us.

I opened my mouth and said something that I'd *never* expected to leave my lips. "Revenge doesn't seem as important, does it?"

Vance looked at me first, as though he were the most surprised by that. Then again, out of all of us, Vance and I probably had the biggest reason to pursue Lorien.

Vance had lost the use of his hand, and in doing so, lost the thing most important to him in his life — his art. And me? I'd lost my wife, the only person I thought I'd ever care about.

So for me to say this was no doubt shocking.

"It's because of Kenz," Hayden said softly. "Before I didn't see a future, didn't see any reason for going on beyond making Lorien pay for what he did. That doesn't feel quite as important anymore."

My phone vibrated, and it was funny how I already had it in my hand as though I expected it. That went to show how comfortable I'd gotten with Tor and how he communicated.

She made me realize how empty a life lived only for revenge is. She makes me want more.

Vance had said nothing so far, and when he leaned forward with a soft curse, I couldn't even guess what he'd end up saying. "I thought art was all I had, all I cared about, the only thing worth something in my life. After Kenz, though? I feel like she showed me there was more out there for me."

"So what does that mean?" Hayden asked. "It's easy to say something but figuring out what we do is different. This isn't as simple as just letting Lorien go, since he's got his sights on Kenz."

"It'd be nice if he'd just fuck off," I muttered. "But I agree—it doesn't seem like he's going to do that."

If we keep going on like this, he's going to get her eventually, Tor texted.

"That *won't* happen," Vance snapped out.

"Of course it will," Hayden offered up. "I've worked on protection details enough to know that if a person really wants something, if they won't back off, it's only a matter of time until they find a way. We can do everything in our power, but eventually, everyone gets lucky."

I thought back to that pit after my wife had died, when I'd attended her funeral, when I'd recognized that she was gone and that it had been my fault. That was a wound that never healed fully, a loss that a person never got over. My wife had been part of my life day in and day out, even if I'd always hidden my real self, even if I now understood just how empty the relationship had been — all because of me — it had been difficult to forget.

I thought about it when I woke up in a bed alone, when I ate meals by myself, when I fell asleep in an empty bed. I couldn't ignore it when her side of the closet was empty, when the scent of the fancy coffee she liked didn't fill the house in the mornings, or when I no longer saw her shoes by the door beside mine.

The loss could tear a person apart, and I'd somehow come out the other side of it alive.

"I can't lose another woman I love," I said softly.

It seemed as though those words sucked the air right out of the room. We'd all come together before without talking much about our own feelings, our own problems. We'd already known what we had each lost, but we'd never been the type to open up and talk about it.

We weren't exactly *sharing hour* men, here.

However, the memory of Kenz leaping from that bike sat like a spot of acid in my brain, burning down through the layers, growing worse and worse as it went, impossible to ignore.

"I've been through that once already. Kenz was the one who showed me a path out. She didn't pull me out — I had to do that myself — but she showed me that something else could still be there. No matter what happens, I *can't* go through losing her, too. I can't bury her, can't fail another woman."

Just saying those words had me leaning forward, my chest tight, my breath difficult to pull in. Still, I made myself keep going, forced the words through my narrowed throat. "Seeing her fly off that bike, not knowing if she was alive, if she'd broken her neck, it took me back to the explosion, back to when I'd realized my wife was dead. I want Kenz, I want a future with her, to see her grow gray, to see how she changes each year, and always protect her, but I'm terrified that that is just my own selfishness. If it comes down to giving her up or risking her life…"

I drew my hands into fists so tight that my knuckles ached. "I don't want to let her go but I'll do it if it's best for her."

"How is she safer without us?" Vance asked. "Even if we backed away from her, that doesn't take Lorien's target off her."

Nem could keep her safe.

My hands trembled as I looked at the words Tor had texted, especially because I struggled to argue with the fact no matter how much I wanted to.

"Are you sure about that? I mean, if we can't protect her, how could she?"

Hayden sighed softly before speaking up. "We are just the four of us, and we're here in Lorien's space. Even if his mother took away her support, he still has people he knows here. If she returned to California, if she was given over to Nem, the Quad and Jarrod— she'd become a far more difficult target. They have power and status and control there. Nothing is for sure, but Nem would have a far better chance at protecting Kenz than we could."

"And we just write her off? We just forget all about her? Can you do that?" Vance asked as he stood, the first real signs of panic I'd seen in him.

I shook my head. "No. With Kenz safe, we could focus on Lorien."

"I thought you didn't care about revenge," Vance said.

It isn't about revenge anymore, Tor texted. *It's about removing a threat to Kenz. We've been forced to split our attention, to always keep one hand on her, but if she's safe? We get to take the gloves off.*

Vance pressed his lips together, frustration clear on his face. However, Vance came from a different background than the rest of us. He'd known about the darker side of the world, had seen it only from the POV of the rich, but he hadn't existed in the depth of that filth like the rest of us.

He still retained more hope than we did, didn't recognize just how ugly life really got. That made it more difficult for him to come to terms with how easily people were killed.

"And if we get Lorien out of the way?" Vance asked. "If we succeed in making sure he isn't a threat to Kenz anymore? What then?"

"You mean if we survive it?" Hayden pressed, driving home the point that going after Lorien was hardly a sure thing.

We had our own power, our own skills, and we were a force to be reckoned with. However, we still had chains on us, morals we couldn't let go of. Lorien had none. He would burn down an entire city to get what he wanted, which meant going up against him meant accepting that there was a good chance it wouldn't end with us standing.

That fact hadn't bothered us before—in fact, we'd welcomed it. As long as we got rid of him, our future hadn't mattered.

Didn't it figure that we actually had the chance to face him when we had something we wanted to return to?

"Yeah, I mean if we succeed."

I turned my gaze toward the stairs, thinking about Kenz there, in her bed, asleep and wounded and so vulnerable. "I have a feeling that if we do this, if we get Nem involved, I don't think Kenz is going to forgive us. I don't think Nem will let her go again. I doubt we'll have the chance to just pick things up again like nothing happened."

If we do this, we're putting Kenz's life above not only our own lives, but above our future together, too.

I nodded at Tor's words, again amazed that the man who couldn't really speak could put the facts so clearly in line.

"Pretty much," Hayden said. "So the question is, are we able to give her up?"

I want her alive and happy most of all. Everything else is secondary, Tor texted without hesitation.

Vance sighed, then whispered softly, "If anyone deserves a good life, it's her. I can't stand in the way of that just because I love her."

I wanted to tell them no, that I'd fight, that I'd do whatever it took to keep her. I didn't want to lose this feeling I'd found, the sense of belonging she gave me, the ability to be myself and have someone else accept it. It was a miracle I didn't think possible. However, when I opened my mouth, that wasn't what came out. "I can do anything except bury another woman I love."

Hayden sighed, then pulled out his phone. "Okay. I'll make the call."

And even though I knew this was for the best, that this was what needed to happen, that this was the only way to protect her, I couldn't stop myself from feeling that same sinking, overwhelming grief as when I'd lost my wife.

As it turned out, death wasn't the only crushing loss a person could experience.

* * * *

Kenz

I woke alone, in one of my nightgowns that I sure hadn't put on myself. I might have been more embarrassed if I wasn't so sore, well, everywhere.

I had bandages on my arms and one leg. I got out of the bed and dragged myself to the bathroom, I found many more scrapes all over me. It brought me back to when I'd leapt from the motorcycle, the split second before I'd hit the ground, before I'd rolled and felt the tearing of my skin.

Talk about a memory I'd rather forget.

Especially the way Lorien had spoken to me, how he'd sworn not to give up.

I lifted the nightgown to see the scrapes that went up my thigh, all the way to my hip. Each time I moved, the scabs pulled, burning. Most didn't seem that deep, but they'd still take a while to heal, and I doubted I'd get away without any scars.

"Bet that hurts."

I looked into the mirror to find Char behind me, his arms crossed and his shoulder against the doorframe of the bathroom. He had the expression I was used to, one that always seemed both mildly annoyed and mildly amused, as though he teetered between the two feelings and wasn't sure which one would win.

Yet just seeing him made me feel safe. It pushed back the memory of Lorien, of that fear, as if those things hadn't happened.

"It's not bad," I said softly, then realized that I still had the hem of my gown up and nothing on beneath it.

I rushed to drop the dress and cover myself, my cheeks heating.

Char chuckled before heading into the bathroom. "I've seen everything already. There isn't much of a reason to hide it now, right? Besides, who do you think put you in that?"

I frowned, looking at the gown that had gotten picked. It was black and silk, without embellishment. The soft fabric slid easily against the scabs without catching them. "I figured it was Tor."

Char stopped just behind me, then pressed his fingers against my lips. I parted them for him, trusting him without reservation. Two pills touched my tongue before he handed me the water bottle he had in his other hand. I used it to wash down the pills, not even bothering to ask him what they were. If he'd given them to me, I knew they wouldn't hurt me.

Char's lip curled into his half-smile before he leaned in and brushed his lips to mine, as though a reward for me taking my meds like a good girl.

"Those should help with the pain."

I flushed at his comments, at the way he touched me, the way he made my heart race. How was it that he could turn me mindless so easily? I leaned forward, not wanting the moment to end, to have him steal away my worries a little longer.

Unfortunately, it seemed that wasn't his plan, because Char chuckled and pulled away. "You're way too tempting, kitten. Come on, get dressed and come on down. You've got to be hungry, and Tor cooked."

I went to tell him I didn't care about food, that I had other things I was *far* more interested in, but the loud growling of my stomach answered instead.

Char dropped his gaze and went silent for one long, mortifying moment, then let out a bark of laughter. "Yeah, that's what I thought. So get dressed and come down."

I expected him to swat my ass as he turned, but he paused before making contact, then rubbed gently. *Is that because of the scrapes?*

I smiled as he left, charmed again by that kind side of him. He seemed so surly, so rude, but then he did things like that which reminded me that he was always looking out for me.

So I hurried and changed, both because of the thought of food and seeing the others.

Ten minutes later, I sat in the backyard along with Hayden, Tor, Vance and Char. They all looked safe, which let me breathe more easily. Even though I didn't think anything had happened to them during our run in with Lorien, I couldn't have been sure.

Seeing them let me rest easy.

I had a large plate balanced on my lap, and despite the fact it was two in the afternoon, it turned out breakfast was delicious any time of day. "Seriously, Tor, how do you cook this well?" I took another bite of the perfectly cooked omelet, the cheese inside warm and gooey with pieces of mushroom and onion throughout.

He shrugged and gave me a smile, one that said he was glad I liked it.

"So," I said, ready to ask finally about what had happened after I'd passed out. No one had brought it up, which struck me as weird.

Maybe it had been because they didn't want to upset me? Maybe they wanted me to relax and not think about it? To be fair, they didn't have a full idea of what had happened, did they?

"Don't worry about that," Hayden said, cutting me off before I could get more than one word out.

"But, don't you think it's sort of important?" I pressed.

Tor reached out with his phone, which made me realize I hadn't brought mine with me. I took it, then read the note typed out on the screen. *You were in different clothes. We found the ones you were wearing before.*

My breath caught as I recalled the way I'd shaken when I'd changed clothing, when I'd stripped out of everything I'd had on before then changed into the dress he'd given me. The fear that had swamped me there wasn't like when I'd faced off against my father, when he'd held a gun pointed at me. Instead, it had been like a glimpse into my future that I hadn't wanted.

I held my breath to steady my voice, then let it out slowly and handed the phone back, looking him in the eyes. "He didn't do anything. He just made me change in case I had a tracker on. He even turned his back." I snorted softly, despite knowing the sound wasn't all that convincing. "A weird time for him to be caring, huh?"

A hand rested on my shoulder, and I turned to find Vance there, offering me a smile as though to tell me it was okay. He reached up and swiped a finger beneath my eye, which was when I realized that I'd been crying.

Great job being tough, I thought, scolding myself.

A movement to my other side made me shift my gaze just as Char stole one of the small pastries from my plate. "Hey!"

He shrugged before popping it into his mouth with a wide grin. "Look, you can cry or you can eat. If you choose to cry, well, you miss out on your food."

Hayden sighed, leaned over, then dropped a new pastry from his plate to mine.

When Char reached again, a snap drew all our attention Tor's way. He lifted one eyebrow, then took a knife from his pocket and rolled it over his knuckles in a smooth motion that implied he was *far* too familiar with that particular weapon.

Char laughed then pulled his hand back. "Lucky little pastries, defended by Tor."

I stuck my tongue out to taunt Char, surprised by just how relaxing the afternoon felt. There was a strange tension in the men, one that implied something was on their minds.

I'd ignored it because, well, who could blame them? After what had happened with Lorien, it had to weigh heavily on them. They were often protective—especially Hayden—and I'd ended up hurt and nearly abducted on their watch.

I had to assume they weren't taking that well.

Which had me ignoring the tension and smiling wider, trying to get them past it, to reassure them that everything was okay.

After we ate, I went to gather the plates. When I reached for Vance's, he waved me off and took mine instead. "I've got them." He took the plates from the others as well, then walked in toward the kitchen, leaving the rest of us there, in the yard.

The sun felt wonderful, and the loose dress I wore helped not to pull at the scrapes that still ached when I moved too much. It wasn't the same one Lorien had gotten me, of course, which made it all the better.

In fact, I hadn't seen the one I'd worn from him. I'd bet after they changed me out of it, they'd destroyed it. Part of me wondered if they didn't have some ceremony where they burned it like an effigy. The idea alone had me chuckling.

"What are you laughing about?" Hayden asked.

"Nothing important," I assured him, not wanting to ruin the mood. "So what now?"

"What do you want to do?"

The question took me off guard. It wasn't that they never allowed me to do what I wanted so much as they didn't normally ask it so officially. Typically, they simply asked for my plans for the day, expecting to sort their days around what I had to do.

Those times it had been about my plan and schedule, but not about what *I* wanted. This time, they asked me directly.

"I don't know," I admitted, feeling put on the spot.

"We shouldn't really go anywhere," Hayden hedged, his tone saying he didn't like giving me any restrictions. "But if you need something, one of us can go grab whatever it is. We could pick up something for dinner and spend the day here doing whatever you want."

I thought back, then smirked at him, unable to help but poke at him a bit for fun. "Well, I *do* need a little art practice."

He smiled, as though that idea was somehow exciting to him as well. "That's fine. You can spend the whole day painting if you want."

"The thing is, my life art class was a little rough because *someone* kept glaring. And since you didn't seem to like me using someone else as a model, how about you pose for me?"

He froze, just as I expected. It had been a joke, since he wasn't the sort who would happily strip down and just stand there for me. In fact, before he even responded, I could *hear* his response, telling me he was too old for that, that his body wasn't like the guy I'd looked at earlier.

And just like I heard his answer without saying it, I came up with my own.

My reaction came by way of a memory, of how he'd looked the morning we'd all slept together. His tan skin, the dark hair on his chest and at his groin, the scars that covered his body as proof of the fact he put himself in the way of danger to protect others. He might not have looked much like the man who had modeled, but I also hadn't *reacted* the way I had to that model.

I'd felt nothing for the model, had stared at him only to take in the lines of his body, detached and professional. He'd been no more appealing than a bowl of fruit or a pitcher used as reference. In fact, I doubted I could actually draw Hayden like that, because I'd be distracted for far less appropriate reasons.

"I mean, if you really needed me to," Hayden stuttered, the reaction beyond adorable. "I think Vance would be a better choice, though."

Char busted out laughing, going so far as to basically roll over, to the wood of the deck, holding his stomach.

Hayden shot a glare at Char, a look similar to the one Tor had given Char earlier. *He gets threatened by everyone, doesn't he?*

Even if it was a fair reaction, I couldn't stop myself from laughing right along with Char. He'd broken that weird tension between us, made things comfortable again. It made me remember just how much I enjoyed being here, with these men.

This was why I'd leapt from that motorcycle, because I'd wanted this back, because I hadn't wanted to lose moments like these. I hadn't wanted to lose *them*.

"I was just kidding," I said.

Hayden sighed heavily. *Are you that relieved?* "That was just mean."

"Be glad," Char said from his spot, still lying on the deck. "Because I have a feeling you wouldn't have gotten out of that painting lesson with your dignity intact. Shame on you, Kenz, for lusting after a professional model that way! Poor Hayden could file sexual harassment charges on you."

I twisted to find Char smirking at me, his expression like that of a little boy who was having the time of his life. It reminded me of how young he really was, and right then, all I wanted was to see more of that carefree smile, to see him happy and relaxed.

Which told me *exactly* what I wanted to do.

Anything, so long as it's with them.

* * * *

The sun had set and dirt smudged my cheeks.

"You know," I said, "my mother and father would have had a meltdown if they saw me like this."

"Like what?" Hayden asked from my side, where he sat on the edge of the flower bed. He'd helped me with all the work, just like the others, and between all five of us, we'd planted the entire other flower bed. Instead of flowers, however, I'd picked vegetables.

"With dirt on me. My mother would have said this was work for the gardeners, and my father would have lectured me on getting dirty and not looking lady-like." That took me back to both of them, to the people who had raised me, the ones who had created me.

It was strange, because I struggled to think fondly about them, but at the same time, I didn't hate them as I perhaps should have.

"What's with that look?" Char asked.

"I was just thinking about how I wish I had memories like this with my parents. I don't have a lot of memories with either, really. My mother died when I was still pretty young, and she was busy when she was alive. My father never really cared about spending time with me, so even though he only died a year ago, we didn't really spend much time together." I thought about my own words, then laughed at my own foolish thoughts. "Isn't that sad? Even after what my father did, I wish I had good memories with him."

"It's not sad," Vance said. "I know what you mean. My parents aren't the best—I mean, you met them—but that doesn't mean I don't wish I had better memories. I think all kids want that, no matter how bad our parents fuck up."

I turned my gaze toward the garden we'd created, the plants making me smile. I'd never really grown food before, since my apartment wasn't a good place for it and I'd never lived anywhere else where it was possible. The idea of planting, of taking care of those, of eventually harvesting and using the food it grew?

"Your face is like a roller coaster." Char chuckled lowly. "Every few seconds it changes and you think of something new. What is it this time?"

I didn't bother to try to hide my smile. "I feel like this is creating a future for us. We'll get to take care of these, to help them grow. Char and Vance can help me with the weeding, and Hayden can help with watering—since he won't forget it—and Tor can cook the vegetables when they're ready. I guess, I like the fact that we're doing something that feels like building a future."

I lifted my gaze when no one spoke, only to find all four men looking at me silently, a strange expression on their faces. It reminded me of that same hesitation that they'd had, a tension that they'd tried to hide.

"What is it?" I asked, suddenly worried my words had come on too strong. Maybe I'd scared them off? Men didn't like to talk about a future, so perhaps I was getting ahead of myself? "Sorry if I was rushing things," I went on, my voice dropping to an embarrassed whisper. "I didn't mean to get ahead of myself or anything."

Still, they said nothing, the silence almost painful. Vance opened his mouth, as though to say something, but his gaze rose instead to look behind me, toward the house.

It wasn't a subtle glance, and that forced me to pay attention. I turned around to find the last person I expected standing on the deck, just in front of the house.

The looks the men had given me about the plants suddenly made sense. They hadn't reacted not because I was moving too fast, but because they'd already known that we would never get the chance to take care of those plants, to harvest them, to enjoy them. They weren't the future I'd thought, but rather a goodbye, a last good memory.

Because Nem standing there, looking at me like she was, without the men reacting could only mean one thing.

They'd contacted her and planned to send me away.

Chapter Fifteen

Kenz

How was it that seeing Nem could feel so strange? For a while there, just seeing her face made me happy since she reminded me that I wasn't alone in the world anymore.

However, in the time since I'd been with the men, since I'd last seen her, a lifetime had seemed to have passed. In many ways, I didn't even feel like the same girl, the one who had clung to Nem out of fear.

"Oh," I whispered, the word the only thing I could think of to say.

"Kenz," Hayden started to say, but I shook my head, pleading with that one gesture for him to be quiet. The pain that tore through me was overwhelming, and it would take almost nothing for it to shatter whatever control I had.

Nem walked forward, her red hair like dancing flames, her looking exactly as she had the last time I saw her. From behind her, the Quad entered the house as well.

It was like my past reaching out to snatch me back, just when I'd thought I'd found something solid, something I'd craved for so long.

Thrown away, again.

I let out a laugh, one broken and full of pain, then shook my head. "I guess I should get my things, huh?"

"This is for the best," Char said from behind me, his voice lacking any of the playful tone it had before.

And just like that, it snapped the cold exterior I'd tried to hold on to. I wanted to be my mother, to accept something I didn't like with elegance and grace, to appear unaffected no matter how deeply it hurt me.

However, here I was, forced to remember that I didn't have all of that. Instead, I had a lot of my father's temper as well.

"Don't you *dare* say that to me." I spun on my heel to look at Char—no, to look at them *all*. "You went behind my back and made decisions about me, about my life, without even talking to me."

"You would have never agreed to this," Hayden pointed out. "If we'd told you, you'd have just argued with us and ruined the time we had left."

"So that's what today was? Just a final farewell? And you thought that would be better?"

"I don't like this either," Vance said, taking a step toward me. "I didn't want to do this, but after what happened? Lorien is out of control, and you being here is only going to threaten you more. One of these times, we won't be able to protect you."

"I've had people deciding my life for me all along, but I thought I finally found a place where I got to choose, where people actually respected me enough to give me a choice. Instead, you're no different than everyone else, just doing whatever the hell you want without listening to me at all. In the end, you treated me just like everyone else does, like I'm just a thing you can shuffle around as you please with no thought to what I want."

Vance reached out for me, as though to set his palm against my cheek, but I couldn't stand the thought of his touch. I smacked his hand away before he could make contact. He sighed but dropped his arm without trying again. "It's not like that."

"Of course it is." I took a step away from them and looked down, because the sight of them was too damn painful. It felt like having to watch my entire world fall apart around me, as what I wanted most dissolved, falling like sand between my fingers.

"You could have died," Char said, his voice strangely empty. "When you jumped off that motorcycle, you could have died. I don't want to lose you, but it's better you have a good life somewhere else than you die here."

"*You* could have died!" My voice rose, and I didn't give a damn that it had turned almost hysterical. Sure, I didn't love the idea of Nem or the Quad seeing this mess, but I couldn't stop myself. This might be my last chance to talk to the men I was hopelessly in love with, after all. "Lorien had a gun. He almost shot Hayden through the door in the office. He could have shot any of you from that bike. You want to sit there and say this, but any of you could have died, too! I know you don't value your lives, but I do, yet I'm still here. In fact, the odds of you getting seriously hurt are far higher than mine, since Lorien doesn't give a damn if you live but he wants me to survive."

The reality of what we'd faced off again, of what had happened, hit me. They were so damn worried about me, but they didn't really understand what I wanted at all, did they? They hadn't ever really accepted or heard me.

It made me want to collapse, to scream, to do *anything* to make my voice finally heard.

No one listened to me. No one ever heard me. I was some ghost in my own life, drifting through the world with no agency. They all did what they felt was best, treating me like some delicate toy put high on a shelf for my own safety.

And I *hated* it.

I took another step backward, ready to leave. I didn't want to bring anything with me, couldn't stand the idea of another moment here. Anything I took would only remind me of what I'd lost, would break my heart all over again each time I saw it.

"Don't leave like this," Hayden said, his voice almost desperate. "We're going to deal with Lorien. I swear he won't be a problem for you, no matter what."

"You think I care about that?" I shook my head, unable to stop the tears anymore. They ran down my cheeks, burning like acid. "You'll do whatever you want no matter what—you always have." I glanced around the yard, toward the house, so many memories swamping me.

I'd lived in so many places in my life, moved from one to another, to wherever was convenient. None of those places had ever felt like home. Hell, I'd started to think no such feeling existed, that people just made it up, that no one felt that relaxing, welcome sense of where they lived as being important.

Yet I'd found that feeling here for the first time. Maybe it hadn't started that way, but it'd turned into that eventually. Over my time here, it had turned into that welcoming place where I could let down my guard and relax. It wasn't the house that had caused it, and no matter how hurt I was right now, I couldn't deny the truth.

It had been the way Hayden fussed over me, the way he always watched out for me. It was Vance's flirtatious nature, the way he made my heart race. It was how Tor's silent company eased me, and the rare smiles he gave me. It was even Char's teasing and the quiet bits of kindness he gave out, even if he would never dare acknowledge or admit to them.

That had made this place special to me, yet here I was, thrown out of it, cast out of the only place that I'd ever truly wanted to stay.

"If I'd known just how much this had hurt..." I whispered, then dared one last look at them. "I wish I'd never come here at all. I wish I'd never tried to make a life for myself. If it was going to end up like this, with me finally finding a place where I was happy only to have it taken away, I wish I'd never known it was even possible."

All my attempts to keep some sort of control went out of the window with that, and my legs gave out as my tears came faster, turning into broken sobs. Strong arms caught me, but one inhalation told me it wasn't *my* men.

Not mine anymore, are they? Hell, I guess they never really were.

"Come on, Kenz, let's go." Dane's voice made me cry harder, as though it reminded me that I'd truly lost the men I loved. He hugged me to his familiar chest, then pulled at me. I followed his lead, letting him guide me.

Of all the ways I thought this might end, I never once thought they'd just throw me out.

But I should have, right? This is how it always goes for me…

Nem

Colton's voice in my ear before we'd arrived, telling me, '*Don't kill anyone,*' rang in my head as I stared at the men who had just made my sister cry.

Dane had walked her out, and no doubt was already on his way to the hotel room we had booked in town. We'd taken two cars to ensure we could all fit comfortably and to accommodate anything Kenz needed to bring with her. However, Kenz hadn't seemed to want to bring anything with her.

The men were less impressive than I'd have thought, given they'd somehow not only managed to get my sister—who hadn't shown much interest in anyone—to fall for them but also got her this upset.

For that, I'd expected models or men who were larger than life. Instead, they appeared disappointingly normal.

In fact, I doubted I'd have looked twice if I'd run across them in public.

"You must be Nem," came the familiar voice I'd heard over the phone.

I turned my attention to the man who spoke, the oldest of the group, dark eyes at least implying he had some brains on him. "You're Hayden, the one who called me."

He nodded, then gestured at the other men, telling me their names one at a time. We'd arrived here without a great deal of information, since getting here had been first in my priorities.

Well, other than a less than pleasant call to Jarrod, who evidently knew all about this, the asshole.

"Is Kenz safe with that guy?" Char, the redhead, asked. His hair was the only redeeming thing about him that I saw, the shade similar to my own. His gaze was still locked on the door, as though he could see Kenz and Dane.

"She's safer with him than she has ever been with you." I walked farther away from the house, each click of the heel of my boot against the wooden deck loud in the silent backyard. "Dane, Rune and Bray will take her to where we are staying and ensure her safety."

"And you're comfortable here without your security?" Hayden asked, the sharpness of his gaze making it clear that he was dangerous. Bray had managed to look up his information easily, and he sure did move the way a bodyguard would. "I'd think a person with as many enemies as you have would keep more people with you."

His words might have sounded like a threat from anyone else, but he struck me as far too noble a man for that. In fact, a part of me disliked him for that reason alone. A man who cared about getting his hands dirty wasn't a man capable of protecting my sister.

I offered him a smile, the sort I knew unnerved others. "I'm a woman who can take care of myself. I don't require bodyguards for that. However, even if I did, I can assure you that Colton here is more than capable of doing so."

The man in the back, the silent one with the golden eyes, Tor, stared not at me, but at Colton.

And wasn't that the look of a man who seemed to know exactly who Colton was? It made me curious just who he was. His expressionless face, his stance, it all said he wasn't afraid.

"You mentioned Lorien. Is that a problem I need to take care of?"

"No," Hayden assured me. "We'll handle that. We just needed to make sure Kenz is safe, that she isn't here."

"She had bandages on her arm, and the way she walked implied those aren't her only wounds." I didn't need to add a threat to that — I was pretty sure my voice alone made the danger clear.

Vance, the blond playboy in the back, answered this time. "It's why we called you in. I don't want to see her get hurt again."

"You want to tell me what happened?"

Hayden sighed, then gestured at the chairs on the deck. He sat on the sofa across from them, the action heavy as though he wasn't worried about me in the least. I doubted it was because he wasn't aware of my history or reputation, but more that he thought I'd have no reason to harm him.

That really all depends on what you say right now.

I took the seat, but Colton remained standing and behind me. Likewise, Tor stayed on his feet, the two like an odd, deadly mirror of the other.

"I gave you a general idea of what happened. Lorien is a dangerous man who is determined to have her as his wife."

"And you've done nothing about this problem?"

"I wouldn't say nothing," Char said, seated beside Hayden, a creepy smile on his face that wasn't in the least bit real. "We were able to find out his identity and stop him from buying her at an auction. In addition, we drove a wedge between him and his mother, which removed most of his backing and support."

"And you didn't realize that when you back a tiger into a corner, they tend to swipe?" I shook my head at the gross misunderstanding.

Then again, I thought back to Kyler, to Kenz's father, and how I'd done the same. I'd pushed him, bit by bit, inch by inch, until he'd reacted in a way I hadn't expected. The truth was, playing games like these led to reactions no person could ever fully predict.

People were just too difficult to fully predict.

"So why not have me clean up the mess?"

"Why would you do that?" Vance asked.

"Not because I care about you at all, I assure you. However, if Kenz is endangered by this Lorien bastard, wouldn't the smarter choice be for me to handle it? I imagine the Quad could quietly take him out. Would that not resolve this?"

Hayden shook his head. "You can't do that."

"And why is that? Because, I can assure you, I'm fully capable of it."

"For a few reasons. One, I contacted you because I want Kenz safe. I'd rather you use your resources to protect her rather than splitting them. Two, if you attack him, it makes it clear where Kenz is, thus putting her in danger again. If you simply take her back to California, or better yet, hide her somewhere, it'll take Lorien far longer to narrow down her whereabouts. Lastly…" He paused, then slumped forward, folding his hands together and resting his elbows on his knees.

"Kenz has lost too much already. If you—any of you—were harmed going after Lorien, she'd blame herself. I can't be responsible for taking anyone else away from her."

I sat back, staring across the short distance to take him in. He struck me as honest—frustratingly so. I lived my life around criminals, around liars and thieves, and this man before me made me want to yank back, as though his earnest nature might just infect me somehow.

Honest people were dangerous, driven by needs that I neither had nor understood. It was why Sasha always made me uneasy, why I struggled to connect well with Kenz no matter how much I adored and cared for my sister.

We were just too different.

However, Hayden's words made sense. I didn't like it, since I'd been the sort to deal with my own problems, but this wasn't really *my* problem.

And if Hayden and the others could take out Lorien, it solved any issue I might have. Kenz would be safe, and she wouldn't have to be exposed to these men or those dangers any longer.

"Well, despite what she said, I'd like to see her room and gather a few belongings for her. Could you show me the way?" I rose to my feet.

Char did so as well, then nodded at me, his smile just as unnerving as it always was. "I'll take you there."

I glanced at Colton, who had studied the men the entire time. He looked at me, waiting for my choice. If he'd had any real worries for my safety, he wouldn't just sit back and wait to see what I thought—he'd have insisted I remain with him. If he left it up to me, it meant he didn't believe I was in danger.

Which meant I had no issue going with the red-headed man and his fake smile. "Lead the way," I told him, leaving Colton behind.

Tor

Vance and Hayden both made themselves scarce, as if they didn't much care for spending time with Colton.

I understood that—Colton was like me.

We tended to make people nervous. Something about being around a killer made normal people uncomfortable. Even if they didn't know why they couldn't meet our gazes, if they had no idea who or what we were, they still felt it, as though they could smell the scent of death on us.

It was different from men like Hayden, men who had killed, who would kill if they had to, but who didn't make a living with that as the goal.

Even if I hadn't known exactly who Colton was, I'd have spotted that stain on him, the same one I saw in the mirror each time I saw myself.

"You know me," he said softly. "I can tell by the way you stare at me."

I shrugged but didn't try to respond. What was the point? What was there to say?

He came closer, then leaned down and stared at my throat. The action was slow and allowing him anywhere near my vulnerable areas wasn't something I enjoyed. Still, I didn't react, refused to show any level of worry or fear.

He studied the front of my throat before standing up and giving me a half-smile. "I thought as much. Our world is rather small at the end of the day. That scar is light, almost invisible, but not quite. You're the silent killer, aren't you?"

I pressed my lips together, not caring for that nickname. It was overly dramatic. Still, it was just as difficult to argue with or deny, and a part of me enjoyed the idea that he knew about me.

Colton was the sort of name few people uttered and survived, so him knowing about me made me want to stand up taller.

Because Kenz cares about him, and I want those she cares about to approve of me.

But why? It wasn't as though I expected any future at this point, so what did it matter if her pseudo-brothers respected me or not?

Colton moved a few steps away, then lowered himself onto the swing. "I know sign language," he said. "It's a good skill to have when people like us work in the dark and the quiet so often."

I glanced up toward the house, then used sign language to communicate. *I'm surprised you're okay with Nem going in there without you.*

"Nem is a force of nature herself. She doesn't need me to protect her. Besides, the moment I saw you, I knew I wanted a chance to talk to you."

Why?

"Because we see the world differently from the others. It's the way it works, because we deal in death, that we can see things others miss. Your friend Hayden, he sees the world as something worth protecting. Vance sees it as something to taste and enjoy. Char sees it as something to hide from and manipulate. You, however? You see it as I do. So tell me, this Lorien, how big a problem is he really?"

I thought about everything we'd been through, all the ways that Lorien and my life had wound together since I'd passed on that contract, since he took it, since the names on that list had started to keep me up at night.

He is, I signed. *He isn't in it for the contract.*

"So why do it? It's a good way to make money, but if you don't care about that, what's the point? It isn't exactly easy or safe work."

He sees it all as art. He thinks that killing people is some artform of his. He's well-known for leaving a lot of collateral damage behind.

Colton pressed his lips together in displeasure, the sight reassuring. While I'd never heard Colton was the type to kill innocents while doing his job, seeing his unhappiness at hearing Lorien was that type helped assure me he was different. "And why would a man like that be after Kenz?"

He was her advisor at her college. It seems like he ended up with some obsession with her. He believes she's his soulmate. In fact, he's gone out of his way to even win her over and to protect her.

"That makes this even more difficult," Colton said softly. "If he just wanted her for her name, people like that are a lot easier to deal with. People like that are practical. They see things as risk and reward. If they're shown that the risk is too great or the reward too small, they'll back off. However, someone driven by something like love?"

It isn't love, I signed back, my hands flying so fast I was amazed he caught it.

He lifted his hand to calm me. "Are you sure? Love—it's confusing, isn't it? It's hard to pin down and impossible to prove. No matter what I think about his feelings, he believes in them. His feelings are as real to him as yours are to you. That's a lot harder to deal with, and it makes a person a lot less likely to give up. Knowing Lorien is that type — he sure is a problem."

I nodded, agreeing at least to the last part.

"Do you really think you all can handle him?"

I didn't tell him yes right away. Colton was a colleague, in a strange way, and I felt the need to offer him the truth. *I don't know*, I admitted. *I know that I won't give up, though.*

"For revenge?"

No. It was for revenge at first, but not anymore. Now I just want to remove the threat from Kenz. I want to keep her safe.

"But after turning her over to us, I doubt she'll ever forgive you. You want to know a secret? Not just about women in general, but about those Hester girls? They hold grudges. Kenz has wanted to belong so badly for all the years I've known her. I remember when she was little and she chased after all of us, always trying to keep up, always wanting to belong. In fact, I remember when she asked if she could join the Quad when she grew up." Colton's expression softened in a way that I hadn't thought him capable of, and I knew he saw her as she'd been back then.

Jealousy stirred inside me, not because I thought he saw her romantically, but because he had a connection with her that I lacked, because he had a long history with her that I didn't.

He went on. "Letting her come out here alone wasn't easy. Do you have any idea how many nights I stayed up late, worried? I tried to talk her out of it, wanted her to stay closer to home, but she wouldn't listen. She looks fragile, and I know I often see her as the little girl she used to be, but she's tough. She wanted to live on her own, to make her own way, and she did what she had to to make it work. Still, in all that time, she never really got close to anyone."

She doesn't seem to have any real friends here.

"Yeah, she doesn't make friends. I think she's too afraid of having to lie to them, of putting them in danger because of her. It's why it surprised me so much to see her that upset earlier. Girl was downright broken-hearted."

Yeah, I know.

"At least you look just as unhappy. If you were all smiles, I might just have slit your throat over it. Seeing that girl cry makes me stabby."

I never wanted to make her cry. I sure as hell hadn't ever wanted her to regret meeting us.

No, not just meeting us, but regretting having moved to Florida, for her to regret having spent time at that school, having gone out on her own. Because of us, she wished she'd never done what she used to be most proud of.

We'd not only ruined all that, made it so she couldn't continue in her school, but we'd tainted her entire time on her own.

Colton sighed, then leaned forward to stare right at me. "Deal with Lorien. This all rests at his feet, at the end of the day, so make sure the son of a bitch pays *dearly* for every tear that girl cries. You do that? We're good."

And finally, something I could do. If he'd asked me to make Kenz happy, to fix what I'd broken with her, I wouldn't have had a clue how to do it.

Taking out Lorien, though? Making sure that asshole took his last breath? If that was for Kenz, that sounded just fine to me.

I'd happily use my vast skills to get rid of him, especially because I had a reason far better than revenge.

For Kenz, I could do anything.

.

Chapter Sixteen

Char

Nem was an enigma I couldn't get a real read on.

"Staring is rude." Nem took items and carefully packed them in two large duffel bags that she'd brought with her. She picked the things she took with great thought, and the way she did it suggested she knew her sister well.

It was strange, given the fact they'd barely spoken since Kenz had been with us. I'd thought them estranged, yet here Nem was, going through Kenz's things without hesitation.

I smiled widely, surprised by how uncomfortable that mask felt. Perhaps I'd gotten so accustomed to not using it around Kenz and the others that it chafed more than it had previously, or maybe I'd just not noticed the discomfort before. "You strike me as strange."

"Oh really?" She gathered the paint brushes from Kenz's art supplies, placing those in one of the bags. "How so?"

"You fit what I'd heard about you. Tough, terrifying, takes no shit from anyone."

"Don't you find mob bosses are like that in general? I'm not sure why that seems strange to you."

"That isn't the strange part. I just struggle to connect *that* with Kenz's sister. She's about as far from that as a person can get. So with you two being related, I thought you'd be more similar."

"Well, we don't share a father."

"Right. Your father is Jarrod."

Nem turned and lifted her eyebrow, the expression showing she hadn't expected me to know that much. She recovered quickly, then went back to sorting through Kenz's art supplies. "Well, at least you aren't entirely useless, I suppose."

I thought the conversation would end there, but to my surprise, Nem continued. "The truth is that Kenz is an anomaly. She takes after neither of her parents in a lot of ways. Our mother was tough and serious. She cared about family and had a temper to burn the world down if pushed. Both of her parents were cunning and secretive and perfectly suited for life in the world of crime. Kenz, however, has never been like that. Despite the fact she grew up around such people, she kept her softer side, her kind side. In many ways, it's amazing that she could keep it, given how the world has tried to strip it from her."

"You sound as though you care for her." My own words surprised me.

Because of the rumors I'd heard about Nem, a part of me had wondered if she had a heart at all. Even when she'd seen Kenz crying, she hadn't been the one who had hugged her, the one who had reassured her. In fact, she hadn't said a word to Kenz.

"That surprises you?"

"It wasn't exactly a warm reception when you saw her," I pointed out.

Nem turned toward me and leaned against the desk. "In case you've failed to notice, I'm *not* a warm person. Anything warm in me died when I did. However, that doesn't mean I don't care for my sister. Everything I have in California, the power, the money, the position, I'd happily give it all up for her sake. I'm not the sort of sister who can speak sweetly with her, who can wipe her tears when she's hurt, but I am the type who can and will destroy the person foolish enough to make her cry. Maybe that isn't a normal love, but it's what I'm capable of."

What caught me the most weren't the words Nem said, but rather the shadows in her eyes, the way she pressed on despite the clear pain.

That was Kenz.

"Maybe you're not as different as you think," I found myself whispering.

"Oh really? And please do tell me how you think you know that? You, who has met me for all of five minutes and known my sister for such a short time? What grand expertise do you think you have?"

"Kenz works *so* hard for other people. Even when she's hurting, even when she's struggling, she never lets it show. She buries it down so she doesn't trouble those around her, so she can take care of the people that matter to her." I thought back and laughed softly—a real laugh, not even a forced one—when I thought about the time she'd brought me a snack. "One night, when I could tell she was exhausted from class, I told her to go to bed. I was up working late, but an hour later, there was this knock on the door. She came in, a plate with snacks and a cup of coffee in her hands. She was dragging her feet, about ready to pass out on the spot, but instead of going to sleep, she took care of me."

The memory went further in my head, to the fact that she'd sat on the couch in my room, then all but collapsed into sleep right there as I'd worked. She'd looked so innocent in her sleep, her body just giving up the good fight, but even that close to exhaustion, she'd thought about me.

"That's her sweet side," Nem said, her severe expression having lost some of its edge, as though speaking about her sister had eased her and allowed her to let down her guard. "It makes me worry about her, but it's also her strength. It's what makes her special."

"You do the same thing, though. Maybe not the same way, maybe it looks different, but it's the same drive. She told me that you went back to save her, that you were willing to give up your revenge against her father to save her. You came out here without a second thought, knowing there was a danger, all to protect her. Even when you're hurting or worried, you still put that aside to take care of her. Maybe you two aren't as different as you think."

She frowned, her gaze on the floor as though she worked through my words, looking for some way to argue against them. "I think she's who I could have been if I hadn't been broken so young. She's the person I could have been, and I don't want her to lose that. I know calling me wasn't what you wanted, that you all knew what it would mean, but the fact that you still did it…"

She lifted her gaze, and for the first time, those silver eyes of hers didn't make me think she might be plotting my death. "Maybe that girl is rubbing off on all of us, making us better people, because I know you called me despite the consequences, because you thought it was best for her."

I thought about Kenz, about that sweet smile I knew I wouldn't ever get to see again. It fit, though. Kenz was a light that shattered the darkness, that reached into the deepest pits that I'd thought couldn't be escaped from. She changed the world around her just by being who she was.

She could make a woman like Nem give a damn about someone else, could get her to soften and smile. She could get Jarrod to act like a father, could get killers like the Quad to behave like doting big brothers, and she could make me give up what I thought mattered most to me all because she forced me to recognize how much more she mattered.

"That sounds like Kenz," I said with a soft, empty laugh.

"I've spent enough time around death to see it coming. You don't think you'll survive Lorien, that you'll make it back out alive. I'm not going to stop you or tell you to do things differently. All I'm going to say is that I hope you make it back. Who knows, if you do survive, if you ever see Kenz again, maybe I won't want to kill you for breaking her heart anymore."

If only that were possible.

* * * *

Kenz

My eyes hurt, and I knew I looked a mess. I might have cared if I'd been anywhere else, but Dane, Bray and Rune had seen me at far worse times.

Besides, I couldn't stop myself. The tears that had started at the house, when I'd realized that the men I loved had turned their backs on me, hadn't stopped until I'd run out of them.

And Dane hadn't let me go the entire time. He'd sat in the backseat of the car with me while Bray had driven, and when he'd brought me inside the large hotel room on the top floor, he'd just sat and kept his arms around me.

It felt so familiar that it almost hurt more. Dane smelled the way he always did, and his comforting hand rubbed over my back, as though to tell me I could cry just as much and as long as I wanted.

Something touched my arm, and I forced myself to turn my head toward it. Rune stood there with a bottle of water held out to me. "It'll help with the headache." His rough words made me laugh, even if the sound was downright pathetic. They really knew me, didn't they? They knew that I always got headaches after crying.

And as much as I hated it, I'd been a big crybaby during a lot of my life.

Here I am, doing it again, proving I haven't grown up all that much.

I forced myself to smile and took the bottle.

"You finally coming out of my chest?" Dane asked, his charming smile the same as ever.

Though, it mostly reminded me of Char, now, and no matter how much I hated to admit it, Char was better at it.

"It's time," I said as I twisted the top off the water and took a big drink. The cool liquid soothed my sore throat, as though to tell me that things kept moving forward. No matter how devastated I felt, I could keep going. "I can't just sit here and cry forever, right?"

"That's right," Dane agreed, then looked down at his black shirt, at the mess I'd made of it. It had mixtures of tears and snot, the entire thing evidence of my heartbreak. "I liked this shirt," he muttered.

"Yeah, well, you were the one who decided to hug me when I was crying. That makes it your problem."

"You used to be such a sweet kid," Dane complained. "You're crotchety in your old age."

"*My* old age? Coming from *you*? Aren't you getting senior citizen discounts now?"

Dane pressed a hand to his chest, mock horror on his face. "You should respect your elders, young lady!"

The theatrics helped ease the aching in my chest, and for the first time since leaving the house I'd grown to love earlier, I felt almost happy. Or, at least like I might smile.

Fabric landed in my lap. I touched the soft and familiar cotton covered in cartoon ice cream characters. I looked up to find Bray standing there, his arms crossed, silent.

These reminded me so much of the ones he'd bought me before, when I'd still been in school, when he'd come to see me overseas. I held the pajamas, reassured by them, as though Bray used them to remind me that I still had a place.

"Thanks," I said.

He nodded, then sat on one of the chairs at the dining table, turning it around to face us. He stared at me but didn't speak. He didn't often say more than needed, yet that hadn't bothered me ever. In fact, I recalled how much I enjoyed spending time with him when I was younger, because I could talk nonstop and he'd just nod or offer up short, one- or two-word answers while just letting me go.

"We can plan a time to get all your things," Rune said. "Colton and I could pack 'em up so you don't even have to go back."

The idea of going back to that house broke my heart, but the idea of sending them was just as bad. "There's nothing important there other than the photo album."

"What about your art? I'm sure you've got your sketchbooks and paintings there," Rune asked.

"I can always redo it."

Rune frowned, lines in his forehead that said he didn't care for my response. "You love your work, Kenz. It's worth saving."

"I don't think I can look at the things from there." My chest tightened even thinking about it. Each brush stroke I'd added held too many memories, as though my own feelings had bled in with the paints and I couldn't ever separate them.

"We'll get it all and put it in storage," Bray said, his voice even despite the tension. "You might want it later."

I shook my head. The idea that I could ever look back fondly on this didn't seem possible. It all hurt too much, and I doubted time would change that.

"You've been through a lot." Rune sat down on my other side. "Can't believe you didn't call us."

"Can we save the lectures for later?"

Rune tossed his arm over my shoulder, the action reminding me of so many times in the past. "Oh, trust me, we'll fucking talk about it."

"Wonderful," I muttered.

Silence took over as I drank my water, trying to come to terms with what had just happened. It was hard to understand it, to even accept it.

"It was such a nice day," I whispered to myself. No one spoke, as though leaving me room to continue if I wanted to. Maybe it was pathetic, but I couldn't stop myself from going on. "They called you yesterday, didn't they?"

"Yeah," Bray answered. "We hopped the first flight we could."

"It makes sense why they were weird today. They knew you'd show up. They wanted to give me some nice last day, I guess." I thought about our breakfast together, about the way they'd let me pick whatever I wanted to do. It felt like that last big trip to an amusement park before parents told their kids about a divorce.

It didn't make me feel better, though. Instead, it made me feel as though they'd tainted something precious to me. The day, which had been so wonderful, crumbled because they hadn't done it just because. It wasn't just us being together, but them trying to ease their guilt, as though one good day would make up for the pain they were about to cause me.

"I was really happy," I admitted.

"You want me to kill them?" Rune offered, and boy did that take me back. He'd offered that often when I was younger, anytime I'd gotten upset about anything. *You want me to kill that teacher? I could make that bully disappear.* I hadn't realized as a kid that he was serious, but I knew it now, and it warmed me all the same.

"No." I brought my knees up and wrapped my arms around them. "As mad as I am, as much as I wish I never came here or met them, I don't want them hurt. I'm pretty sure that would be a lot worse."

Dane snorted softly. "That almost seems like you love them or something."

I set my chin on my knees, curled into a ball, unable to even respond. Admitting it to them was too difficult, but I couldn't deny it, either. The truth was that I was hopelessly in love with them.

After they'd thrown me away, though, it was just too hard to say it out loud. In fact, it made me feel pathetic.

"Fuck," Rune cursed, his voice low. "Well, now I think it's a damn good idea to kill them."

I elbowed Rune in the side, met with hard muscle that told me he probably hadn't even felt it.

"Fine, I won't kill them *yet*."

"If you even think about laying a finger on them, you and I will have a problem," I said.

"Ah, there's that feisty girl I know," Dane said. "Pretty sure I like you better hissing than crying. Perk up and big brother Dane will take you drinking and to a strip club."

"Thanks, but I don't think booze and naked women will solve this."

"Booze and naked women solve *everything*. And if they don't? You're not using them right."

A smacking sound made me twist to find Rune pulling his hand back and glaring at Dane. "Don't talk to her about things like that!"

The interaction made me smile, even when I didn't feel much like smiling.

"So, no killing them, but what if we hurt them just a little?" Dane asked.

I pushed up and off the couch, surprised by just how tired I felt. Then again, it had been an exceedingly long day. "Thanks, but I think I'm going to shower, get into these pajamas, and go to sleep. Tell Nem I'll talk to her tomorrow."

"We've got a flight planned for tomorrow evening, so you should sleep in," Bray said. "Your room is the third door on the left."

I offered a soft thanks as I headed out of the room.

"What about flat tires?" Dane called out as I went down the hallway toward the room Bray had indicated. I didn't acknowledge his words, but he kept going, in true Dane fashion. "I could send poisoned pizzas to their place."

"She doesn't want them dead," Rune reminded him.

"Just *barely* poisoned!"

I shut the door to my room, closing out Dane's nonsense and the inevitable fight among the Quad. It was the first time I'd been alone since everything had happened, since I'd had my world pulled apart again.

I took my phone from my pocket, but when I found it with no messages, no missed calls, my heart sank. It really was over, wasn't it? They wouldn't half-ass something like this.

They'd cut ties with me, and even though I had their numbers still, even though I could reach out, I knew it would be pointless. It would only hurt me more when they ignored it.

So I held the phone tightly, then crawled into the bed, too tired to shower, to change, to do anything but curl around the phone and close my eyes.

Now alone, I let the pain wash through me.

I had no idea love would hurt this damn much.

* * * *

Nem

Flying took it out of me, or perhaps it was my age. In my early twenties, I'd felt as though nothing could slow me down. As I reached thirty, however, I didn't feel quite so spritely.

Or perhaps it's because I'd been so focused on revenge before that I never noticed my own exhaustion. I'd hardly felt alive back then, which meant being run down didn't feel any different.

Someone handed me a mug, and when I lifted my gaze to find Bray there, I smiled. At least, until I looked inside the cup. "What is this?"

"Chamomile tea."

"Who drinks this shit? I want coffee."

"It's after midnight. You don't need coffee at this time of night—it'll only make it harder to sleep."

I narrowed my eyes, annoyed by the fact he didn't fear me. *Everyone* feared me, yet Bray ignored my glare as though I were some little girl making a pointless threat.

When it seemed I wouldn't win this fight, I took a sip of the tea, surprised to find it less objectionable than I'd expected. It even had a lovely sweetness to it, suggesting that he'd used honey.

I glanced toward the hallway when I hadn't yet spotted Kenz.

"She went to sleep after she calmed down," Dane said.

I took the cup of tea and sat on the couch beside Dane, Colton sitting in a chair and Rune pacing. It was strange, but I had an ease I hadn't experienced in a long while.

Why? Was it because I had Kenz here, as well? Having her close, knowing she was safe, let me relax in a way I'd struggled with ever since she moved.

"Is this how parents feel when their kids come home on holiday?" Colton asked.

When I looked toward him, he had his gaze pinned down the hallway, no doubt thinking the same as me.

"It's nice having her back," I acknowledged. "Like finding something that's been missing, like getting to take a deep breath finally. How is she?"

Bray answered, his voice careful and without inflection. "She's changed." After he said that, he frowned as though he didn't care for his own answer. "She's always wanted to do as she pleased, but she bent to the will of others. She'd argue with us, but in the end, she'd do as she was told."

"That shows she's smart," Dane said. "She knows that she should listen to us because we know better. We have more information."

As he said that, however, it didn't sit right. It took me back to the many times in my life I'd had people telling me how to live my life, how to dress, how to act. Even still, I *felt* those judgmental looks from others. They rarely dared to say anything—at least to my face—but I still felt it.

How often had that ended up with people thinking it would be best if I simply gave in? If I listened to them, if I behaved myself, if I did as I should?

Yet I wouldn't be where I was if I did that—I wouldn't be *who* I was.

"I didn't really think she'd do okay here on her own," I admitted.

"Me either," Rune agreed. "Honestly, I thought we'd get a call that first week of her crying and asking us to come get her." He smiled slightly as he thought about it, a sadness to his expression implied he was disappointed she hadn't. *Never figured these men would want to play hero, but I guess for Kenz, even villains can want to be different.*

"She's actually done pretty well," Dane said. "Her place is clean, she's healthy, she's got fantastic grades, she's handled her money well. She's been a lot better off than most kids her age."

"To be fair," Colton added on, "she's been on her own a lot before this. Kyler left her to her own for years, at boarding schools, while he worked. I know it's easy to think of her like a little kid still, but she's been responsible for a while."

"Responsible isn't the problem with her," Dane muttered. "It's that she's too naïve, too sweet. She's too trusting. If she was like us, if she was willing to kill people more often, I wouldn't worry so much."

I frowned, thinking about that, about how willing she was to forgive people, to see the best in them. "Yeah, but if she did that, would she ever spend a minute with any of us?"

At least the Quad hesitated at that point, a reminder that the very people we worried about around her were really us. If Kenz was a less sweet person, she'd have wanted nothing to do with any of us.

And hadn't I thought that was the best choice before? At first, after Kenz had been hurt, I'd expected to send her away immediately. It would have been safest to help her leave, to give her the means to start over somewhere else and have no more contact with her.

My presence in her life only opened her to danger, yet I hadn't been able to cut those ties.

Kenz's willingness to have a relationship with me, with the Quad, with Jarrod all showed she had a strength to her, even if she didn't see it herself.

"I can't fucking believe she was going through all this, and we didn't even know," Rune muttered. "We're supposed to watch over her, but we sure fucking failed."

"She's smart," Colton said. "She knew if she said a word we'd come down and deal with it."

"That's exactly why she should have said something." Rune drew his hands into fists as he continued to pace. "I mean, from what it sounds like, she went through a fucking lot, but she said nothing?"

"She was abducted, sold at an auction, bought by four men, targeted by a well-known killer and attacked a few times." As Colton listed out the actual things Kenz had suffered through, it really hit me.

I'd known some of it, but I hadn't heard it all together like that, hadn't truly recognized just how quickly this could have gone bad. I knew better than most how easily one bullet could change everything, how one wrong move could end a life.

Yet I'd dealt with my own petty problems in California while my sister literally fought for her life here, without my knowing anything.

It burned. When I'd come back, all I'd wanted was to save her from the life Kyler had planned for her, to give her a chance to pick her own path, to protect her. The fact that I'd failed so badly at the one thing that had truly mattered to me hurt.

A heavy hand grasped my knee and squeezed, and when I turned, I found Dane with an unusually serious expression on. "It'll be okay. We're here now, and we'll make sure nothing like this can ever happen again."

"She won't like that," I pointed out.

"So? I'd rather have her safe and mad at me than happy with me but dead. Sometimes you have to do things people don't like for their own good," Dane answered.

And despite the fact that those very words could have left my mouth as well, they didn't sit right. They mirrored the things Kyler had said to me when he'd planned Kenz's wedding, the things I'd heard so often about me.

So could I really force Kenz into a cage like everyone else in her life had done to her?

Hadn't I risked everything to keep that very thing from happening?

Chapter Seventeen

Hayden

Not a single minute of good sleep last night.

As it turned out, no amount of coffee could overcome a complete lack of sleep. After Nem and Colton had left, when it became real that Kenz was truly gone, the house had seemed empty.

It had felt as though all the life had drained out of it.

I hadn't spoken to the others yet. We'd walked by each other like ghosts, like phantoms no longer alive or part of the world. It was strange how it could go back to what it had been before so quickly. It hadn't bothered me before, but after having Kenz around, I noticed it.

She's probably eating breakfast now...

The thought hit me, and I worried for a moment if she had something to eat. Where was she? Was she lonely? Was she crying? Would those assholes with her make sure she ate?

I took another drink of my coffee to try to shake away the questions. I'd contacted Nem for this exact reason, to get Kenz somewhere safe, somewhere away from us. It was why even if I'd wanted so badly to call her after she'd left, to check in, to at least message her and tell her I was sorry, I didn't.

Instead, I'd removed her number from my phone, the same as Char, Tor and Vance had done. I'd kept Nem's contact information — I still needed to be able to update her in the event of problems — but the ability to easily reach Kenz would pose too great a temptation.

Better to head that issue off.

I walked from the kitchen after topping off my cup to the dining room, only to find a large towel spread out and Tor with his pistol taken apart. It was a strange sight, as he'd started doing this work in his room after Kenz had started to live with us. I guess he hadn't wanted her to see his weapons up close.

It felt like a reminder that she was gone, that things had truly changed.

"Good morning." Char's cheery voice took me by surprise, and when I turned, I saw a smile that had been absent for a while. *So instead of being depressed, he's gone back to his mask, huh?*

I nodded toward the kitchen. "There's still at least a cup in the pot left over if you want any." I left the other part unsaid, that I'd bet he hadn't slept any better than I did.

Everyone had dark circles under their eyes as proof of that.

Char went into the kitchen just as Vance came into the room as well, looking even more run down than the rest of us. Then again, Char, Tor and I were used to being up late for jobs, but Vance wasn't. Stress probably got to him worse than us.

He sat at the table, all but falling into the seat. His gaze moved over the gun as he wrinkled his nose. "I hate the smell of whatever you use to clean that thing."

Tor lifted his gaze for only a moment, as though to make it clear he heard Vance and just didn't care. Sometimes that petty side of Tor made me laugh.

Char came back into the room, holding a cup of coffee. He smelled it slowly, as if to savor that scent, then took a big drink. A grimace said it was likely too hot, but he still swallowed it down. "So who's free in two days?"

"Two days?" Vance rubbed his eyes, leaning back in his chair. "Friday night?"

"That's right." His cheerful tone got my suspicion up.

"I'm free," I said.

Char looked over at Tor, who nodded as he went about reassembling his pistol. Vance also gave a half-hearted thumbs-up.

"Very good. See, this ghastly face of mine isn't because I was up late moping. Instead, I actually made some use of my time. I've been reaching out to contacts, since Lorien had quite a few people less willing to keep their mouths shut now."

His words had me fully turning toward him now, a spark of hope inside me. Did this mean he'd found something? "Do you know where he's staying?"

"Sadly, no. He's too careful for that."

"So why do you look so proud?" Vance asked. "That expression should be saved for when you actually do something useful."

Char shrugged, then took another drink of his coffee. "Well, what I *did* do was use my contacts to plant the story of a very important meeting. You see, we are going to be sending Kenz off because it's too dangerous here, but the only good way to do it would be to give her to a transporter."

"And how is that supposed to help us?"

Char gave me a look that implied I was quite possibly the dumbest person who had ever lived. "An exchange like that is tricky, and one of the best places to do it would be somewhere with amazing security, used to dealing with the more underhand parts of society."

A bad feeling crept into me, and it didn't help at all that Char appeared far too pleased with himself. There was only one place I could think of that might fit the bill, and the reasons for picking it weren't lost on me. "You're talking about the auction house."

He pressed his lips together as though impressed. "And here I worried your brain was just for decoration. That's right. I've already made sure to leave enough of a trail that there's no way Lorien won't catch wind of it."

"And you think he'll take that bait?" I asked.

"People take whatever they want, and he wants this to be true. He's been banging his head against the wall, this whole time, too. He'll be there."

I stared down at my hands, the reality hitting me all at once. We'd planned to deal with Lorien, to make sure he couldn't endanger Kenz again. That was still my plan, but this felt so final.

"If he shows up there, if he targets him..." Vance didn't finish the thought.

He didn't need to, though.

"Bradley won't turn a blind eye," I answered. He was merciless when it came to his rules and his auctions. We'd all gotten off easy the last time, mostly because he didn't want a scandal. However, if we showed back up, if we turned his precious auction into a bloodbath, he wouldn't let us off so lightly again.

Char's smile disappeared, a glimpse of the real man he tried to hide. "If we do this, we'll ensure Lorien is dealt with, that he can't ever target Kenz again, but we won't make it out alive."

No one spoke again, as though the true weight of the choice had finally hit us all.

If we did this, if we went through with it, it would be the end. We could take Lorien out, save Kenz, but even if Lorien didn't take us out—Bradley would.

Could we trade out futures for Kenz? Give up the years we might have left to buy her those years?

The answer was so obvious that I almost laughed. There was only one choice, really, only one thing we could do.

"Okay. Let's do it," I said.

It'll finally all be over. I just wish I got to see Kenz happy one more time.

* * * *

Kenz

It was funny how time eased all pain. No matter how badly I'd just wanted to keep sleeping, to ignore all the pain in favor of unconsciousness, eventually, my body refused to sleep anymore.

So I'd slept in late, then gotten up the next morning, finding new clothes in my room, waiting for me, telling me Nem or one of the Quad had left them there for me. I'd showered with the hottest water possible, ignoring the way it stung on my wounds, especially because I'd taken off the bandages on my arm and thigh.

The clothing left for me was obviously an attempt to work around the scrapes. It had a tank top so as not to aggravate my arm, then a long, loose skirt to make allowances for my thigh. They were both black — it implied Nem might have picked them out herself.

After all that, when I worked my hair into a French braid, I realized how strange it was that I could do this.

My chest was a hollow pit, yet I'd dressed like normal. My life had fallen apart, but my fingers still moved in accordance with the practiced motions, like nothing had changed.

Noticing it didn't make me feel better, though. It didn't make me feel as though things would get better, that I'd heal and go on and someday look back at this like some bittersweet memory. Instead, it felt like a reminder that I had to keep doing this, keep moving no matter how bad it hurt, no matter how little I wanted to.

Just forced into another life, another path, following someone else's plan.

A knock on the door made me grip the counter of the bathroom, telling myself to suck it up, to do what everyone expected from me, to keep going. One deep breath later, I stepped out of the bathroom and called for them to enter.

Colton opened the door, his expression careful and guarded as he looked over me, as if checking to ensure I was still okay. It made me laugh, because I had no doubt people had come in during the night to ensure I was both safe and still there.

I offered him a smile I didn't feel to reassure him. *I'm fine. I'm always fine.*

He pressed his lips together but didn't call me on the smile. "Come on—food's ready."

I nodded and followed him to the dining room, recognizing how nice the hotel room was. The night before, I'd been far too tired and upset to take proper stock. Now, however, the fancy furniture, the expansive views—they were far more obvious.

And yet, I felt as uninspired as ever.

I took a seat at the table, the rest already there. The fact they could appear so well put together when I doubted they'd gotten much more sleep the night before was impressive.

Not that I cared how I looked, at least beyond not wanting to cause them to worry. I'd created enough problems for them already, hadn't I?

A plate already rested at the open seat for me, and the smell of food hung heavily in the air. Nem and the others ate—we weren't the type to feel the need to wait on manners.

I pulled the silver lid off my own plate, setting the large cover on the center of the table. There, on the fancy white square plate sat an omelet, the yellow surface of it appearing perfectly cooked and the scent mouthwatering.

And yet...it left me cold. It only reminded me of the food Tor had cooked, the way he'd left the bell peppers off mine because he'd known I hadn't liked them. I knew, logically, that this food was at least as good, yet it appeared as appetizing as spoiled milk to me.

When I felt a pair of eyes on me, I lifted my gaze to find Nem staring at me.

I didn't want to cause any more trouble for anyone, so I picked up my fork and forced myself to nibble a little off the end. It tasted about as good as I thought it would, and my stomach rolled as I forced myself to swallow.

"We aren't going to leave for another two days," Nem said.

Those words made me frown. "Why? You seemed in a rush yesterday."

"Things change. It seems your *friends* have a plan coming up. It'd be good for us to stay here, off the radar, until they're done."

The use of 'friends' made it clear she meant, and I sat up straight at the mention. "What do you mean?"

Nem's red lips curled into a smirk, as though she liked the fact I showed some spark. "That got your attention, did it? I heard about an hour ago that they've got something set up. If we get spotted flying out of town, it might mess with their plan. It makes more sense to just stay here until they've finished."

"Until *what's* all done?" I gripped the fork in my hand, squeezing tight as anxiety ran through me.

"They've set up a trap, from what I understand."

"What sort of trap?"

"They've planted the story that they'll hand you over to a transporter to get you away and hide you. The handover is supposed to take place tomorrow night at the next auction."

The mention of the auction made my heart race, my palms sweating immediately. If the men's house felt like home, the auction house was my own hell. The darkness, the thick bars of the cage, the way the lights on the massive stage blinded me, it all came back to me.

Except…I couldn't let myself focus on that, so I closed my hands into tight fists. "Are you serious?"

"So they say," Nem said, shrugging as though it wasn't her problem.

"That's a horrible idea," I argued. "Lorien is *way* too smart to fall for something like that. Even if he *did* believe it, if he went with it, if they attacked him there…" My voice trailed off as the truth hit me.

If they attack Lorien, Bradley will have them killed.

It meant there was no way out for them. Even if they did everything right, even if they got the upper hand and took Lorien out…they would still die.

I'd thought the auction was the scariest thing, but it turned out worse things existed in the world—like the idea of losing the men I loved.

"They can't do that," I whispered, fear gripping me and making it hard to pull in full breaths.

Bray spoke next, no food left on his plate, his tone of voice flat as though this didn't involve him at all. "They aren't foolish men. They know what this course of action will lead to and they're still choosing it. If this is their plan, you should sit back and accept it."

"Even if it's a bad idea? Even if it's dangerous and stupid?"

"Even if it is, what are you going to do?" Dane asked, his tone gentle, as if he knew damn well what he had to say would insult me. "There isn't anything for you to do about it, and if you got involved, you'd just cause more trouble. If you try to interfere, you'll just give them more things to worry about. You'll only cause more problems."

I dropped my gaze, the words hurting more than I thought they would.

It took me back to all the times when I'd felt useless, when I'd been unable to do a damn thing but watch as others decided my entire life. I recalled when my father had pointed that gun at Nem and pulled the trigger, when Jarrod had taken that bullet. I remembered when Hayden had gotten hurt protecting me, when Vance had been willing to get shot just to keep me safe.

How many times in my life had others suffered for me?

It made me feel useless and pathetic and I *hated* it. Dane's words brought all that impotency back up. It poured alcohol into the wounds I'd carried around, the feeling that I was supposed to just sit back and accept that I couldn't help.

I couldn't fight, couldn't protect the things I loved, couldn't do anything for those who mattered to me.

"I know this is hard, Kenz," Rune said, his voice so gentle that it sounded strange, like it didn't belong to him at all. "But sometimes the best thing you can do is just sit down and wait. Just be a good girl, and we'll have you home in a couple days. You can get back to your normal life with us, then."

Be a good girl.

Those words rang in my head like a bell, one that crashed against the insides of my skull. I'd heard that my whole damn life.

My mother had said it, my father, all the men in my life. They'd all told me to be quiet, to behave myself, to do as I was told, to *be* who they wanted me to be. Even Nem, even the Quad and Jarrod, they all wanted me to be good, to listen, to trust them and not make a fuss.

And I'd accepted it each time. Even if I scoffed, even if I hated it, I'd folded and bent to their whims.

No more.

I shook my head, then stood. "No."

"No?" Dane repeated that as though the word made no sense. "I don't think anything we said was a yes or no question."

"I'm not going to just stay here and behave myself. I'm not going to sit back and let them risk themselves like this."

"And if you get yourself into trouble?" Colton asked. "If you rush into something you're not ready for? What then?"

"They're already doing that for me. They're doing something they *know* is dangerous because they want to protect me, and I'll be damned if I sit here and do nothing in return. I might not have the same skills you do, but I'm not useless."

Bray looked toward Nem as though for help. "What are you going to say about this? We aren't actually going to just let her run out and do something stupid, are we?"

I expected Nem to stand up, to tell me I was being unreasonable, to send me to my room like a child being scolded by her parent for her foolishness. Instead, she smiled, still sitting back. "I say it's about time."

The fact that with so few words Nem could draw the complete focus of the Quad, all at once, was nothing short of astounding.

These men faced anything without flinching, yet Nem could throw them so easily?

"Excuse the fuck outta me?" Rune said, his phrasing enough to make me laugh at any other time.

Nem didn't acknowledge him—or any of them—and kept her gaze on me. "It's about time you stopped listening to others and did what you wanted, what you think is right. You're my sister—we share blood. We may be very different, but neither of us were ever meant to be mindless dolls. It's good to see you stepping up."

"So you won't stop me?"

"I don't like it. I want to lock that door and keep you here, insist that at the very least, you take our help, but I accept that that isn't a good idea. I told you before that I came back for one reason—to free you, to give you your choices back, your life back. It was all for nothing if I take them away now. So no, I won't stop you. I know you're strong, that you're smart, and if you put your mind to this, you can do it. If you're set on saving them, if you've got your sights on Lorien, well, he's fucked."

I stared at my sister, at the way she held herself still, tension running through her. It made it clear that she didn't like this, that she struggled against her own instincts, but she still did it. She still sat there and opened the door to my own cage, giving me the ability to make my own choices.

So I nodded, stepping away from the table, my mind going so fast that I struggled to make sense of all the ideas I had. I said nothing else, rushing back to my room. I'd need things, which meant packing, first.

In the room, I grabbed the few things I'd need. My phone, my new glucose reader, some cash, just the essentials. I tucked them into the pockets of my loose skirt. Within a few minutes, I'd done everything I could and went back to the living room.

Nem and the Quad all stood there, by the door, and my heart sank for a moment. Would they stop me now? Had they changed their minds?

It doesn't matter. I'll go through them if I have to.

Dane held out his hand, passing off something to me. It took a moment for me to realize it was a bank card. "There's plenty of money on this. Use it if you need anything."

Next, Rune shouldered him out of the way, then took my hand. He slid a set of rings onto my fingers that connected, and it took a moment for me to recognize them for what they were—*brass knuckles*. They appeared fancy enough that anyone seeing them might not recognize just how dangerous they were, especially with the rough, sharp edges on the outer side. "If anyone fucks with you, you use this, okay?"

Bray took my hand and gave Rune a glare, as though he didn't care for the weapon. Instead, he reached into my pocket and took my phone, then took another from his own pocket. After a few moments, he held the new phone out to me. "This is my personal phone, and it will receive your calls, now. If you need help getting into anything, press this button here."

He showed me the screen, an icon with a black square on the home page. "It'll hack into most things, and it'll connect to my laptop so I can help with anything beyond what it can do automatically." He didn't say anything else, taking a step back as though he'd said all that needed saying.

Colton next came up last, his hands in his pockets. "I'd love to give you a gun, but I know you won't actually shoot anyone. Instead, I'll give you this." He slid a necklace over my head, the pendant a pretty silver oval. He grasped the edges of it and pulled, allowing it to open. Inside sat two pictures, one on each side. The left had an image of my mother, and the right had Nem and the Quad.

I frowned and looked up at him, the item surprisingly sentimental for him.

He made a soft sound before offering me a rare half-smile. "You forget what you come from sometimes. I thought this might help you remember." He tucked his hands into his pockets as though uncomfortable before turning his gaze away.

The four of them looked at me, shifting their weight as if they wanted to say more, but backed off before doing so. It left only Nem between the door and me.

"I'm surprised they aren't stopping me," I admitted softly.

"Oh, they want to, don't get me wrong. I'm sure I'll catch hell for this." She let out a soft laugh, the sound strange from her. It had less edge than usual, less hardness. Still, she offered me a half-smile and went on, "I know you always think that you're not as strong as me, that you're somehow less than I am. I see it when you look at me, like I'm a goal and you fall short. I want you to realize I have never once seen you that way. Believe it or not, neither do they." She nodded toward the Quad, who stood a few feet away as though to give us some semblance of privacy.

"Then why are you always trying to protect me?"

"Because that's what we are—who we are. We're violent and difficult and live in the darkness. It's our place to protect others. You? We don't do that because you're less than but because you're more than that. No matter what has come your way, you've survived it all, you've kept your kindness, you kept your soul. I've never thought you were less than I am, and I don't want you to think that, either. So I'm letting you go because I know better than anyone else just how tough you really are. So go on—go do what you need to do and prove it to everyone else, too."

I nodded, swallowing down my tears and throwing my arms around Nem for a quick, awkward hug that she didn't seem to know how to react to before I rushed out of the door.

First things first.

I took out the phone Bray had given me and dialed a number I knew by heart. If I was going to save the men I loved, I couldn't do it alone.

Chapter Eighteen

Kenz

I hadn't expected to ever face this man again. So far, he'd been there for some of the worst moments of my recent life, so if I did see him again, I didn't think it would be because I came to him.

Yet here I was.

Bradley Chains. The auction boss. The cold, heartless man who had started so much of this. He wore his fancy, expensive well-tailored suit and looked at me with the same hard eyes he had before, as though none of this mattered to him beyond the bottom line.

"I didn't expect to see you again, Ms. Fox, and I certainly never saw you coming here yourself. You seemed unwilling to endure my company before—I wonder what has changed."

I sat across from him in a large office, one in a busy, tall modern building. Finding his information hadn't been all that difficult, making me suspect he was one of those hiding-in-plain-sight sort of men. By day, he was Bradley Chains, land developer and property magnet. By night? He ran auctions that sold anything a person could desire—even people.

"I needed to speak to you," I said, struggling to meet his gaze directly. It took me back to that cage, to when I'd first met him, to how terrifying he'd been.

"So I assume, since you came so far, and alone. When I first received word that you wished to meet, I had assumed you would have those men surrounding you. In fact, I wasn't sure the meeting was worth having given the trouble they have caused me. However, upon discovering that you would come alone, I couldn't turn that down. What, pray tell, is so important that you would risk speaking to me alone when you so obviously do not want to be in the same room as me?"

"I need your help."

He let out a soft, unkind laugh. "I am not the sort of man who helps people. Surely you know that already."

"I don't expect you to do it for nothing, but this will benefit you as well."

He folded his hands on his lap and sat back, a subtle smile playing across his lips. "Well, I can say this is entertaining, if nothing else. So what is this favor you want?"

I forced myself to look up, to meet his gaze directly. He had eyes that were just as dark as I recalled, and his facial hair was well groomed. He looked every bit the part of a rich, successful businessman, his gaze shrewd.

Even if he laughed softly, if he acted as though this were all a game to him, that expression showed just how serious and capable he was.

It also told me to tread *very* carefully.

"I want you to sell me again."

The lifting of his eyebrow might not have seemed like a large reaction, but it went to prove his surprise. "That was probably the last thing I expected to hear you say," he admitted. "I thought you might come to ask me to deal with Lorien, to beg me to intervene, perhaps even to tell me how I owed you something due to what you went through."

"I'm not the type to beg," I said. "I'm not here because I think you'll help me out of the goodness of your heart. This world isn't made by that. This world is made by give and take, by what people need and what others can offer. I wouldn't be foolish enough to stand before you and expect charity. Instead, let me put it this way. You offered to Hayden and Lorien that if you re-auctioned me off, you would waive the auction fee in exchange. I'd like to do that again."

"And why?"

"You offered this."

"Yes, but it was turned down. You weren't interested in working with me then. When things change, I want to know why. Why now? What happened that made you think this was the right time?"

"I tried to let the men handle this, but it's clear they can't sort this out. They'll end up killing one another to get this over with, and I don't want that on my shoulders."

"You're here alone, which means you could escape, right? You could run away and hide and let them destroy one another. Why are you here, then, willing to sell yourself instead?"

"Because I don't want anyone dying because of me."

"So you're willing to trade your freedom for their lives?" He shook his head as though embarrassed by that. "That is pathetic. No wonder you've found yourself in this position. Foolish people end up at the mercy of the strong. It would be for the best, perhaps, for you to sell yourself off just so you don't end up in this sort of position again."

His comments might have hurt me before, but Nem's words rang in my head, working like a shield for me. I didn't have the same kind of strength as Nem, but that didn't mean I didn't have my *own* type.

So I stared right at him, unwilling to back down. "I might not be able to stand up against the likes of people like Lorien, but that doesn't make me helpless. I'm strong enough to do this, to stand tall and do what needs to be done to protect the people I care about."

Bradley tipped his head, his smile fading. "So you hope that your men will win the auction? There won't be any cheating this time. We will hold a new auction, and you *will* be awarded to the highest bidder. Because this has already caused me a headache and threatened my reputation, I can assure you, the person who wins *will* get you and I will put all my power and authority into assuring that whoever wins keeps you this time. You are signing yourself up to giving your entire future to the winner of this auction, and there is no guarantee that it will be the person you want." He spoke slowly, as though truly wanting me to understand the risks, the potential effects of this choice.

However, I'd gone over it. "Trust me—I've thought about this more than you have. I am well aware of what could happen. However, doing this will keep the peace. It will protect everyone involved."

"Everyone except you," Bradley pressed.

"There are things that are worth risking everything for," I said. "If giving up my life or freedom is the only way I can protect the people I love, I'll do it."

He said nothing at first, as though he had to come to terms with my words, like they weren't what he'd expected. "You know, when I first saw you in that cage, you seemed a very different person. You trembled, refused to meet my gaze, you were like this frightened little rabbit. I'm surprised that that woman facing off against me now is the same one. When I saw you there, I didn't expect you to survive a week after the auction, thought this world would have crushed you."

"That's because you didn't know everything," I said softly. "You thought that was my introduction to this world, to violence and crime and people like you."

"I saw your history—you were raised rich and spoiled."

"Rich? Yeah, spoiled?" I laughed softly and shook my head. "No. Not so much. Do you take my offer?"

He pressed his lips together, and I got the sense he wanted to say no. Why though? This would solve all his problems, would give him everything he wanted, but he hesitated.

Could he actually not be as bad a person as I think?

That seemed impossible, given he was willing to sell people without batting an eye.

The direction or fluidity of his moral compass wasn't my problem, however, so I pushed that aside.

He let out a sigh, making me suspect he'd seen that I didn't plan on giving up. "Very well. I'll hold a special auction, open to any qualified bidder, in two weeks."

"Make it tonight. You have an auction already, right?"

"We won't have many people willing to bid," he complained. "Selling a woman brings in a certain type of buyer, and there aren't always a lot of people willing to buy such a product. We need to give buyers time to make the appropriate plans to attend."

"No need. Trust me, you'll have more bidders than you can deal with, and I'll sell for more than you can imagine."

Bradley let out a soft laugh. "You've got guts, I'll give you that. As a businessman, I want to tell you no, but you've caught my interest. Even I enjoy a good bet, after all. Very well — since time is of the essence for you, I'll adhere to your requirements. I will refund the money spent to purchase you last time, and at ten o'clock tonight, Mackenzie Fox will be sold to the highest bidder again."

"Almost right," I corrected him.

"Almost? What is it that you feel isn't right about that?"

"Mackenzie Fox doesn't exist. Make sure when you announce me, you use the right name — Mackenzie Williams. By the end of tonight, someone will get to own the only living heir to both the Hester and Williams bloodlines."

The widening of his eyes said he'd finally recognized my true worth, that he knew that name, that he figured out who and what I really was, and I knew instantly he'd do as I wanted.

Wasn't it funny? After all the years when I'd wanted nothing but my own freedom, where living my own life had mattered so much to me, here I was, willing to sell it all.

Of all the things I thought might destroy me, I sure hadn't expected love to be the one that got me in the end.

* * * *

Vance

The tension in the room felt strange. I'd lived in the spotlight, always under the pressure of the opinions of strangers, but that felt different. That had been normal, just a fact of life for me.

This was different.

I wasn't a man who knew much about danger or violence. I'd spent my life creating art, enjoying my fortune, living as I pleased. I'd had bodyguards, at times, to ensure my safety, but danger had been a far thought in my mind.

This time, though, we were unlikely to walk out of this again.

It had hit me as I watched the others preparing. Hayden, Tor and Char all checked their weapons and ensured they had whatever they needed.

They couldn't bring much with them — security was tight at the auctions, after all, and there was no doubt Bradley would keep a closer eye on us. Still, all that mattered was that we got Tor close enough to Lorien to finish this.

We all had our parts to play — I had to show my face to reassure Lorien that we were there. Hayden would make the rounds near where we'd rented a room for the fake handoff, pretending to watch for signs of danger. Char would blend in as a staff member to keep tabs on Lorien, and Tor would be the one to actually make the move.

The plan, on its surface, would work. We just had to focus on our tasks and by the end of the night, all of this would be finished. It was strange to sit here and *know* it was my last day, that I wouldn't see the sun rise tomorrow. I'd often lived my life as though each day were my last, savoring every pleasure the world had to offer. This was the first time I knew it for sure, though, and I didn't feel the relief I expected.

Maybe it was because I had things I would miss, now. I'd tasted real happiness for the first time, and I found myself reluctant to sacrifice that, even if I knew it was for the best.

A noise on my phone made my heart beat faster, the stupid hope I'd had each time it chimed. Before even looking, however, I knew it wouldn't be the one person I wanted, that it wouldn't be Kenz.

I picked up my phone and frowned when the notification came from a banking app.

Not just any app, either, but the shady one that we had used to pay the auction house for Kenz. I opened the notification, waiting as the phone accessed the highly encrypted files, to find…

A refund?

It showed all the money we'd paid for her refunded back into our account. I blinked as I tried to make sense of that. Could it have been an error? No, an error like that would have occurred right after the purchase, not over a month later.

I opened the note associated with the transfer. *Refund after return of purchased merchandise.*

Return? A cold spark ran down my spine.

Bradley wouldn't return funds like that out of the goodness of his own heart, given I doubted he had such an organ in the first place.

"Char," I said, my voice shaky.

He must have noted the tone in my voice, because he jerked his gaze my way. "What's wrong?"

"We just got a refund for the money we spent on Kenz. The note says it's because we returned the merchandise."

Hayden, who was across the room, checking items in a bag, pulled his phone out before I'd fully finished the statement. He pressed buttons on the phone, then at one last one, activated the speakerphone, the ringing on the other side loud in the deathly silence of the room.

"I was wondering how long it would take for you to contact me." Nem's voice was one I would never forget, and the fact she answered in such a way said she knew something was going on.

"Where's Kenz?" Hayden asked.

"I thought you let her go. In fact, when we spoke last, you assured me you would leave her be for good."

"And you assured me that you could keep her safe. We just received a refund from the auction house. Bradley would only do such a thing if he had her back, if he expected to make that money back another way. So I ask again — where is Kenz?"

Had I ever heard Hayden speak like that? He was usually so calm and collected, and even when he stood his ground, he rarely used such an outright threatening tone.

"You're lucky that Kenz would be upset if I killed you, because I don't allow people to speak to me that way. I'll overlook it this time for her, but be careful, because my patience only lasts so far. Kenz left last night."

"And you just let her do that?"

"She isn't a prisoner. She isn't a pet to be locked up or chained for our ease or comfort. She's her own person, and she makes her own choices."

"Even if those choices put her in danger?"

"You can't protect people who don't want to be protected," Nem said, her voice softening slightly. "You can't force people to behave the way you want and expect them to simply accept it. They will fight back, and it'll eventually fail."

"That sounds like you taking the easy way out. If something happens to her, that will be on *your* head."

Nem said nothing back at first, and it went on so long that I feared she'd hung up. Finally, she went on. "You know better than that. Doing what's right is rarely the same as doing what's easy. Sitting back and allowing people to make their own choices, and potentially their own mistakes, is far more difficult than trying to control them. You made your choices, to face Lorien knowing Kenz would never want you to risk yourselves like that. You can't fault her for making her own choices in response. That girl has a will of steel when it comes to protecting others, and she'll face down the devil himself because, for some reason I will never understand, she loves you all."

Face the devil himself. Those words echoed in my mind, feeling important.

"So where did she go? What is she doing?"

"That I can't tell you, because I don't know. Kenz is aware of my tendency to intervene, so she didn't tell me her plan. She knows to reach out if she needs me, that I will help in whatever way I can, but she's yet to do so."

"So you have no idea what she's got planned? What she'll do? Where she might be?"

"No, I don't. But I trust her. You should, too."

Hayden gripped the phone so tightly I worried that he might break it. His tone was angry when he responded. "If you hear *anything,* call me immediately."

I was pretty sure she would have responded by telling him not to order her around, but he hung up before she got the chance. He stared down at the phone, and I felt the same confusion, the same helplessness.

A single question floated through all our minds, no doubt — *what now?*

"What the hell was she thinking?" Char muttered.

"Should we try to find her?" I asked, an uncomfortable fear tugging at me. I pictured her alone somewhere, frightened and crying. "We could put off the plan tonight and focus on her, instead."

Hayden shook his head. "We can't do that."

His words took me by surprise, given Hayden was by far the most paranoid and overprotective. It meant I'd expected him to agree right away.

He must have taken my silence for surprise, because he continued on. "Lorien is the most dangerous thing to Kenz. If we back out of our plan, Lorien will suspect something's wrong, might realize Kenz is gone. No matter where she is, it's safer that she'd be here."

"So we just ignore that she's missing?" Char asked.

Hayden sighed, and the troubled look in his eyes made me feel guilty. He was as trapped as the rest of us — worse, if anything, since he usually held himself responsible for everyone around him. This couldn't possibly be easy on him, even as he tried to do what was best. "It isn't about ignoring it." His voice came out soft. "We have to focus on what will make the most difference for her. Kenz deserves to feel safe, and the best thing we can do is to give that to her. She'll probably show back up at Nem's in a day or two — let's make sure she has a safe place to return to."

I wanted to argue, but how could I? Hayden was right. We'd made our choice already, and Kenz running off didn't change it. Finding her would be a temporary measure that would only make things harder in the future. The only option we had was to keep moving forward, to remove the threats to Kenz before they could harm her.

And in the meanwhile, we had to hope Kenz kept her head down, that she didn't have some foolish plan in her mind, that she didn't intervene and get herself hurt. If only I had faith that she was that sort of practical person.

Just what the hell are you up to, Kenz?

Chapter Nineteen

Kenz

Back here again, huh?

It was strange how different it felt, now. I was back in that damn cage, the same one as before. Bradley had offered not doing that, given this time I'd turned myself in willingly.

However, something fitting had me repeating the same as before. At least I wasn't drugged this time.

Small miracles.

"You look surprisingly good." Bradley's voice had me turning in the cage to find him there, dressed as he usually was. It was strange just how different I felt about him as well. Instead of him scaring me, I almost saw him as a partner in crime. Or, perhaps, it was better to say he was a hyena to my lion. He would kill me if he saw an opening, but so long as I left scraps for him, he'd happily take them.

"This is better than last time." I glanced down at my outfit, the dress far different than the one I'd been given before. "I'm surprised this one is so much classier."

"Well, the last time your worth was mostly in your health, your age and your body. We wanted you to appear sweet and innocent and attractive. This time, however, your bloodline and power will attract bids. You should know selling is all about presentation and packaging."

I rolled my eyes at the way he said *selling*, the term bothering me. It was fair, I suppose, but it still chafed. "Did everyone come?"

Bradley nodded. "Lorien has checked in, as have Tor, Hayden, Char and Vance. None have given any sign that they know you are here. It appears your plan is working."

"What plan? You're giving me too much credit. I'm just here to keep them from fighting and getting themselves killed."

"Isn't that cute? So willing to give yourself up for other people?" He grasped one of the bars of the cage, leaning in closer. "You know, if I were a different man, you might actually have some appeal. People like you are rare in this world, and I am a man who likes rare things. If we had met another way, if I had lived a different life, who knows? I never expected that a woman could move so many others, could change so much, yet you've managed it. That is rather impressive. It makes me wonder just what else you may be capable of."

"Well, I'm sure glad we didn't meet another way," I told him, for once not afraid. Not of him, not of my future, not of anything. I'd put this all in line, had created this situation, and for once, I had no questions, no worries. I'd done what I did and now could only follow it through to the end. It was funny that it freed me in a strange way, and because of that, I allowed myself to speak as I wished.

"No? Am I so terrible?" He tilted his head as though honestly curious.

"I don't know you, but I know that I wouldn't give up what I feel for the men I love, not for you, not for anyone."

He stared back, then chuckled finally, as though my words didn't bother him. "Fair enough. Well, Ms. Williams, it was nice to meet you. I suspect that no matter how this plays out, whatever happens, I am unlikely to meet another like you. Believe it or not, I wish you the best and I hope that this turns out to your advantage."

It was strange, because I got the sense that he meant it. He might not lift a finger to help me, but he truly wanted this to go my way. He nodded once more, then turned his back and walked away, leaving me to wonder just how much else rested under that exterior.

All I knew for sure was that whatever woman had to deal with him in the future would have her work cut out for her.

The auctioneer — the same from before — came up to the cage, his smile just as creepy as the last time. "I never expected to see *you* again, but I'm not that sorry. Are you ready?"

"As ready as I'll ever be," I muttered, then nodded.

No backing out now, nothing else to do but see this to the end.

It's time.

Tor

Being at the auction had my attention focused, and I was ready to react at any moment. I'd been here before — many times, in fact.

Sometimes there was no better way to get items than to come to a place like this, than to buy things from the shadows. I'd gotten information, key cards, necessary files. I'd learned that people could buy anything at the end of the day.

However, this time the items up for sale didn't matter to me. Instead, my focus remained only on looking for Lorien.

He took the bait, so far as I knew. It appeared he'd checked in, though people entered through so many different places that there was no good way to find him other than this.

I had an earpiece that connected to the others, and occasionally they'd speak up to tell me their locations. The mic for it hooked to my collar and was sensitive enough that it could pick up even my whispers.

Still, I hadn't caught sight of the man himself.

It made me wonder where Kenz was. Even after Nem's call, after knowing she'd disappeared, I couldn't stop thinking about her. We'd heard nothing from her, had no idea where she'd gone, what she'd planned.

A part of me hoped she'd given up on us all. Perhaps she'd finally realized that we would get her killed, and she'd turned around and left us all. As much as that would hurt, knowing she was safe, that she'd left before having to suffer through the pain of our deaths, was enough for me.

Because *none* of us were walking out of this auction house. Bradley wasn't the sort of man who would let go something this obvious, which meant so long as we spotted Lorien, this would all end today.

Still, I wished I could see her one more time, that I could see that smile of hers, that I could hear the way she whispered my name.

In fact, I even wanted to whisper hers again, to suffer through the pain of using my voice just to say her name, to tell her I loved her from my own lips. Not words on a screen, not written, not signed. No, I wanted to *say* it.

But that's not going to happen.

I'd given that chance up a long time ago. Perhaps I'd lost it with the first life I'd taken, as though the universe had decided I no longer deserved anything good.

And yet, I'd gotten time with Kenz, and even if it hadn't been forever, it was more than I expected or deserved. I could end this, knowing I'd kept her safe, and close my eyes happy with that much.

About half the items had already gone up for auction, and the excitement had grown steadily through the night. They always saved the best items for the end, to ensure that people remained and to increase the odds of something catching their eyes.

I moved through the dark rooms, checking the public spaces, searching for any sign of Lorien. As a higher bidder, a VIP, he usually bid from his own private room. However, that wouldn't help anything if his goal was to find us. It was strange, how we circled each other, searching for each other while trying to stay hidden.

More items went up—a priceless statue, the diaries of an old head of the FBI rumored to include a massive amount of previously unknown government secrets, an arranged marriage to a princess from a small kingdom in the Middle East—and they were all snatched up quickly.

Still, I found no sign of Lorien.

I stood in the large central auditorium, near the back, trying to ignore the stress that increased like the winding of a clock.

Movement across the room drew my attention, my instincts and skills honed to the point that at times they alerted me before my conscious mind caught up. This was one such time, my gaze zeroing in on a figure moving. They wore thick glasses and hunched forward, their movement that of an elderly man.

However, after a moment, I recognized the reason for my attention. While they walked with a cane, the movement wasn't *quite* right. They didn't rely heavily enough on the cane, and the slight drag of the opposite leg didn't appear regular enough.

It had me moving in that direction as the auctioneer offered up the final item on the list—a vase that was over three thousand years old. It had people bidding, using the small tablets that allowed them to bid without drawing attention to themselves. Only their numbers flashed on the large screen as the auctioneer called them off.

As I neared the person, my certainty grew. It was Lorien. I had no doubt about that at all, his features clearer, his movements all calculated. I reached into my pocket and wrapped my fingers around the blade that I'd snuck in.

No weapons were allowed, but that hardly stopped men like me or Lorien. I had no doubt he had weapons of his own, after all.

I got just beside him, so close that I could *taste* my win. I pulled my blade, aiming for his throat, wanting it over quickly. Not because I gave a damn if he suffered, but because I didn't want to risk anything going wrong. Succeeding was far more important than my own desire to see him suffer for what he'd done.

When I attacked, however, Lorien responded just as fast, mirroring my moves, proving how evenly matched we were. I moved in close, lifting my knife to slide it across his neck. One good swipe would handle the problem once and for all.

Lorien must have anticipated it, because his hand caught my wrist a breath from my goal. He shifted, and with the same sense he used, I brought my free hand down, catching his wrist just as the sharp point of a knife pressed against my side.

It felt as though each action had taken forever, but I knew we had ended up in this position in only a split second. Despite others surrounding us, no one had taken notice because of the speed we'd used. We both paused to take inventory, to recognize we'd ended up on equal footing.

Which was fine by me. I didn't mind one bit dying here so long as I took him out with me. I would *never* let him get close to Kenz again, wherever she was.

"And now, a special item of the night," the auctioneer called out, his voice ringing through the auditorium, silencing the chattering that usually happened at the end.

A special item? That had never happened before, and something about it caused unease inside me.

I allowed my eyes to flick toward the stage as something was rolled onto stage, a large piece of black fabric over the square mystery. Lorien did the same, as though he felt the same discomfort.

"You'll be excited for this one, I'm sure! It is unlike anything we've sold before. All pertinent information is being transmitted to your tablets now, so feel free to peruse it. You will have five minutes to make your decisions before I open the bidding for our final item, the last heir of two powerful bloodlines, a powerful tool for any looking to further their position, Mackenzie

Hester-Williams." The auctioneer pulled the sheet off, and sure enough, my greatest fear stood there.

Kenz, back in a cage, being sold yet again.

Talk about déjà vu.

Chapter Twenty

Char

The sight of Kenz on stage made me wonder if shock alone couldn't stop a person's heart.

When she'd disappeared, I'd thought she'd left. I'd thought she might show up at our house sometime later. The one place I sure as fuck hadn't expected to see her was in a cage getting auctioned off.

Again.

Just how many times could one little girl get herself sold?

To the far side of the large central room, where Tor had encountered Lorien, the two men stood still. It seemed Kenz had managed to surprise us all. They shoved apart, with Tor taking off toward a side door, no doubt heading for a way to get to Kenz. Lorien leaned down, grabbing a bidding tablet he must have dropped in the struggle with Tor.

What got me moving was the auctioneer speaking up again. "All right. Bids open now, starting at one million." Immediately, the large screen above the stage lit up with numbers as people bid. It went up in twenty-thousand-dollar increments.

Well, it seemed that people knew exactly how valuable that woman was. *And yet they don't know the half of her worth.*

That got me moving, and I quickly bid as well. Maybe this was for the best…maybe we could win this? If Bradley put her up again, this time without any of us cheating, he had to follow through with protecting such a bid.

Which meant our only hope at this point was to win, because if we didn't?

Someone else would.

The amount ran up quickly, exceeding two million, five million, ten million. All auctions had a time limit included to ensure they didn't carry on too long. That was ten minutes total. It meant we were likely to run out of time before we ran out of money.

Still, each time I bid, Lorien or another would bid again, driving the price up again and again. I wanted to look up, to see Kenz, but I couldn't. I had to focus on the tablet, my finger hovering above the bid button, pressing it so fast but still failing some of the time to land the next spot.

Please, let me win. This was the only thing that mattered, the only thing I needed this badly. I had to win. This was Kenz's life on the line, and nothing had ever meant more to me.

Lorien's number felt like a mocking voice, laughing in my face each time he got the top spot, but he wasn't the only one. Countless other numbers, ones I didn't recognize, took spots as well.

It felt like I was failing, like I was already losing Kenz. What did Lorien matter if I failed here? If Kenz was bought by fuck only knew who? Bradley wouldn't make this easy on us if someone else won, knowing we wouldn't just sit back and accept it.

The timer counted down on the top of my tablet. Ten seconds left. The price was up at thirty-eight million, having kicked out quite a few bidders so only about four of us kept going.

I took the top bid when we hit thirty-nine million, five seconds left, my finger waiting to press that button again.

Four. Three. Two.

The screen flashed, a new number, one I didn't recognize — 9260 — taking the top spot with a bid of two-hundred million. I hit the button as fast as I could, not caring that the amount had jumped so high, sure that between the four of us we could make it work.

The screen went dark, fear eating away at me. Did I win? Had I hit the button in time? Did it accept my bid? Had Lorien managed instead?

I lifted my gaze to the top screen at the stage where it would list the winning bidder, where the auctioneer would announce it.

The auctioneer looked down at his own tablet, an unsettling smile across his lips before he walked to the cage that held Kenz. He set a hand on the bar, beaming out toward the audience with a level of charm that showed what a threat the man could be. "Wasn't that exciting? This item sold has taken the top spot for the most expensive thing we have ever sold at this auction. The winner, who will be granted exclusive ownership of McKenzie Williams, with all the rights, risks and benefits that go along with that, is bidder 9260."

The tablet slipped from my fingers, crashing to the ground as my knees gave out.

I'd failed.

And now some stranger owned Kenz.

****

Hayden

I struggled to keep myself in check as I walked into a large back conference room at the auction.

We'd lost.

That kept repeating in my head, probably because I couldn't come to terms with the reality of it. After how hard we'd worked, after all we'd risked, all we'd done, in the end, we'd lost.

Even if Lorien had won, we could have killed him, could have removed him, but now?

Some other person had bought Kenz, taking it all out of our hands.

Bradley must have recognized just how unhappy everyone would be, because as soon as the auction ended, a few burly security guards had come to *escort* me to a room. I saw the same thing happened to Tor, Char, Vance and Lorien—that asshole looking as though he'd dressed up like an old man.

The room was huge, with a heavy oak table in the center and fancy antique chairs surrounding it. It all looked so professional, so legit, but I knew the truth, the ugliness beneath it all.

It didn't matter how Bradley dressed this place up— what happened to Kenz proved what it really was. *Inhumane.*

I took a seat between Vance and Char, with Tor on the other side of Vance. They all appeared unharmed, but all on edge. Then again, no doubt we were all on the same page—looking for an opening where we could do something, *anything*, to resolve this.

Lorien sat across the table from us, far enough that even if I leapt over the table, it would be a struggle to reach him before the man security guards stopped me. I had no gun—they were harder to sneak in than blades—but I'd bet Char had one.

Still, killing Lorien wouldn't solve this problem, would it?

He wasn't our only—or arguably our biggest—issue at the moment.

Though, judging from his expression, he was no happier about the outcome than we were.

I guess we can agree on that if nothing else.

A door on the opposite side of the room opened and Bradley walked in, his chin held high, no fear on his face.

Which seemed rather arrogant. In this room were *five* angry, capable men who wanted to tear him apart.

He undid the button on his suit jacket before lowering himself into a chair at the head of the table, then finally seemed to take note of us. "I am choosing to overlook all the problems you have caused me." He paused to look first at Tor, then at Lorien. "And do not think I missed the altercation between the two of you. Luckily, no one else noticed and you all seemed more interested in bidding than continuing that, so I can pretend it did not happen. However, I assure you, any other infractions of my rules will be met with severe consequences. You all seem to believe you are above my law, that you do not need to adhere to the same rules as everyone else. I assure you, that is not the case."

"Where's Kenz?" Char asked, not bothering with his normal fake smile. If anything, his words were nearly sharp enough to wound without any other weapon.

Bradely let out a tired laugh, as though he were tired of dealing with us and our foolishness. "She will be here shortly. I am being nice and allowing you to see her once more before she is handed over to the winner of the auction."

"And you think we're just going to allow that to happen?" Vance asked. "That we're just going to sit back while you give her away?"

"I hate to agree with that derivative playboy, but I'm forced to here. I have no idea what you pulled here, but I'm not about to allow my soulmate to slip through my fingers, not again," Lorien said.

"She isn't your soulmate," I snapped.

"That has nothing to do with you." Lorien waved my statement off as though it were entirely unimportant.

And just like that, we fell into an argument between us, with Lorien claiming he loved Kenz while Vance, Char and I argued that he didn't.

Bradley spoke up, but to no avail.

Something struck the table hard, but it wasn't just the sound that silenced us all. Instead, it was the fact that we turned our heads to find that Bradley hadn't done it, but rather Kenz.

Seeing her made my chest tighten, and I wanted nothing more than to rush over, to pull her into my arms, to kiss her until I forgot the time apart, the future, the things we still faced.

When I went to do just that, however, the guards pressed in closer behind me like a reminder of my place, keeping me in my seat.

For now.

Kenz offered a strained smile to me, seeming to plead with that look for me to behave myself. "You need to quit fighting," she said, her tone scolding.

"What are you doing here?" Lorien asked. "I thought you were getting handed over to a transporter—not that you were getting put up for sale again. What sort of trick is this supposed to be, Bradley?"

"It wasn't me," Bradley said with a shrug. "If you want to know what happened, ask Ms. Williams here."

That had me swinging my gaze back to her, the meaning clear. The desire to kiss her was replaced by the desire to put her over my knee to teach her not to do such foolish things.

"He's right," Kenz acknowledged, but didn't sit like Bradley had. "I met with Bradley and offered myself up to sell—not as Mackenzie Fox, but as my real self."

"Why would you do that?" Lorien asked, his tone sounding almost...hurt?

"Because I knew what you all had planned here. I knew that this wouldn't end, that you would either kill each other or get yourselves into trouble so that Bradley had you killed. Either way, this wouldn't end, not until you were all dead."

"That was *our* choice to make," Char said. "We were willing to pay that price for you!"

"It was your choice, and it was my choice to do this." She didn't appear afraid, but maybe she was just hiding it?

No, not Kenz. She didn't hide what she felt well. More likely, she was so worried about us that she hadn't thought about her own future. She was the sort of woman who could put her own happiness aside for others.

And again, I knew there was no other woman in the world like her, no one who could ever make me feel like this again, no future without her.

"This is touching and all," Bradley said, though his tone suggested he didn't find it touching at all. In fact, he sounded as though he didn't care in the least about any of this. "But we need to keep this moving. Ms. William's agreed to this in exchange for allowing you *all* to leave alive. She offered herself as payment for the trouble you have all caused, as a form of consolation to resolve our issues. Since you all could not find a way to work out your problems, she found one. If, after leaving today, you all want to kill one another, I don't really care. It is no longer my business. However, if any of you so much as approach her buyer, if you try to contact her, if you do *anything* that is against the wishes of the winning bidder, rest assured you will not live through that day. Do I make myself perfectly clear?"

"There is *no* way I'm agreeing to that," Lorien snapped.

"I'm going to have to side with Lorien on this," I offered up. "I'm not going to ignore Kenz being sold off like a piece of property. Not a chance."

Kenz spoke up, her voice lifting before anyone else could argue. She didn't waver in the least, her words strong, her chin held high. "If you love me, you need to listen to me, to trust me. I knew what I was getting into here. I understood the risks and I accepted them. If you really care about me, if you love me like you claim, you need to actually *hear* me. Trust that I know what I'm doing."

I wanted to open my mouth and tell her to hell with that. It was like trying to hold two opposite ideas in my head that I couldn't seem to square. I trusted her, I loved her, but that was the exact reason that the idea of sitting back as I lost her, as she was subjected to fuck only knew what, that was impossible.

"Okay," Vance said.

I swung my gaze over to Vance, about ready to ask him what the hell he was thinking, when he went on.

"How many times have we asked you to trust us? To believe in us? You've put yourself in our hands so many times when you had no reason to believe in us. The least we can do is to offer you the same. I'll agree to follow what Kenz wants. This is her choice—I'll trust her."

Tor knocked the table with his knuckles, then nodded when we looked his way.

Char cursed under his breath, the words vulgar enough to impress any sailor. After his string of curse words, he nodded. "You've proven yourself time and time again. I'm not going to lie and pretend I'm good with this—because I'm sure as fuck not okay with it— but I'll sit down and shut up and trust that you can make your own choices. If this is what you want? I won't get in the way."

The agreement of the others forced my hand, made me think about what they'd said, about the reality. Kenz had risked a lot to put herself here, to save us, and she'd known what the results might be. I hated it with everything I was, but if I ignored her wishes, how was I any different than Lorien? I drew my hands into fists, then looked at Bradley. "I agree to do as she asks but let me make myself clear. If she *ever* reaches out to us? If she asks for help? If she needs anything? Neither you nor anyone else will be able to stop me from doing whatever I have to for her."

Bradley smiled in return, no signs of anger or annoyance at my response. In fact, he seemed rather pleased by it. He really was a mystery, wasn't he? "Fair enough," he answered. "Lorien?"

Lorien's gaze darted around the room, no doubt going through it all, looking for another option, a new path to what he wanted. If he wasn't what he was, I might have almost pitied him. After having been so assured of himself, of his abilities, he'd lost time and time again.

"The next words out of your mouth will determine what happens to you. If you want to fight me on this, you will not leave this building alive. So if your life or future means anything to you, I suggest you remain quiet and accept your place," Bradley threatened.

Lorien's face flushed, the anger obvious, but he said nothing. That impressed me more than anything else, because it was damn clear what he wanted to say.

"Go get the winning bidder and bring them in," Bradley ordered one of the guards. The man nodded and exited the room, leaving all of us and a hell of a lot of tension behind.

After another few silent minutes, the door opened, and the person who walked in made me sit up straight.

What the fuck?

Chapter Twenty-One

Kenz

"You're bidder 9260?" Bradley asked, and I didn't even bother to turn around.

I didn't need to. I had absolute faith. I'd been let down so many times in my life, had people fail me, but it hadn't jaded me. Instead, it had taught me an important lesson.

I hadn't learned not to trust anyone—I'd learned to figure out who to trust.

And I had zero doubts that I could trust Jarrod, so when he answered, "Yeah, I am," I smiled.

The men had their eyes opened wide, clearly wondering what the hell was going on. *Just hold on a little longer.*

"And you are?" Bradley asked. "I don't recognize you, and I know everyone who could afford such a bid."

"You got your money, so clearly I can."

"Fair enough." Bradley tilted his head and tapped his finger against the top of the table. "So, can you tell me who the new owner of this young lady is? I don't normally ask much about our buyers, but this is a case I feel a special connection with."

Jarrod smiled, the expression familiar to me. It was sharp, and would likely worry others, but to me? It felt safe. "I'm merely an intermediary, bidding for a third party who was unable to attend in person. All the required paperwork has been submitted for me to bid by proxy."

"And the person who you were bidding for?"

I turned around to face Bradley and smiled brightly. "Me."

I would have preferred a bigger reaction, for Bradley to appear shocked, even for some widespread gasp. After all, this had been a *pretty good* plan, right? However, the subtle lift of his eyebrow would have to do. "Excuse me?"

"Jarrod Fox worked under my order, bidding in my place."

"We are clear that the money must come from the bidder."

"And it did. I have all the tracking information to prove that every last dollar of that two hundred and fifty million came from *my* accounts. I was left all the money from the Hester and Williams lines, everything from my mother's family and everything my father owned. I can think of no better way to spend it then buying and ensuring my own freedom."

Lorien spoke, his voice weak, his expression dark as though he couldn't figure this out, like he tried desperately to make sense of it and couldn't. "You can't do that. You can't just buy yourself."

"Why not? I agreed with Bradley that the proceeds from my sale would go to the auction house to pay for the continued protection of that asset, given the likelihood of people interfering. The money has already been paid, it's been proven that the money and winning bid came from me and my funds — through my proxy. It's done."

"It's not *done*," Lorien said, his voice low and angry. "You are *mine*. You are my soulmate, and you will always be mine. Tricks like this don't change that, won't save you."

I leaned forward, putting my hand flat on the table, staring hard at him. Every other time, I'd cowered away from him, afraid, uneasy. He'd stalked me, terrorized me, tried to take everything I cared about away, and I'd just given in over and over again.

I refused to do that anymore, so I faced off against him, refusing to give a single inch.

"It's already done," I told him. "You went up against me and you lost."

"You are *mine*," he repeated. "They think you belong to them, you think you belong to yourself, but you're all wrong. You have always been mine — you just need to realize it."

I leaned forward farther so I could look right into his eyes, ensuring nothing was between us, nothing that would soften my words or allow him to misunderstand just how serious I was. "Do you have any idea how often I've heard that in my life? That I belonged to my father, to my mother's line, to the men who wanted to own me? I believed it for a long time, that I had no future except the one created for me by others. I'm done with this. I don't belong to them" —I gestured toward Hayden, Tor, Vance and Char— "and I don't belong to my parents, or my sister, or the Quad, or Bradley, or

Jarrod or you. I belong only to myself, and if two hundred and fifty million is what I have to pay to ensure it remains that way — well, I'm happy to pay it. I do not now, have not ever and will *never* belong to you."

He pressed his lips together and I had only a split second to recognize the signs. It was a shift of his weight in the chair, a jerk of his gaze, a twitch of his muscles. Those occurred to me just before he moved, lunging forward at me.

A guard reached out, but Lorien twisted, slicing a blade in a wide arc through the air, cutting deep into the man's throat. This time, he didn't seem focused on killing him, which meant when the guard staggered back, there was a good chance he'd make it.

Lorien didn't slow in the least, closing the short distance between us, wrapping his hand around my throat and shoving me down, pinning me against the table. He held the same blade to my throat, just above his grip, his eyes full of mindless anger.

It seemed as though no one moved, no one even breathed. One twitch of that hand and he could kill me, slicing so deep that nothing could save me.

It meant despite Jarrod in the room, despite Hayden and Tor and Char — some exceedingly capable and dangerous men — none of them could make a move. He could kill me before they could intervene.

He stared down at me, his hand around my throat shaking. "You were supposed to be mine," he said. "I spent my life alone, thrown away by the people who were supposed to care about me, but when I saw that first painting of yours, I *knew* you were my other half. You saw the pain in the world, suffered the horrors of it, but you still found beauty. You and me? We're the same."

"You can't own another person." I forced the words out even though the press of his hand made it difficult. He hadn't cut off my air, but he'd restricted it slightly. "You can't love someone if you try to own them, to force them."

"It's the only way to get something," he said. "I've had everything taken from me, forced to watch as others get the things I should have. If I didn't take the initiative, I'd have nothing at all."

"That's not true. If you hadn't looked at me like something you could manipulate, if you hadn't done all this, how do you know what could have happened?"

He narrowed his eyes until he stared at me through small slits. "You're saying that if that hadn't happened, you'd have accepted me? You really expect me to believe that? Because people like me, we don't get what we want, not unless we're willing to take it. You should know that—you're the same. Both of us were underestimated, were hurt by the people who were supposed to love us. You would have never accepted me no matter what."

I wrapped my hand around his wrist, trying to get him to loosen the grasp *just* a little, to give me the space to breathe a bit easier. "You don't know that! I thought for a long time that no one could really love me, that I wasn't strong enough to stand on my own, to survive, but I was wrong. If you hadn't done what you did, could things have been different? Maybe. All I know is that I can't love someone who treats me like this."

"Why them?" That question came out a small whisper, a tremble to the words. "Why not me?"

"Because they'd do anything for me. They've risked their lives for me, they were willing to give me up to save me and they trusted me when I asked them to. Are you really asking me why not you? *Look* at what you're doing to me."

He dropped his gaze to his hand, wrapped around my throat, as though it were the first time he'd recognized it was there. What flashed through his eyes was a muddied mess of emotions. Anger, regret, horror, but they switched so fast that it seemed as though he couldn't truly experience any of them.

His hand loosened just a bit, letting me pull in a deeper breath. However, as quickly as it happened, as that hope sprang up inside me, it disappeared. He tightened his hand even more, cutting off my air entirely. "I do love you, but love isn't always the pretty thing you think it is. If you don't understand that now, it's fine. Maybe in our next life you'll figure it out and we can find some happiness then. The sooner we get there, the better." He whispered the last part just before he lifted his hand, sliding the dagger in his palm so he held it with the blade pointed down, toward me then lifted it up.

It seemed that somewhere in his rage-addled mind, he'd decided that burying that blade into my heart was the right choice. Was that some weird matter of romance?

I had no idea, but whereas I had been willing to accept such things before, I no longer was. Too many times in my life I'd given in, but that was over. I had things I was willing to fight for.

So I curled my hand into a fist and lifted my arm as he swung the knife down. I struck his forearm with the brass knuckles Rune had given me, the sharp edges digging into his muscles. It altered his swing, causing the dagger to strike the table just beside my face.

He was off me just that fast, and I rolled to the side, gasping air into my burning lungs, each breath painful after his tight grasp. I pushed myself upright and turned to find Jarrod there, his arm around Lorien's throat, holding him still with ease.

And *boy* did Jarrod look like one pissed-off father. In fact, it was astounding Lorien still lived, but I had a feeling he'd done that for me.

I walked toward a struggling Lorien, his face bright red, a sure sign that Jarrod pressed on his airway.

"How sad that you chose this path," Bradley said as he also rose from his chair, strolling toward Lorien as though this hadn't been the crazy event it was. "You could have walked out of here, but instead, you behaved this way. That was your choice."

"She's mine," Lorien spat, his voice strained and crazed. "I won't give her up, not ever."

Bradley crossed his arms, standing to my side. He peered down at me. "He's forfeited his life. He knew what the cost was to his actions, yet he acted anyway. He isn't even regretful for it now. In short? He's signed own death warrant on this, and given you're the official owner of yourself" — Bradley let out a short laugh at that, as though still amused by my play — "I give his life to you. Using this feels fitting." He pulled the blade Lorien had attacked me with from the table, then pressed it into my hand.

I turned my gaze toward the men — who were all on their feet, watching. The violent desire in their eyes was something I understood well.

They all wanted me to do it. They wanted me to take this blade and plunge it into his chest, to end the problem immediately and permanently. It was what they would have done, what Nem would have done, what both my parents would have done. In fact, it was what every person in my life would have done.

I'd wanted for so long to be like them all, and here was my chance. Except, when I looked at Lorien's face, when I watched him struggle, I no longer found that desire.

I held the blade up, waiting until Lorien locked his gaze onto it. "I could kill you here and now," I told him, "but that isn't who I am. I said that I'll pick my own path, and that includes now." I opened my hand and let the dagger fall to the ground. "You're not worth changing who I am for, and I won't let you control my future, not for a single moment." I turned toward Bradley. "He's yours to do with what you want."

Bradley chuckled, then nodded, gesturing for his men to take Lorien away. Amazingly, Lorien said nothing else, seemingly shocked by the turn of events. Perhaps he'd thought that, if nothing else, I'd take his life, that I'd end things. He'd probably even thought that if I killed him, we'd have some connection forever, that I'd at least remember the ghosts of this moment, haunted by the memory.

Instead, I'd walked away, and he had to deal with the consequences of his own actions. He could take the coward's way out. I wouldn't have wanted to be on Bradley's bad side—I doubted Lorien would last long in that position. Whatever happened to him, though, it wasn't my problem, not anymore.

"So, we're done here?" I asked.

Bradley smiled, then bent to pick up the dagger I'd dropped. He moved it in his hand, rolling it around in his palm, his comfort with it telling me he was certainly not just a businessman. That was the way a person who had used a blade enough times touched one. "So it seems. This isn't the way I expected this to go, but if nothing else, you've kept me quite entertained. Take this, Ms. Williams, as a token to remember what happened here."

"Like two hundred-and-fifty million isn't enough to remember," I muttered.

He snorted but still pressed the blade into my hand. "Even so — you overcame Lorien. You faced off against him and won. If nothing else, take this as proof of that. You've earned it." He turned his gaze to the side, toward the men, then smirked. "Now, I suspect you all have some catching up to do, and if I don't wrap this up, I doubt your men there will behave themselves much longer." He nodded, then took a step back. "You and I are bound now, Ms. Williams, so I look forward to a long and productive future for us both." With that, he walked out, his guards leaving once he'd gone.

Jarrod peered around, then shrugged. "Well, as glad as I am to see you safe, I have zero desire to see that makeup process between you all, so I'll take my leave. Call me tomorrow, Kenz." He walked over and pressed a kiss to the top of my head, then strolled out without another word.

It left me there with only Hayden, Char, Vance and Tor. I turned toward them, a strange fear overtaking me.

After so much, after all we'd gone through, what if they no longer felt the same? What if without the danger, without the stress, we had nothing between us?

I forced myself to lift my gaze, steeling myself against whatever I found there. The moment I did, everything shifted around me.

I found strong arms caging me in, and aggressive lips crashed against mine. I jerked backward, afraid the blade still in my hand would cut the person who had grabbed me, but they seemed entirely unwilling to let me go.

"You're a fucking idiot." Char's angry voice would have made me laugh at any other time, but his kisses kept me from doing it.

Just as quickly, someone else caught my chin, turning my face, and softer lips took mine. This kiss was coaxing and oddly sweet, passionate but teasing at the same time. I didn't need to even open my eyes to know it was Vance, his skill and confidence impossible to confuse for anyone else. Plus, I could feel the way he used his right hand, his damaged one, and he held my chin tightly with the fingers he still had.

For one brief moment, I wondered just how long we had in this room. Could I get away with locking the door, stripping them down, and drowning myself in them? *Bradley owes me at least that much, doesn't he? Two-hundred-and-fifty-million dollars ought to buy me a couple of hours here.*

Vance pulled back, his soft laugh warming my lips. "Just wait till we get home, Kenz, and I promise you all you can take and more." He offered one more kiss before pulling away.

Hands wrapped around me from behind, one slipping around my throat, but where it had terrified me from Lorien, I relaxed against the strong chest behind me. Tor used his thumb to turn my head to the side, so I looked over my shoulder, and found his lips pressed to mine. His kiss was sweet and gentle, as though I were precious to him, like each touch was a way to worship me. He broke the kiss, then trailed his lips against my ear just as his rough, soft voice whispered, "*mine.*"

My head felt cloudy, my body heavy, as though the stress from the day stole all my energy. Just as I reached out, my legs weak, a familiar body caught me.

Hayden wrapped his arm behind me, pinning me against him as he stared down at me. His dark eyes bore into me, intense and unwavering. "Let's go."

"Go where?" I asked.

His lips tipped up to one side. "Home, because I missed you a hell of a lot, and there isn't *nearly* enough sound proofing here for what I plan to do."

And those words, which should have scared the hell out of me, only excited me.

If that didn't prove just how hopelessly in love I was with these men, nothing would.

Epilogue

Hayden

The ringing of my phone had become a source of endless annoyance for me. Had I ever dealt with so many calls?

No, because I usually worked in the field.

Now I had to hear petty complaints and deal with clients and employees all from the suffocating walls of my office. We'd set this one up in the house, since I hated the idea of having to leave to do paperwork. I still had the main office of the company located elsewhere, but the drive to get there felt pointless, so I avoided it whenever possible.

The phone rang *again,* and I managed to give it a glare that would have scared off any smart human before picking it up. I didn't bother to even look at the caller before answering. "Hayden."

"You sound grumpy," my office manager, Laurie, said. "That means you're probably reviewing the upcoming schedule, doesn't it?"

I wanted to deny it, but my gaze found the open spreadsheet on my monitor, lines of colors filling different sections as I worked to find the proper person for the proper job. "Why are people so damn difficult?" I muttered as I stared at the mess.

Figuring out who could do which job, who worked well with who, who hated who, it was all so much drama.

"It's part of the job," Laurie said without giving me a speck of pity. Then again, that was why I'd hired her, because she could handle a bunch of difficult men without batting an eyelash. Hell, she could probably go toe-to-toe with the likes of Nem.

"Part of the job is also doing your damned job. I wish more of our employees would do that instead of deciding they don't like Alex, or Nicole chews too loudly, or whatever other bull has them complaining. This would be so much easier if they all just did as they were told."

Laurie chuckled, a clicking in the background suggesting she worked on her computer at the same time. "You'll get it done—you always do."

"This job used to be easier," I said. "I didn't have to do all this."

"Because you were out in the field. If you don't like this, then go back to taking jobs yourself."

"I can't."

"Why not? Clients are *always* asking for you personally. Do you have any idea how many hours you pay me just so I can apologize to clients and explain that you no longer take jobs yourself?" She snorted softly, then added on, "you could probably buy a yacht with all that money."

"That tells me I overpay you."

"You sure? Because when I went to see old Mrs. Yorli, she was wearing a negligee because she thought you'd come yourself. Do you have any idea how fake boobs look on an eighty-year-old? Because it's not good."

Before I could stop myself, my brain thought about that very thing and I shuddered. "Expect a nice bonus this Christmas," I said.

She laughed, the clicking stopping as though she'd given her full attention to our conversation all of a sudden. "I know you took a step back these last five years, but you're actually involved now. Why don't you take any more jobs yourself? Are you just getting too old?"

"Forget that bonus," I muttered softly. "No, I'm not getting too old. My joints aren't what they were ten years ago, sure, but they do the job just fine."

"So why? You were always so devoted, so quick to put your all into it. That's why so many clients ask for you, why they come to us, because they trust *you*. You always made sure they not only were safe, but that they felt safe. That's the thing too many bodyguards forget. They think the body is all that matters and they make clients nervous or uncomfortable. You always knew just how to make them feel secure, though."

I thought back to the years I'd spent putting myself in danger to protect others, and I smiled. They were good memories, things I was proud to have done. "Maybe we should add some extra training to help our bodyguards develop those skills."

She sighed—*loudly.* "So is that your way of telling me you won't take any more jobs?"

"Pretty much."

"At least tell me why."

"You know why."

"Yes, Kenz is very pretty and far too young and good for you, but how is that any reason? We have lots of married bodyguards working."

I looked over at the picture on my desk, the one that showed Kenz smiling brightly as she'd snapped a selfie of the two of us. My face was stiff and uncomfortable—selfies weren't something I'd done much of—but Kenz had still loved the picture. When I'd seen it, I had gone ahead and had it printed then put into a frame. Whenever she came into my office, I always put it face down because I doubted I could survive the embarrassment of her seeing it.

When Vance had spotted it, he'd laughed and told me that printed-out pictures were for old people.

Old. I scoffed at the word that was at the same time both true yet hated.

"I risked my life for a lot of people over the years," I said softly. "I don't regret any of it. I'm proud of how many people I've helped, and each scar on me is like a reminder that I protected someone. The thing was, I didn't have anything back then, anything worth coming back to. I didn't see my life as worth anything more. Now, though? I've got something with it. I think about leaving Kenz, and I just couldn't do that to her. I couldn't put her through that. I don't want to miss out on the years I've got with her. It means I'm not really fit to do protection work anymore, and you know what? I'm okay with that."

Laurie said nothing at first, the silence stretching out. Then again, I'd worked with her for so long that few people knew me better than she did. After that pause, she chuckled softly, the sound warm. "Yeah, I get it. Okay then, I'll take care of things here."

The door to my office opened, and Kenz came in like a whirlwind, items clutched in her arms, her voice already mid-sentence. "Since I doubt you've eaten lunch, I brought a picnic!"

Laurie's laugh grew louder over the phone. "You go take care of your girl. I'll hold down the fort here. God knows you deserve any happiness you can get." She hung up, not waiting for my goodbye.

Kenz froze when she actually looked at me. She lowered her voice so it was barely above a whisper. "Are you on a call? I'm so sorry! I'll come back later."

"It's fine," I assured her. "It was just Laurie and I'm already done. Besides, some lunch would be great."

The hesitation on her innocent face disappeared, and again she flashed me that bright smile that made getting up every day worth it. Damn, some of the time I was reminded how different my life was now, and I couldn't stop myself from wondering just how I'd lucked out.

I had countless scars on my body that could have killed me, ones I'd happily taken, but ones that had nearly kept me from this—from meeting her. It made me recognize something had to have been looking out for me, protecting me so I could get here.

Kenz came into the room and placed the picnic basket on the desk, beside my keyboard. The fact she'd not only gotten lunch for me but gone through the trouble to pack it like this made me chuckle.

I grasped her hips and pulled her closer, so she sat in my lap.

Her cheeks flushed but she ignored it, didn't try to get away. No, not Kenz, she wasn't the type to try to escape. Instead, she leaned forward and opened the lid of the picnic basket and pulled out the items inside.

The action caused her ass to grind against my lap and I was reminded of one of the benefits of having a home office…

"I picked up those canned coffees you like and made sandwiches!" Each thing she took out proved how well she knew me and just how much she paid attention. The sandwich had no lettuce on it, and the coffee was made with milk but no sugar.

I really can't ever deserve her.

I pressed a kiss to her shoulder, the skin bared from her tank top. Salt clung to my lips, a sign of the heat that had grown as we'd moved into summer.

She shivered, always so responsive, but then froze. The way she went still made me stop, worried I'd somehow crossed a line. She was usually up for about anything, but given how young and inexperienced she still was, I always made certain to never push her.

I moved back to see where she looked, then cursed myself.

"That's nothing," I said, reaching out to hide the item.

Kenz moved faster, though, snatching the picture before I could flip it down. She stared at the picture of the two of us, and the uneasiness inside me grew.

While I adored the picture, even I understood how lame it appeared.

Kenz was significantly younger than I was, smiling and sweet and with so much life ahead of her. Me, on the other hand? My hair had started to gray at the temples, and I'd taken as much life as I'd protected over the years. I was jaded and my back ached when I woke up in the mornings and it was so difficult to see her beside me.

So I wondered for a moment if the picture was the last straw. Would she see it and realize how different we were? Would it be the end?

Kenz dragged a finger over the picture, then turned her face slightly, a bright smile over her pink lips. "I didn't know you printed this out. Can you get another one for me?"

I frowned. "Vance said kids your age don't print out pictures."

She shrugged. "Not as often, but I like this picture. It was so hard to get you to take one with me like this, so it's important to me. I want one in my room, too."

And just like that, I knew I was helpless against her. It didn't matter if I feared our future, if I was worried about our differences, I couldn't ever make that matter, not against her. She won against me, always. Her sweet smile and her strength and her kindness, it took me down each time.

So I caught her chin and kissed her, deeply, pulling her against me more.

"But, the food," she complained softly but didn't push me away, didn't stop me.

"Later," I promised her. "First? There's something I want far more." I reached down her front, to the button of her slacks, then paused to give her the chance to tell me no.

Except, like always, Kenz didn't reject me. Even if she should have, even if she could do better, she twisted and kissed me back, giving herself up the same way she always did.

And right then, I knew I'd made the right choice. I'd spent my life protecting others, but now my path was clear. I would spend every day of the rest of my life protecting the woman I loved — her mind, her body and her happiness.

Nothing else had ever mattered more.

* * * *

Char

I rolled my head, trying to ease the aching in my neck. I'd spent far too many hours dealing with nonsense on a case I hadn't even wanted to take. It had required weeks of work, of delving into old files, of questioning so many people that had meant me taking on half a dozen different roles.

However, in the end, I'd gotten what I'd needed. The asshole who had been coaxing young girls into sex work was done for. He didn't know it yet, of course. In fact, the petty part of me enjoyed the idea of him having his last night of freedom, having no damn idea that his entire life would fall apart come tomorrow.

"You look happy," Claire said as she fitted another puzzle piece into the image on the table. The old woman who I'd met years before, who I still visited weekly when I came by the retirement home she lived in, was a surprising but fitting enemy for me.

"I'm always happy."

She snorted, the sound decidedly unladylike. "That's not true. You're always smiling, but that's not the same thing."

"Do people usually smile when they aren't happy?"

"Not normal people, but you haven't ever been normal," she pointed out, sorting through the puzzle pieces. "Of course, you're happy now."

That took me by surprise. Not that she'd come right out and say it—she'd been that way in all the years I'd known her.

"You're crazy," I muttered, letting my forced smile fade away. I'd found that I did that more, too. I didn't make myself be that cheery person as much anymore.

I still did around strangers, but I let it go when around those I was close to. I let them see the real me, the one that I'd thought no one could possibly accept. When at the house with the others, I let my snarky, asshole personality shine and no one even seemed surprised anymore. Likewise, here, I let it go after spending a bit of time.

It still wasn't comfortable, perhaps, but it felt more normal as the days went by. I didn't feel quite as on display as I had, as though just waiting for someone to reject me due to my behavior. Slowly but surely, it had felt more normal.

"Speaking of happy," she said, her lips pulling into a conspiratorial smile, "how is that lovely young woman of yours?"

I wanted to keep a poker face, but her speaking of Kenz like that made my cheeks heat. I'd never had a family, which meant I'd never dealt with doting parents or grandparents embarrassing me about who I dated. It seemed I lacked the skills to ignore such affectionate mocking.

"Well, that look tells me things are going just fine," she added on. "I'm glad. She stops by every week to visit, and she just lights the place up."

"She comes by here?" I sat up straighter at the information.

"You didn't know? That surprises me—I figured you were the type to know what she was doing at all times."

"I don't keep her locked up," I protested. "She goes to school and does what she wants." Besides, despite her real identity being known, Bradley kept a close eye on her as well. It meant she didn't have to worry much about her safety anymore, and the way she smiled when she left the house meant I couldn't stop her, even though there were times I wanted to. "I just didn't realize she came *here.*"

"Of course she does," Claire said. "She likes to come and talk. I think she misses her family sometimes."

I understood that, though I didn't like it. I couldn't give her everything—no one could—but I hated the thought that she didn't get enough from us.

She lifted her gaze and smiled widely. "Speaking of…"

I turned my head, knowing what I'd see before I even did so. Sure enough, stepping into the large rec room was the woman herself. Kenz hadn't seen me, didn't appear to be looking for me. She wore a loose black dress with a large bag slung over her shoulder. The way she could make the air in any room seem lighter amazed me, even now, months after interacting with her.

Her long dark hair was loose, and she seemed to float as she paused to say hi to each person she passed. And in response? Nothing but smiles.

"I don't deserve her," I said softly, not even realizing the words had escaped me until Claire laughed.

"Do you want to know the real secret? No one ever deserves the person they love. It doesn't matter who they are. I think it's because we see the best in someone else and the worst in ourselves."

That felt easy to say for her, but she didn't understand, clearly.

"You know," she said, her voice lowering, "I told her the first time I met her that you weren't as bad as she thought—that you weren't as bad as you thought. I'm glad that she sees it, too."

Before I could argue anymore, Kenz looked toward our table, and the moment her gaze landed on me, her smile widened more, as though nothing was more important or exciting than her realizing I was there, too.

She headed our way, then gave me a quick kiss before sitting at our table. "I thought you were working all day."

"I was," I admitted. "But I finished up a little earlier than I thought and realized I hadn't stopped by in a while. I hear *you're* visiting pretty often?"

She didn't give me a look that implied she felt bad about that. Instead, she shrugged. "I like coming by. Plus I always walk away with cookies. Apparently, I'm pretty easy to bribe."

Her words warmed me, especially because I knew they weren't true. She didn't come for the cookies, but because this place mattered to me, because she was kind, because she was the good person I'd never thought I could be.

One of the newer residents walked by, their face pinched into unhappy lines. I watched them go, unable to shake the feeling something was wrong.

"She got here a few days ago," Claire explained. "She hasn't said much, but clearly something's wrong."

Another resident, Harold, sat in the chair to the side of Kenz. "I heard that she had a house she's lived in her entire life, but her kids pretty much pushed her out of it so they could sell it since the market's high."

I narrowed my eyes, watching as the woman walked with no problem at all. She didn't seem old enough to need the help a place like this required, and her expression went along with the idea that this move hadn't been her idea.

"So they're selling her house from under her?" Kenz asked, that sweet voice of hers heartbroken already. "That's horrible." She turned her gaze toward me, a question there.

It made me want to laugh, that pleading she had. No, not just that. She didn't look at me as though she had to beg, just like the others at the table. Instead, they looked my way as though I were not just a problem, but rather the solution. I wasn't just a surly, unpleasant conman they needed their guard up around.

Instead, they looked at me like I was a hero, someone who could fix this, who could make things right.

It melted me all over again for Kenz, who accepted and understood every part of me — the ugly ones I used to hide included.

So I smiled back at her, the look real, then nodded. "Yeah, let's go get her house back."

Kenz leaned over and wrapped her arms around me, then took my lips in a kiss that was probably entirely inappropriate for the location, but fuck if I cared.

Kenz was my whole damned world now, and I'd con anyone out of anything if it meant keeping her.

* * * *

Tor

The sun had long past disappeared beneath the horizon by the time I reached home, when I spotted the porch lights of the house like an oasis in the desert.

I'd hoped to get back much earlier, but the job hadn't gone perfectly, which was a fact of life for people like me. Instead of the quick in-and-out I'd planned for, the target had ended up in a panic room.

Breaking into a panic room was a quick way to a ruined schedule.

Still, some relief hit me as I glanced at my watch to find the time at two in the morning. Kenz would be safely asleep, which meant I didn't have to see her.

Not that I didn't want to see her. Each time I left for a job, the craving to see her bright smile, her dark eyes, it ate away at me. I didn't keep her photo on the phone I used for jobs—the last thing I would ever allow was for her to end up in danger if something happened to me—which meant I had to suffer through that absence.

However, I always avoided seeing her at first when I came back from jobs, terrified she'd look at me differently.

I unlocked the front door and turned off the security system so I could enter. I reactivated the exterior sensors and doors once inside, then headed for my room. The hallways remained dark and silent, making it almost feel as though I lived alone again, like the past months hadn't happened.

And, in a turn of events I would never have expected, I found that I didn't like that quiet.

I put my gear away first, locking it into the safe in my closet. Tomorrow I could go through it all, clean what needed cleaning, replace what got used. I had already disposed of anything that might connect me to the job anyway.

I stripped down, tossing my clothes into a laundry basket in the closet before going into the bathroom and turning on the shower.

The first bit of hot water to stream over me, to wash away the dirt and sweat from the job, let me sigh heavily.

There were times I thought about quitting. Not because I disliked my job, not anymore, but because this heavy fear had grown inside me, day by day, and I struggled to carry it any longer.

Would Kenz turn her back on me? She'd accepted what I did so far, but perhaps that understanding could only go so far. One time, when I returned, would she look at me differently? Would she flinch away from me?

I leaned my arm against the wall, hanging my head forward, letting the water strike the back of my neck and roll down my body. My mind felt as though it sparked, moving from one idea to the next but unable to make sense of any of it, and I couldn't even track the passage of time.

"Tor?" The soft voice startled me, making me turn to find Kenz standing at the edge of the large shower. Her expression suggested it wasn't the first time she'd called my name.

I said nothing, staring back at her, unsure what to do.

Her gaze moved over me, no doubt taking in the new marks I carried. Few jobs went through without at least a little damage. This one had left me a bruise on my side and a new cut on my arm. Nothing serious, but her careful gaze locked on each one.

"You were in here so long the water went cold."

It had? I furrowed my brows as I realized for the first time that, yeah, the water coming from the shower head stung from the icy temperature. Still, I didn't move to turn it off.

Kenz sighed and moved into the shower, reaching past me to twist the handle of the shower off. It got her arm wet, but she didn't seem to notice. "Come on," she said, grasping my wrist without hesitation. "Let's get you in the bath so you warm up or you're going to get sick."

I didn't fight her when she tugged me from the shower, then started the large standalone bath. It took me back to when she'd been on her period and I'd run a bath for her, when I'd sat with her in the room, having what might have been our first real conversation.

How things change.

When the water got high enough, she urged me over the edge of the tub, then into the water. It burned my skin, but I'd bet that had more to do with how cold my skin was from the shower rather than the bath being too hot.

I closed my eyes, unsure what to say, afraid to do anything to break the moment. It was like coaxing a small animal over, knowing that if I did a damn thing, it might get startled and take off.

Water splashed, and I opened my eyes when something touched me. Kenz got into the large tub, granting me only a glimpse of her bare skin before she sank into the water and bubbles along with me.

She sat across from me, causing me to sit up and cross my legs to make room.

Had I ever actually taken a bath with anyone? Not since being a kid, at least.

"You were supposed to wake me up," she said, her voice quiet over the water still filling the tub.

She handed me one of the same types of crayons that we'd used in the bathroom before. It made me smile, that she'd thought about that.

She always did, though. Kenz never made me feel less than, as though my struggles with speech posed a burden on her even if I knew they had to. She accepted that limitation, accepted all of me.

It was late, I wrote.

"So? I've been waiting for you. I want to see you when you get home. I missed you." She didn't say that as though to scold me, to nag, but instead seemed to just want me to understand.

Still, I couldn't quite let go of the worries that ran through my head.

Kenz sighed, then reached out and caught my wrist, much like she had before. She tugged softly, using her other hand to help steer me where she wanted me.

Which turned out to be against her, my back to her, a reversal of how we normally would sit. It felt strange, made me uneasy. Her body was smaller, and me sitting in front of her struck me as weird.

And I tried hard to ignore the sensation of her bare breasts against my back.

She grabbed a washcloth and gathered bubbles on it, then ran it along my arm, careful to avoid the newest cut. "You've been acting more distant whenever you get back from a job." Her voice came out a whisper beside my ear.

I pressed my lips together, seeing no good reason to respond.

She moved to clean my other arm, the steady rhythm of her heart soothing. "I don't like when you're distant.

It makes me feel lonely, like you're slipping away from me. When you avoid me like this, it hurts."

I flinched at her words. Of all the things she could have said, that was the worst, the last thing I'd have wanted. So I picked up the crayon from the ledge of the tub and wrote the words I hated having to write.

I don't want you to see me afterward. It feels like you can see what I did, that you can see the blood on my hands. I'm afraid that one day, you'll see that and walk away.

By the time I reached the end of the statement, my hand trembled. Having bad things happen was a fact of life, but somehow it felt worse when I caused it. So being the one to actually tell her this, to put those facts into her mind, it turned the general fear into a very specific terror. What if, by telling her this, she recognized it and agreed?

Kenz sighed, took the washcloth, and used it to wipe the words away. Colored water streamed down the wall in its place. "I know who and what you are, Tor. I know people think I'm naïve, but I'm really not. I know when you leave, someone will die. When I'm waiting for you to come back, I know that seeing you means there is at least one less person out there."

Her saying such things had me holding my breath, hating that she even had to know that. It didn't seem fair, like I tainted her just by being here, by being near her.

Except, she didn't stop speaking. Instead, she wrapped her arm around me, holding me tight. "But I also know *you*. I know that you only take contracts with people who the world is better off without. I know that because of what you do, the world is a better place. There are dirty jobs that have to be done, things that are messy and unpleasant and I *see* the toll it takes on you.

So I'm not going to walk away because of this. I know you—I know your heart and the man you are and just how much you value life. You cherish it enough to risk yourself and make the hard choice to take it sometimes." Her soft lips touched my shoulder in an affectionate kiss, as though to try to pair her words with actions to prove their truth.

And something I would never ever thought possible happened. That weight I'd carried, the fear, it dissipated. Perhaps not all at once, and I had a feeling it would rise again from time to time, but the hold it had before was broken because of Kenz's words.

She didn't just look the other way when it came to my job. She didn't accept me in spite of them but rather *because* of them. She saw me as someone good, someone who added to the world rather than taking away from it. It eased that fear of mine that she would grow unable to ignore the lives I took one day.

In accepting me entirely, Kenz had given me a precious gift. She didn't pull me into the light—I didn't belong there, could never live there—but neither did I pull her into my darkness. Instead, she stood on the edge between the two worlds and reached out to me, the only person who could touch me there.

It made me beyond grateful, humbled and amazed that a person like Kenz could exist and, more so, that she could fall for me as she had.

So I twisted, unwilling to just accept her affection, wanting to make sure she understood just how much I cherished her. I leaned against her, rewarded by the shy expression she wore, the way her cheeks pinkened from both embarrassment and the heat.

I cupped her cheeks, staring into her dark eyes, wishing I had the voice and words to tell her exactly how much she meant to me. When I knew anything I could say would be inadequate, I did the only thing I could.

"I love you, Kenz," I whispered to her before leaning in and taking her lips in a kiss meant to prove just how much this woman meant to me.

* * * *

Vance

The cute girl in front of me would have been *exactly* my time not so long ago. She batted her fake eyelashes and set her hand on my arm as she leaned closer, smiling in the way that promised me whatever I wanted.

And the old me would have taken her up on it no problem. In fact, I'd have found her attempt adorable and been on my phone renting a room before she had to give it any more effort.

However, things were different, now, so I took a step backward, hedging the line between making my rejection clear but not humiliating her.

I have a reputation, after all. It wasn't fair to embarrass her much for thinking I'd jump into bed with her. I'd been that person for a long time, after all.

"Work on getting outside of your comfort zone," I told her, keeping my voice gentle. "You usually do landscapes, so try some portraits. You'd be amazed at what you discover if you try subjects you normally ignore."

Her smile fell, and I got the sense she rarely experienced rejection. Not much of a surprise there, given just how pretty she was.

"Okay, Professor Moore," she said, then moved away and gathered her things. She wasn't a bad kid, just a girl used to getting her way when it came to men. She had the talent to succeed in art, but I wondered if she had the drive, the desire to do the work that it would take.

However, only she could decide that.

"Isn't this a surprise?" The voice had me turning from the podium where I had my things back toward the main area of the classroom, unsure I'd heard them right.

Sure enough, when I turned, the sight of my mother took me by complete surprise. It felt like seeing a doctor at a bar, where I struggled to make sense of her in this context.

She walked toward the front of the now empty class, her low heels loud against the wood floor. She had a dress on, one that made her look every bit the aristocrat she was. Enough fillers and plastic surgery could make any person look good well into their senior years, and my mother proved that point and then some.

I leaned my hip against the table at the front of the room then crossed my arms. "I think you're a little old to start school, don't you?"

Her smile was half-hearted, as though to say she heard me but didn't find me as funny as I did. That seemed pretty on par for our relationship, though.

I was forever being myself and they were forever wishing I'd be anyone else.

"How did you even know I was here?" I asked when she didn't seem willing to start up the conversation. For a woman without a job, my mother sure kept busy. She wouldn't waste her time to visit me for no reason.

"Do you really think I don't know what my own son is up to?"

"Beyond the things that piss you off? Not really. You've never seemed all that interested in my life."

That took me back to all the times they'd failed me as a whole. How many exhibits and awards had I attended on my own? Or sometimes with the most recent flavor of the month on my arm?

My parents had certainly never seen a reason to come, not even back in high school, seeing me as the lesser child, at best the *spare* that might need to exist but little past that.

No matter the pain that pushed through me, though, I refused to let my mother see it. I pushed it down and reminded myself that no matter how much that hurt, that was no longer my life.

My mother stopped just before me, her gaze lowering to my hand.

I let out a soft laugh as it became clear. "So that's it, huh? You saw the interviews?"

She lifted her gaze, snapping it back up and managing to look *embarrassed* by my words. That wasn't a look I often saw on her face. "Everyone saw the interviews. You did a tour and were on every magazine cover and primetime show."

"So you're here to, what? To complain about bad press for you? Or did you just feel like you needed to put in facetime to look good?"

The rough edges of her expression softened, something unusual for her. She didn't respond at first, either. After a long enough time that I started to fidget, she spoke, her voice barely over a whisper. "This isn't about looks, Vance. I may not have always been a good mother, but I'm still your mother. I just wanted to see you, to see if it was true."

Her words took me by surprise. When she'd spoken to me over the years, it had always felt as though she'd measured her words against some imaginary recording device, like she decided what to say based on how well it would play later. She'd often said the right thing for the moment, but not the *true* thing. So many times it hadn't felt like I had a true mother, but rather a cardboard cutout who did the things required but never really *saw* me.

That wasn't the case now, though. Now, she spoke to me like a person, like a flawed woman hurting and regretting choices she'd made.

And years ago I would have flipped her off and walked out.

Now, though?

"It's true," I said and uncrossed my arms. I held out my right hand, the one without a glove, the one with a new prosthetic that actually had some use of the fingers. It couldn't be hidden the way my old one could, but it was far more useful. I still couldn't paint with any level of detail, but it let me teach.

My mother crossed the last few steps between us and reached out. She paused just before she made contact, however, as if unsure if she should touch me.

I held my hand out farther to give her permission.

Her touch was gentle, as though afraid to cause me pain. She took me by the wrist, turning my hand over, touching the line where it shifted between my body to the prosthetic. Her eyebrows pulled more toward one another, and it impressed me that she could even make an expression like that given how she paralyzed her facial muscles.

"It doesn't hurt," I told her when she seemed afraid to touch more than the lightest. "It did, when it happened, but it's healed as much as it can."

"I'm sorry." Her voice came out so soft that I almost didn't catch the words.

"It wasn't your fault," I said. "I've got a lot I can blame you for, but this isn't one of them."

She shook her head, her gaze down, locked on my hand. "I'm not saying sorry about this happening. I'm sorry that I didn't know, that you couldn't tell me, that you had to deal with this alone. I'm your mother. You should have been able to come to me, to tell me about it, to let me help you. You didn't because I never gave you the safe place I should have."

I almost wanted to laugh at the apology I never thought I'd get, the one I didn't even know I wanted. Even if someone said that such a thing was possible, I'd have laughed and said I didn't want it.

Yet…that wasn't how it felt.

Her words poured across the wounds I carried from a lifetime of feeling unwanted, unworthy, and soothed them. They didn't heal them, didn't make it as though the wounds didn't exist, but they did take some of the sting from them.

"It's okay," I said, surprised that I actually believed that. "If there's one thing I've learned, it's that no one's perfect. We're all just fucking things up in our own special way until we learn better. I've made a mess out of my life enough times, and I've been lucky enough to find people who accept me despite that, who forgive me for all my screw-ups. It'd be pretty terrible karma to not give the same to others."

She squeezed slightly at my hand before releasing it and lifting her face toward mine. A smear of black makeup around her eyes startled me. *Are those tears?*

Had I ever seen my mother cry? In all my years, I didn't think so. She was the type to follow the rule that a person never showed their emotions, that they hide them with everything they had. It meant she'd found this important enough, upsetting enough, that she couldn't stop herself this time.

"Will you come to dinner soon?" she asked.

"Thanks, but I can't stand seeing my father," I answered. "But I'd be happy if you came to my place instead."

"You don't need to worry about that. Your father isn't in the house."

I tried to make sense of her meaning. "You mean he's on a trip?"

"No, I mean I kicked him out. I should have done it a lot sooner, really, but sometimes it's easier to stay in one place than move in the direction you should. The news of our divorce should hit the public in the next few weeks."

I had no idea what to even say to that. My parents felt like a staple in the universe, their marriage something impossible to break. It wasn't that I ever thought they were happy, I just didn't expect either to ever do anything about it. People in our world didn't break up—they just had quiet affairs and smiled for the camera when needed.

"What about my brother?"

"He's not happy, but that's really too bad. I'm tired of living my life based on what I should do instead of what I want to do. Seeing you grow, seeing you find your own place in the world, one you picked, it inspired me to do the same. So, please, will you come to dinner next weekend?"

I swallowed hard, wanting to say so much but managing only to nod in response. It felt like an open door that had been locked my entire life, like entry to something I never thought possible.

She smiled, the expression uneasy as though she wasn't sure how to react either, then nodded and left.

I stood alone there, in the large classroom, thrown by the situation, by the future and options I'd never thought I could have.

"Was that your mom?"

Somehow, even Kenz's voice didn't surprise me. She often popped in to see me, and it always made me smile. The fact she might be around when my mother stopped in was hardly a shock.

"Yeah." I looked toward the door where my mother had left. "She's leaving my father, and she invited me to dinner. She also apologized for…well, everything." Even saying it didn't feel real.

Kenz slid her arm around my waist, nuzzling into my side. "Really? That's great."

Years ago I would have rolled my eyes, would have said it was pointless, that it didn't matter, but now? Now I saw it differently. Kenz had shown me that family mattered.

It didn't have to be made by blood, didn't have to consist of people who shared DNA, but no person could survive entirely on their own. I hadn't had family before, but Kenz had created one out of a ragtag group of misfits hell-bent on revenge. She'd formed those bonds, showed me how much that mattered, and now?

The idea of having my mother back pleased me. It felt like finding something I'd missed before. I thought about the future, about children someday, about holidays and celebrations and all the things that had been lonely for me before. The idea of having my mother at those felt good.

I turned my gaze toward the reason for it all — Kenz.

She'd given not only me the chance for a family, but she'd given me a purpose again. The proof sat in this classroom, in the students who had already left, the prosthetic on my hand, the lesson plans on the board.

She peered up at me, somehow able to appear so innocent despite the far-less-than-innocent ideas in my head. "You know, I think you're going to win favorite instructor this semester by the students. Pretty unfair, given you only started teaching at the end of the year."

"What can I say? This face is a winner."

She leaned against me with a playful bump. "You know that's not it. You always listen to the students and give them help. You don't talk over them, don't treat them like they're stupid."

I chuckled at her words to hide my discomfort at the praise. "I never would have thought myself the teacher type. Well, other than in a few role plays."

She made a show of rolling her eyes. "You're such a pervert."

I turned fully toward her, looking down at her lovely face, wondering how I'd ever thought I was happy before she'd come into my life, before she'd taught me how life was supposed to feel. Except, those sorts of words or comments were far too deep for a man like myself, and one of the many lessons Kenz had taught me was to not bother trying to be anyone except who I was.

So I danced the fingers of my good hand along her side, teasing her through the thin fabric of her top.

"That's no way to speak to your teacher, is it Ms. Williams?" I cocked up an eyebrow.

Red colored her lovely cheeks before she responded with a soft voice, "You're such a pervert, *Professor Moore.*"

"What a rude and entirely true thing to say about a trusted educator. Now, why don't we discuss extra credit?"

"I'm not taking a class from you," she complained. "And we're busy! I brought you clothes to change into before the exhibit."

I glanced at the clock, then pulled Kenz tighter against me. "We've got time. I mean, I've got to get naked before I can get dressed, right?" I leaned in and ran my tongue along her earlobe. "Besides, you should know that I am a very serious instructor who puts the proper education of my students above everything else."

She shivered against me, a sign that her resistance was wavering. "I don't think this is what they put in the catalog for education."

"That's their mistake. I bet if they included this, they'd have more students than they could handle. Now, come on, sweetheart, you're not really going to turn me down, are you?" I pulled back just far enough to peer down and into the familiar eyes of the woman I loved more than anything else, the one I owed everything to.

She took my hand in hers — my damaged one, the one I'd thought had ruined my entire life, that had stolen away everything that mattered to me — and she kissed it, trailing her lips along the line between the real and the fake. She never shied away from it, never treated me as though it bothered her, or if she were uncomfortable. Because of that, it no longer bothered me, either. "Okay," she said back to me, giving in. "But not here. Maybe we can go discuss my grades in your office, Professor Moore?"

And just like that, my cock ached and my head went blank, her teasing voice stealing any rational thought I might have had. So I took her hand in mine and headed out, toward my office, ready to show this girl who had saved me every bit of my appreciation.

I owed her everything, and while a couple orgasms wouldn't repay her for all she'd done for me, it sure wouldn't hurt, either. I'd happily spend all my years showing her just how much I loved her — orgasms and all.

* * * *

Kenz

I straightened my hair and smoothed down my dress as I rushed into the art gallery, alone.

Vance had offered to drive me, to arrive with me, but I'd turned him down.

I needed to stand on my own, and that wasn't the general mood I'd give if I showed up on the arm of art superstar Vance More, especially because I felt like 'we just had sex' was tattooed across my forehead.

I didn't regret my quickie with Vance, of course. It was impossible to regret almost any time I spent with him or the other men I loved. That time was too precious to me. However, I didn't want anyone else looking at me as though I'd ridden their coattails to my current place. The news had died down around Vance and I dating — I had a feeling that was partly due to Bray keeping my name out of the spotlight — but I still had a complex about proving myself.

So I'd taken my own car, leaving Vance to change and arrive at the gallery on his own.

The gallery looked as it had the day before when I'd spent hours helping set it up. Each painting was exactly where I'd picked, and the lighting was perfect. There were also already so many people there, all moving around the space, looking at the work and speaking softly to one another.

My heart thundered against my ribs. I'd put my all into the pieces, had stayed up *far* too many nights and gotten countless lectures from Hayden about needing more sleep.

It was all worth it, though, to put together a final exhibit I was proud of.

And I was damn proud of this.

An arm slid around me from behind, and I peered up to find Hayden there, dressed up. He rarely wore a suit anymore, preferring his casual clothing most of the time. It meant I didn't get to ogle him like this often, because he filled out a suit *fantastically.*

He flashed me a smile before telling me, "You're late."

I went to tell him I was sorry, but the memory of what exactly had kept me made my lips clumsy and I couldn't get anything more than a stammer out.

He chuckled and shook his head. "I knew letting Vance work at your school was a bad idea." He pressed a kiss to the top of my head, then pulled away. "The turnout's good. Even better, the pieces are all fantastic."

"You know nothing about art," I pointed out. "Even if my work was horrible, you'd *still* think it was the best thing ever made."

"Fair enough." He didn't look sorry at all before shrugging, as if that was a given.

"You're late." The voice made me wince, taking me back to the times I'd gotten scolded as a kid for failing to be where I was when I was supposed to be there. I turned slowly to find Colton behind me, his arms crossed and his dark eyebrow lifted.

I almost went over some excuse until I recalled an important detail. "I'm an adult now. I'm allowed to be late."

He snorted, then offered a subtle smile. "I don't think I like the influence of these men on you. You never used to talk back."

"She always talked back," Dane said as he walked up and slapped a hand against Colton's back. "Just not to you since you like to glower. This girl has always had a mouth that won't stop, though." He turned his gaze to me and grinned widely. "Good job, Kenz. Your paintings are amazing."

The praise made me smile wider, pleased to *finally* get to prove myself, to show off my work. "Where's Nem?"

Dane gestured behind us. *Of course she sneaks up on me.* Some things would never change, like my sister being a step ahead of me at all times. It didn't bother me anymore, though, not since I'd realized we didn't have to compete.

So when I twisted to find her standing there, wearing a black suit and her red hair pulled back and in a bun, I had to blink away a few tears. For so long, I'd thought her gone, thought myself alone. The fact that this wasn't true felt like a gift I'd never expected.

"I'm impressed," she said. "I knew you were talented, but seeing so much of your work in one place like this?" Nem paused, her gaze moving around the room. "It's really impressive. I'm glad you came out here, that you fought for this. Now, if you will excuse me, I believe I see a few of your instructors over that way." Nem took a step that way, and my chest tightened.

"She wouldn't threaten them, right?" I asked to no one in particular.

"Of course she will." Rune strolled up, snacks in his hand to tell me he'd already found food at the event. "It won't matter, though."

"It won't?"

"Nope, because I've already done that."

I rubbed my eyes, a sudden headache bothering me. "Has anyone not threatened someone here?"

"I didn't." Bray took one look at Rune's snacks and scoffed.

"You see—at least Bray controls himself. You could learn a lot from him."

"That's right. I just hacked into the grading information to ensure you had top marks." He didn't stick around—probably knowing he'd get lectured—before he strolled off after Nem.

Colton, Rune and Dane snickered, offering more 'good jobs' before walking off.

"I can't believe them." Even as I said that, it wasn't really true. Didn't I know them well enough to expect this sort of behavior from them? The reality was that in their world, people won by cheating. Of course they'd go that far for me.

That same old warmth filled me as I had to admit, their caring might be strange, but it was real.

Arms wrapped around me, a soft body pressing against me, lips offering a kiss to my cheek so fast that I struggled to identify the person at first.

"Give her room to breathe," Jarrod said. Even though I heard his voice, I knew damn well he wasn't the one being all affectionate like that.

Though it did let me know who it was.

Sasha pulled back, a wide smile on her lips. "I can't believe how wonderful this all is! You are fantastic, Kenz. I had no idea you could do this!"

Jarrod wrapped an arm around Sasha, pulling her against him as though afraid she'd attack me yet again. His gaze was steady, and he didn't offer any such large declarations.

Instead, Jarrod nodded. "Good job." It was funny that even without such flowery statements, his praise struck me just as deeply. It was honest, and it was the way he expressed himself, and I knew he meant it. I gave him a smile in return in thanks—not just for coming, but for so many other things. For taking me in when he didn't have to, for looking after me even when I wasn't his own.

He scooted Sasha off under the guise of looking for a drink, giving me a moment to take a deep breath.

"Aren't you popular?" Char snickered, the sarcastic little comment telling me he'd seen everyone ambushing me. In fact, I'd bet he enjoyed watching it while remaining safely out of sight.

"You're supposed to rescue me, I thought."

"I promise to rescue you from bad guys, not family."

"To be fair, her family *are* bad guys." Vance strolled up to us, his smirk *far* too familiar to the one he'd worn early when he'd toyed with me.

"And you aren't?" I pointed out.

"Harsh," Vance muttered and set a hand on his chest. "I'm not a bad guy. I don't know about the rest of them, but I'm an upstanding member of society."

"Speaking of upstanding members of society." I peered around the room again. "Where's Tor?"

A moment of doubt struck me. Had he decided not to come? I knew he didn't care for parties or crowds, and I would understand if this was too much for him, but the idea of him missing out on such an important event to me still hurt.

Char pointed toward the side, and standing there, 'speaking' to Colton and Sasha, was Tor. He would listen intently, then move his hands to sign back a response. As though he felt my gaze, he turned toward me. The moment our eyes met, the golden of his almost glowing even from that far away, I was struck by just how handsome he was.

He didn't stand out the way others did, perhaps, but that didn't make it any less true. He signed once more to Sasha, who glanced my way with a smirk, before Tor headed over to us.

He captured my chin, then wiped my cheek with a thumb from his other hand. He pulled that hand back so I could spot lipstick on the pad of his thumb. *Thanks, Sasha.*

He smiled, then left a kiss where the mark had been, as though covering that kiss up with his own. When he pulled away, I took a step back and was again surprised by just how good looking all four of them were.

They'd all dressed well, the small act enough to tell me this mattered to them, that they'd found this important enough to put the effort in for. They could have shown up in pajamas and I wouldn't have cared, but them having treated this event with care made me smile, made me feel as though *I* mattered to them.

Tor narrowed his eyes, the action catching me off guard. I turned to find one last person who I recognized, one who I sure hadn't expected.

I took a step that way, but Hayden caught my arm. "Kenz…"

I gave him a reassuring smile. "It's fine. I'll be right back."

He blew out an unhappy breath but released me. "We'll be right here."

I headed over to the guest, who stared at a painting on the wall. It was the last one I'd painted for the exhibit, the one I'd spent the most time on. In fact, I hadn't finished it until just two days previous, all but collapsing when I'd added the final brush strokes to it.

"I didn't invite you," I said.

Bradley smiled but didn't actually turn toward me. Instead, he kept staring at the painting. "We're bound together, you and me. I need no invitation to check in on you. I am surprised you have yet to reach out and ask about the fate of our mutual friend."

I knew who he meant without having to ask. I would have loved to say the moment I walked out of the auction, I never thought about Lorien again, that he neither deserved nor occupied any part of my mind, but it wouldn't have been true. I thought about him often, still woke up from nightmares now and then, but those things were outside of my control. I refused to ask a thing about him. "He isn't my problem," I simply said.

Bradley let out a soft, amused laugh. "Then all I will assure you is that you will never have to worry about him. Of course, seeing just how talented you are in art, I fear you went for too low a bid."

"That is probably the weirdest compliment I've ever gotten." I paused, then added softly, "But thanks."

"This is my favorite," he said, nodding at the painting we stood before. "I went all around the exhibit, but I like this one best. When you are prepared to part with it, I would like to purchase it."

"Really?" I frowned as I looked around the room, catching sight of the other pieces. This was far from my best piece by any real standard.

"Don't get me wrong, your ability is obvious in them all. You captured an amazing amount of softness in subjects who would not be considered soft." He moved his gaze over to other pieces as he spoke.

One of Nem, of Colton, of Bray. On the walls hung paintings of all the people in my life who mattered. I'd given my all to each one, showing what I saw rather than what the world saw.

"You have an uncanny ability to look beyond the surface of your subjects. Everyone can look at someone and see what they show to the world. I understand why Lorien fell for you — you see something else, something deeper, something they hide from everyone else. You bring that out and expose it. He was a fool, of course, but he wasn't wrong about you."

"So why do you like this one?" I peered at the largest of the paintings, that of a cage, the thick bars I'd been on the inside of *twice*. It sat on a stage, in a spotlight, but the cage was empty, the door open. I'd painted it in place of putting my own image there, as a way to represent myself in the exhibit.

"Believe it or not, we all exist inside our own cages. Even those who appear to have it all, they have their own chains. Something about this, about the sight of those chains left behind, that door open, it speaks to me,

I guess." He shook his head, as though waking up, then offered me an embarrassed smile. "I should get going. I didn't intend to intrude—I just wanted to show my support as well. Good work, Kenz. I'm glad things worked out the way they have." With that, he nodded and left, as much of an enigma as he had been the first time I'd seen him.

"We might have to kill him." Hayden set his chin on my head as he came up behind me. Tor stood to my other side and nodded in quick agreement. Char and Vance laughed, but that laugh wasn't an argument.

I looked around the room, taken in again by all the people who had gathered. Nem, the Quad, Jarrod, Sasha, even Bradley. For so many years I'd thought I was alone in the world, forced to do nothing but follow others' lead, listen to them, live the life they wanted me to. I remembered standing in that wedding dress, thinking my future was nothing but marrying a stranger because my father ordered it.

Then everything had changed, and I'd felt stuck.

"Kenz?" Vance cupped my cheek, his blue eyes worried.

I set my hand over his and smiled even as my eyes burned. "I'm okay," I promised him. "I was just thinking about how much my life had changed."

"And that makes you cry? I know Vance is a pervert, but we'll keep you safe from him," Char said.

I laughed and shook my head. "Thank you. I had no idea I could be this happy, that I could have this much. I owe it all to you."

"No you don't," Hayden said. "This is all because of you. You worked hard, you risked your life and everything else. You have what you have because of you, Kenz."

I turned again to face the painting of the open cage, surrounded by the men I loved, the ones who had stood by me, the ones who I couldn't imagine living without anymore.

Maybe they didn't realize it, maybe they never would. I might have been the one to step out of my cage, but they'd been the ones to give me the strength to do it.

And I knew with all my heart that they were the reason I had the life I had. I could never thank them enough, but all the years I had left, the future I never thought I'd get, the happiness I'd found, I'd spend them all with the men who had made it possible.

I wasn't my sister or my mother or my father, and for the first time, I was okay with that. It had taken getting sold at an auction, getting purchased by strangers and having my life risked more times than I could count to get me here, to make me understand my own truth.

I was Mackenzie Williams, and because of the men who loved me, because of how much I loved them, I finally knew exactly what that was worth.

Want to see more from this author?
Here's a taster for you to enjoy!

The Devil's Luck:
A Devil of a Time
Jayce Carter

Excerpt

My name is Loch Lacey, and I am sexually attracted to red flags — the more of them shoved into a vaguely man-shaped form, the hotter and dumber I get.

I'd say that trait would end up killing me, but it already had. Five years ago, I'd let some fuckwit tell me pretty lies and sold my soul for his benefit, which left me spending my afterlife here in the Chasm as my punishment.

And even though I should have known better, a part of me saw the man across the bar, Tyrus, with a flashing neon sign above his head saying *death two here*. I didn't believe in love at first sight but fuck if 'my future bad decision at first sight' wasn't a thing.

Tyrus sat at his normal table in the back. He ran this place — much like he ran many of the businesses here. Whereas most bosses, especially ones with as much on their plate as Tyrus had, would half-ass the actual day-to-day headaches, he never seemed to. He was *always* here.

Right now, he was talking to someone else, his arm out on the back of the bench as if to prove himself in charge. *Talk about posturing.*

Of course, Tyrus was all about his posturing. He liked to play the game and from what I'd seen, he excelled at it.

"Another?" The bartender, Koya, put a new drink down in front of me before I got the chance to answer. Then again, my empty glass suggested I needed more. I didn't have a whole lot of talents, but I could drink most people under the table while staying on my feet. Call it a gift from a life spent trying to escape the ugliness of my reality.

I nodded in thanks, then brought the new glass to my lips. The liquor burned, but I didn't so much as flinch as I swallowed down a gulp.

"Hey there, pretty thing. You new here?" The unfamiliar voice made me struggle to resist the urge to roll my eyes like a petulant child.

I turned on my barstool to find a damned behind me, his body already twisted beyond recognition. He had horns that curled back from his temples and bright red eyes, his face having shifted into a muzzle. When I'd died, five years ago, the thought of talking to something as terrifying looking as him would have sent me screaming. Now, however? I was used to it.

Fangs, feathers, claws, scales? *Big fucking deal.* So long as they didn't drool or spit acid on me, I didn't much care.

"Nope," I answered before taking another drink and peering out at the dim bar again.

The Chasm was *always* dark. Even inside, even with lighting, it never got bright enough. Trying to do puzzles here was a fucking losing battle. It made me wonder if the very air here absorbed the light.

Wouldn't surprise me. Seemed yet another way to remind us all that we were the bad guys and this was our punishment.

"But you still look human—you can't have been here that long," the man added on.

I gave him a side-eye because I'd heard this shit before plenty of times. People showed up in the Chasm in two forms—as damned or as demons. They all looked human at first, but the damned quickly twisted into monstrous forms. They grew fangs and claws and became animalistic. Demons, on the other hand, kept their human body. They had another form, a demonic one, but they didn't have to take that. Demons were rarer and more powerful, putting them above the damned.

I still appeared human because I'd been one of the few who arrived as a demon rather than damned.

"Nope," I assured him. "Been here in this depressing paradise for five years."

"So why haven't I seen you?"

"Because I've been really fucking lucky so far?"

He narrowed his eyes until they looked like some cheap Halloween decoration, nothing but a red spotlight staring out from his not-at-all human face. "You're mouthy for someone who just got here."

"Again—didn't just get here. Why don't you go look for someone who might actually find you charming?" *Like there's anyone who would...*

He leaned in closer, bringing his face just in front of mine. His breath was hot and smelled of rotting flesh. "You need to learn how this world works. People survive by clinging to someone more powerful. You'll lose those looks of yours before you know it, get twisted into something just like the rest of us, so why not sell that pretty little human body while it's still worth something?"

My stomach didn't even roll. Was that how far gone I was already? That even this disgusting thing whispering into my ear in the middle of a bar, suggesting things I'd *never* take him up on, didn't even warrant any stomach churning? Not at least a rumble or threat of vomiting all over him?

I really am jaded, aren't I?

I'd suffered with assholes like him plenty of times, damned who took one look at my unmutated form and wanted to own and break me. I knew what I looked like, which was exactly the same as when I'd died. I didn't have to dye my hair green anymore, since it was like that when I'd taken the bullets that had killed me. I still had the small tattoo on each of my cheeks, hadn't grown more than my pathetic five feet in height and didn't put on or lose weight. Basically? In death, we ended up stuck. It made me feel bad for those who died with not-so-great trends like shaved off eyebrows or shitty tattoos.

On the plus side, I'd shaved the morning I'd died, so no worries about body hair! I had to find the silver lining where I could, or the dreariness of this place would get to me.

"Hard pass." I brought my drink to my mouth again, letting the heavy glass smack him as I did so.

At least that caused him to lean back and give me a bit of space.

"Who are you bound to? I'll just buy your soul off them."

The name caught on my lips. Talk about an answer I hated to give. Then again, that was how the Chasm worked. People didn't wind up here because they were bad people—though, to be fair, most of us were—but because we'd all sold our souls. Just admitting that I didn't own my soul made my mood plummet.

And given I was this far into a bottle on a…Tuesday night? Yeah, my mood was already dragging ass.

"I'll find out," he assured me. "And I can be *extremely* persistent. You'll be mine by the end of the week, and I can't wait to fuck up all that soft human skin. Bet you won't look so pretty when I'm done with you."

"I would personally advise against that," said a deep voice that made the man freeze. He turned slowly, as though if he took long enough, he'd find something other than what he expected behind him.

Except it didn't change. No matter how long the man took, Tyrus still stood there, his dark eyebrow lifted in an obvious challenge.

"She yours?" the man asked, a waver in his voice that made it clear he wasn't rising to that challenge.

"No."

"Then why do you care? Unless you're enjoying her right now, in which case, I'll fucking wait. I don't want to step on any toes."

"Hardly," Tyrus said with so much disgust in his voice that I was pretty sure I should feel insulted. I might not be sultry or sexy, but he didn't need to say that as if I were some rotting carcass. "She belongs to Gorrin."

And there went the color from the man's cheeks. In fact, forget some parting snarky shot—the man was lucky to stay upright as he fled the bar just as fast as his little legs could carry him.

"Coward," Tyrus muttered as he watched the man leave, then turned toward me. "Why didn't you tell him about Gorrin? Mentioning his name would have resolved this instantly."

"Somehow, it bothers me to admit being owned. Imagine that?"

Tyrus leaned against the bar beside me, giving me the chance to see him up close. How was it that someone could look that dangerous, even dressed in a suit, as civilized as a man could appear? He had tan skin and dark features, with deep brown eyes and black hair slicked back in true gangster style. He had facial hair that rode the line between being well-maintained still looking like he had a five-o'clock shadow.

He was terrifying in a wholly unusual way, and when he stared at me, I felt as if he saw me naked.

No, *worse* than naked. I could deal with people seeing bare skin—what did that matter? Plenty of people had seen my tits and I wasn't conceited enough to think they were special in any way. The left was better than the right, but neither were real superstars. Tyrus saw deeper than that, though. He peered into my soul—what a shitty turn of phrase since I'd sold that already—and saw things I wanted to keep hidden.

"You wouldn't deal with people like that if you gained your own power and made your own name," Tyrus added on.

It's always back to this, isn't it? Seemed it was lecture time yet again.

I took another drink, hoping the burning liquor would dull my senses and the conversation. "I'm fine."

"No, you aren't. In the Chasm, the only things that matter are power and connections. You need to obtain both to survive here."

"I'll do that about when hell freezes over, which it hasn't in five years, so I think I'm safe."

"This isn't hell."

"Close enough. I'm not about to go around stealing souls just to make myself more powerful."

"It isn't stealing — it's bartering. When you were still alive and human, did you not exchange money for goods and services? You do the same here. The only difference is that we use souls as currency."

I thought back to how I'd ended up here, to when I'd sold my soul, to that crushing regret when I'd realized it had all been for nothing. The memory threatened to close my throat, but I shut my eyes and took a deep breath to push it all away.

The Chasm wasn't the sort of place to show weakness, and certainly not in front of a Demon Lord like Tyrus.

The four assholes who ran this place — Tyrus, Gorrin, Hale and Yazmor — held the souls of nearly all the damned between them. This gave them the power to stand mostly unopposed. They ruled the Chasm through fear, threats and a good old heaping of violence just to really flavor the whole recipe.

"Thanks for the completely unsolicited advice, but no thanks. I'm good."

"You really aren't. You have stagnated here for five years. You've survived this long only because of your connection to us — that won't save you forever. It is an imperfect defense that chips away each time you use it. Eventually, it will crumble, and you will have to stand against threats on your own. You can either be moral or you can be strong. You will have to choose between the two." With that, he peered at Koya. "That is her last drink. She does not need to be drunk on her way home."

"Didn't think the devil cared."

"I am not a devil."

"Could have fooled me," I muttered as I gulped down the rest of the liquor and slammed the glass down on the bar top.

Tyrus said nothing else before he turned on his heels and headed back to his table. The other man still waited there patiently, telling me Tyrus had left his meeting to intervene on my behalf. It made his words sting more and irritated me worse than the cheap liquor.

And yet that annoyance didn't stop me from noticing the way he filled out his suit. Most men I'd known who wore such outfits mixed different colors. They'd have a black suit with a white shirt and red tie — something to create a balance. Not Tyrus, though. He paired a black suit with a black shirt and a matching tie.

It wasn't how he looked that garnered the fear and respect of others, though. It was his power, his demon form, his absolute ruthlessness that had earned him his place at the top. I'd yet to see that other side of him, and honestly? I never wanted to. Seeing my *own* demon form had shocked me enough when I'd first arrived here.

I peered back at Koya, who offered me an apologetic smile. "Sorry, Loch. If it were anyone else, I'd say fuck it and give you another, but I'm not about to piss the boss off."

"Thanks anyway, Koya." I shrugged and slid from the bar stool, the world shifting as I moved for the first time in a few hours and more than a few drinks.

Guess Tyrus hadn't been wrong about cutting me off.

Koya set something on the bar, and for a moment, I smiled. Had he given in to my meager charms?

Of course not. Instead of more alcohol, a cup made from a small skull sat there, the dark liquid inside no doubt coffee. "Should help clear your head a bit," Koya said.

"Thanks." I picked it up and took a drink. When I'd first arrived, the idea of drinking from a skull would have grossed me out. Funny how quickly things can become normal for people.

Demons and damned and skulls had been nothing more than Halloween jokes for most of my life, but now? Totally average. In fact, a day where I didn't see anyone brutally murdered would strike me as odd.

I headed toward the door, coffee in hand, ignoring the weight of Tyrus' gaze. Something about the way he watched me always let me know it was him even if I wanted to pretend otherwise. No matter how distracted, how busy, I always felt the weight of his gaze.

But I refused to look backward and acknowledge it, because men who were bad for me had already fucked up my life *more* than enough.

I could fuck it up all on my own now, thank you very much.

About the Author

Jayce Carter lives in Southern California with her husband and two spawns. She originally wanted to take over the world but realized that would require wearing pants. This led her to choosing writing, a completely pants-free occupation. She has a fear of heights yet rock climbs for fun and enjoys making up excuses for not going out and socializing.

Jayce loves to hear from readers. You can find her contact information, website details and author profile page at https://www.totallybound.com

Home of Erotic Romance

Sign up for our newsletter and find out about all our romance book releases, eBook sales and promotions, sneak peeks and FREE romance books!